BRIGHT STAR

BRIGHT STAR

ROBERT LOUIS STEVENSON III

G. P. PUTNAM'S SONS/NEW YORK

G. P. PUTNAM'S SONS
Publishers Since 1838
a member of
Penguin Putnam Inc.
375 Hudson Street
New York, NY 10014

Library of Congress Cataloging-in-Publication Data

Stevenson, Robert Louis III.
Bright star/by Robert Louis Stevenson III.
p.   cm.
Book II in a series featuring two ex–Navy Seal divers,
Phillip Drake and Jack Henderson, in a thriller/deep-sea
adventure—Publisher's info.
ISBN 0-399-14444-7
I. Title.
PS3569.T4568B75   1998
813' .54—dc21   98-8714
CIP

Printed in the United States of America
1   3   5   7   9   10   8   6   4   2

This book is printed on acid-free paper. ∞

Book design by Gretchen Achilles

FOR MY MOTHER,

CAROLINE CRANE STEVENSON

1927–1998

For we are lovers of the beautiful,

yet simple in our tastes, and we cultivate

the mind without loss of manliness.

—THUCYDIDES

ACKNOWLEDGMENTS

I wish to thank my agent, Theresa Park, and my editor, Stacy Creamer, for their friendship, support, and guidance during the writing of this book. Theresa, Stacy: you are every writer's dream.

I also wish to thank Todd Ehrlich, recent member of SEAL Team 8 and current member of the SEAL Reserves, for all his support in answering questions about the SEALs and for giving me a sense of what these truly remarkable men are all about.

Without my father, Robert Louis Stevenson II, my parents-in-law, Chris and Neil Pultz, my lovely wife, Sheila, and my darling children, Devan and Caroline, my life would be a dim rushlight indeed. I love you all very much.

BRIGHT STAR

They were cruising along the sandy miles of northern Michigan in late July, the blacktop highway cutting through the dense pines like a sector line. The tinder beneath the green branches appeared so dry and encrusted with sap that the forest seemed on the verge of spontaneous combustion. *Northern Michigan: an arid country of secret lakes and rivers,* thought General Walter P. McKendrick as he gazed through the windshield. Drake had told him that—not the father and friend who had bled to death in his arms in the tall elephant grass of the Ia Drang Valley, but the son.

Gazing into the pines, he thought of his days of running recon in Vietnam. He had been a member of the deceptively named Studies and Observation Group, otherwise known as SOG. An all-volunteer commando unit consisting of Rangers, SEALs, Green Berets, and USAF Air Commandos, the unit was so "black," in the parlance of the intelligence world, that officially it didn't exist. SOG handled the war's most dangerous assignments. Teams of two to four Americans and a small group of indigenous fighters, usually Nungs, would insert by helicopter behind enemy lines to rescue downed American pilots or to pinpoint targets for air strikes along the Ho Chi Minh Trail. Often SOG teams were inserted deep inside Cambodia and Laos to ferret out North Vietnamese strongholds. A lot of teams didn't come back.

Now, lost in reverie, McKendrick felt as though he were behind enemy lines again, the earth shaking beneath his chest, the jungle vanishing before his eyes, flattened by the five-hundred-pound bombs detonating along the Ho Chi Minh Trail. Hugging the ground from his observation post on a hilltop along the Laotian border, he had glanced up at the sky. At 26,000 feet, the B-52s looked like pinpricks: glinting, silent. He had called them in but hadn't seen them coming. No one had—these tiny flashes of light. Only the sudden shriek of bombs falling through the midday sky . . .

Then the shock wave of a passing car broke the spell completely.

"Crazy kids," muttered the driver of the van, who looked like one himself.

Maybe it was the desolation of the surrounding countryside that had provoked this reverie, if that's what it was—these ghosts rising unsummoned from the past.

Or perhaps it was the occasion of his visit.

He recalled the stirring optimism of the Kennedy years and the anxious spellbinding days of the Cuban missile crisis. He and his classmates at West Point had talked about nothing else, unaware that the historical ground was shifting beneath their feet, that the abyss that would swallow their lives, consuming nearly half their class, lay not in the hardened missile silos of the Soviet Union—or in Cuba—but in a little-known region of Southeast Asia called Vietnam.

They turned onto a four-lane asphalt drive, pulling up to a high-tech security booth in the center of a landscaped island. The sign read:

SYSTEMS TECHNOLOGIES

RESTRICTED

The driver punched in a security code as a hidden camera matched the delicate pattern of the young man's eyes to the precise measurements suddenly appearing on a monitor screen. Iris scan. *Amazing,* McKendrick thought. The young man turned to McKendrick and grinned. In the distance, amid the landscaped grounds consisting of gardens and majestic white pines, McKendrick could see four low office buildings clustered around an enormous four-story structure. The buildings seemed to be constructed entirely of bronze-tinted glass.

"There are no power lines leading to the facility," the young man explained.

"You rely on generators?"

"The sun."

Surprised, McKendrick scanned the tops of the buildings. "I don't see any solar panels."

"You're looking at them."

"Where?"

"The windows." The young man beamed again. "Sandwiched between each pane of glass is a transparent sheet of thermal ceramic which converts the sun's heat into electricity. And stores it, too, which is the amazing thing. We could have a year of overcast days and we'd still have enough power to operate."

"No kidding."

"Welcome to the twenty-first century, general."

The steel gate opened. The young man turned right onto a surface drive and sped toward the glass buildings a half mile away. The sun reflected off the windows in a multitude of amber disks. Gazing at the brilliant complex as though it were Oz, McKendrick couldn't help wondering if the ground were shifting beneath his feet again.

"I called your office to see if you got off in time. Helen said you had placed a sign on your door: 'Gone fishing.'"

"Fat chance." McKendrick chuckled, sure that Helen, his secretary, had made the wry remark knowing it would get back to him.

With a bemused expression, Secretary of Defense Richard Elliot gripped McKendrick's left elbow, inclining his head toward an attractive brunette chatting with two men across the room. The cocktail reception had gotten under way.

"Who is she?" McKendrick asked with casual interest.

"I don't have the slightest."

A waiter appeared.

"Anything to drink, sir?"

"Ice water," McKendrick replied absently. Some people are blessed with the most exquisite natural beauty from birth but lack animation. Others are born plain but are gifted with an intellect and personality that make them sparkle. The woman across from them belonged to the latter category. Mid-forties, McKendrick guessed.

A tall black man was heading in their direction. McKendrick and Elliot recognized him immediately. With intense brown eyes, a muscular frame, and the beguiling smile of a magician, William

Lawrence was known to the scientific community as the Bill Gates of the defense industry. Raised by his maternal grandmother in the slums of Detroit after his parents had been killed in a cross fire between snipers and police during the riots of '67, Billy Lawrence won a wrestling scholarship to the University of Michigan and might have gone on to the Olympics and the front of a Wheaties box had he not slipped on a patch of ice one frigid December afternoon, breaking his right leg. Unable to compete, he had spent the rest of his sophomore year messing around in the computer lab. By the time his leg had healed, Lawrence's interest in wrestling had become a thing of the past. It didn't matter; not with the grades Lawrence was quickly racking up in computer science. By his junior year, he was turning down job offers that would have made him a rich man by any standard. But the former wrestler had other ideas.

From Michigan, Lawrence went on to MIT, where he received his doctorate in computational physics in two years. Six months later he founded Systems Technologies, a high-tech research firm specializing in weapons development. Responsible for a number of startling breakthroughs in computer technology, Systems Technologies prospered, making Billy Lawrence a multimillionaire at the ripe old age of thirty. But for all his money, Lawrence chose to lead a simple life. Each year, he directed two-thirds of his annual income to the Charles and Edna Lawrence Foundation. Named for his deceased parents and located in the former Hudson's Department Store in downtown Detroit, the CEL Foundation, as it was known, was a sanctuary for inner-city children, a place where kids could go for tutoring, counseling, a hot meal, financial aid, or whatever else they needed to enter the mainstream of American life.

McKendrick extended a hand. "Sir Lawrence."

"Hey, Walt! Richard! Glad you could make it. Richard, I see you're fixed. Walt? What strikes your fancy? Beer, wine, martini?" Then with a sidelong glance at the brunette. "A little erranty, perhaps?"

Lawrence didn't miss a beat.

"I hear Christmas came early this year," McKendrick remarked, changing the subject, ignoring the smile lighting up Elliot's face.

"Did, indeed, general," Lawrence replied with a grin. "Wait until you see." He looked across the room. The woman flashed a smile in their direction and broke away from the men.

McKendrick felt the sudden calm appraisal of her eyes as she approached. Then she looked at the others.

"Walt, I'd like you meet our lead project scientist—"

McKendrick looked at the woman, startled. "You're Dr. Reynolds?

"Surprised?"

"No . . . well, yes. I've been reading your reports for months. I didn't expect—" The words were out before he knew it.

"A woman?"

"No, it's not that . . ."

She smiled graciously, sensing his embarrassment. Then she extended a hand. "It's a pleasure."

With a sly look Lawrence tapped Elliot on the shoulder and said, "Maybe you should kiss it, Walt."

Guffaws. Even Julia Reynolds restrained her laughter.

McKendrick glowered at his two companions. "It's a pleasure to meet you, too," he said. He looked at Lawrence and Julia. "So, when's the unveiling?"

"Twenty minutes," Lawrence remarked, pleased by the heightened aura of suspense that the cocktail party had generated.

"Unless we get clobbered by Gödel's boomerang," Julia added.

"Excuse me?" McKendrick inquired.

Lawrence smiled. "One of Julia's coinages. We use it a lot around here."

"Well, now I'm truly lost," McKendrick said, good-naturedly.

"Me, too," Elliot admitted.

"I'm sorry," Julia said, smiling at both men. "When you spend most of your life concentrating on such esoterica as inertial reference gyros, pointing and tracking apertures, and fire-control logics, you become a trifle batty. Have you ever heard of Kurt Gödel?"

"The name sounds familiar," McKendrick remarked. He looked at Julia, intrigued. "He was a scientist, right?"

"A mathematician. Born in Brünn, Austria-Hungary, in 1906. Gödel addressed the problem of axiomatic consistency in a thirty-page paper which overturned a century of effort by other theorists to establish axioms that would form a rigorous basis for mathematics. Gödel's theorem ranks with Einstein's relativity theory and Heisenberg's uncertainty principle as one of the hallmarks of modern science. What Gödel says is this: Within any rigidly logical mathematical system, there are propositions that cannot be proved or disproved on the basis of axioms within that system; therefore, the basic axioms of mathematics may give rise to contradictions. In other words, gentlemen, there's no such thing as a closed system. You may interpret that optimistically, if you wish: the idea that all is never lost. I tend to think of it as a cautionary tale: Just when you think you've done everything right, the unexpected may come back to haunt you. Hence, Gödel's boomerang." She smiled at the group in a mixture of triumph and self-deprecation.

Elliot and McKendrick looked at each other speechless.

They were seated in a small amphitheater, looking down at a black curtain and a stage. Following the cocktail party, McKendrick and Elliot had filed in with the rest of the group and had taken their seats halfway down and to the right of the center aisle. There were fifty people in the audience, all familiar faces in the defense establishment—high-ranking Pentagon, NASA, and Defense Department officials who, like McKendrick, had flown up for the demonstration. They were baby boomers for the most part, people inured to rapid technological change. Yet a delicious sense of high anticipation filled the air. The cocktail party had lent an intimacy to the evening, people chatting with the kind of learned grace that reminded McKendrick again of the Kennedy years. Glancing at Elliot seated beside him, he had to remind himself that he now served a president and secretary of defense both fifteen years his junior. It seemed less a personal milestone than a Rubicon crossed. Still the urbanity of the group was stirring. Nice the way civility somehow managed to trickle down.

The audience hushed as Lawrence and Julia took the stage. Lawrence bantered with someone in the front row, Julia joining in the laughter. They made a formidable partnership: Julia directing the engineering department at Systems Technologies while Lawrence concentrated on computer research. They understood enough of the other's area of expertise that they were equally adept at representing the company during official visits and were able to key off each other's discoveries to form a synergistic union that had led to a number of startling innovations, mainly centering on the fields of laser technology, solar power, and miniaturization.

Julia looked up at the audience with excitement, then spoke quietly to Lawrence who moved to center stage. McKendrick enjoyed watching her, considerably more at ease now that he was buried in the audience. He had been impressed by what she had said about Gödel. How many people did he know who could talk about that? *Now this is a woman I would like to get to know better.* In mid-August she and Lawrence would spend a week at the Kennedy Space Center. He would have to spend a couple of days there, too. *Hmmmm. Ripeness is all.* He settled back into his seat, doting on the exquisite possibility of romance. It was a long time since he had made love. Indeed, he had been in a dry spell for so long that he had come to believe it might run the course of his days, an alarming prospect. Part of the problem was work—he rarely had time to pursue a relationship. The other problem was casual sex—sport fucking, as he called it, a practice he had written off long ago as the callow predilection of boys. Not that he wasn't tempted from time to time; an errant breeze tossing a summer dress, and he was ready to plow the fertile fields. But after a long and distinguished career in the Army, McKendrick wanted to settle down. He wanted a wife and all the blessings that came of a good marriage. He wanted the Beef Wellington.

Lawrence cleared his throat. Then, with Julia at his side, the computer genius looked up at the audience with the confident grin of a born athlete, and the show began.

"For centuries nations have dreamed of forging the perfect defensive weapon, a weapon so powerful that it would guarantee a lasting peace by making war untenable for the other side. Today, thanks to Dr. Reynolds and the engineering staff here at Systems Technologies, that weapon is no longer a dream. It is a reality."

With an impresario's flourish Lawrence held out an introductory hand to Julia, who glanced at him in happy expectation as she took center stage.

"Thank you, Billy." She smiled at the audience. "In the eighties the U.S. embarked on the Strategic Defense Initiative, commonly known as 'Star Wars,' to create an umbrella of laser satellites that would shield the United States from nuclear attack. Unfortunately, the requisite technology for a 'Star Wars' defense could not be attained, despite enormous research and funding. Ladies and gentlemen, what you are about to see represents five years of the most concentrated research in the field of laser technology that the world has ever seen."

She glanced at Lawrence once more, her features composed, a mixture of contentment and self-assurance, as he rejoined her center stage. Then together they faded into the darkness as the curtain rose and the lights dimmed.

McKendrick settled back, expecting to see a movie screen. But what he saw instead was something altogether different.

They were gazing down through a wall of smoked glass into the dark interior of a four-story building, a testing facility built on a grand scale. Metal sensors by the hundreds dotted the concrete floor, sparkling like distant stars. But the audience's attention was quickly diverted to the sapphire object hovering high up inside the dark structure. Like a compact sun, a satellite hung suspended beneath the vaulted ceiling, its solar panels arrayed upward, its faceted lower half as pendulous as a diamond. Pulsing with blue light, the satellite gleamed with the intricate sophistication of a finely wrought toy.

McKendrick leaned forward to get a better look as the satellite's sapphire aura intensified. Then with a sudden crack, a thousand needles of light struck the sensors scattered about the concrete floor. The audience flinched. Caught by surprise, McKendrick repressed an urge to hit the deck.

"My God . . ." Elliot muttered out loud.

Shocked by laser fire, the sensors seem to rise and shimmer like a mirage—or like a soul departing after death, McKendrick thought, recognizing the irony of what he was seeing: a weapon designed to save lives by providing a ghastly premonition of death. He glanced at Julia: the ancient dialogue of Eros and Thanatos. Lawrence's husky voice drifted up from the stage.

"What you see is not a glimpse of the future but the linchpin of the most advanced strategic weapons system that the United States has in its arsenal. Once deployed from the space shuttle *Atlantis,* scheduled to launch one month from today, this weapons system will allow U.S. forces not only to pinpoint enemy ships, tanks, planes, submarines, artillery, and missiles but also to 'paint' up to a thousand targets at once, employing state-of-the-art computer technology to simultaneously coordinate a multiple-beam, high-energy laser attack that will clear enemy forces from the battlefield within minutes. Indeed, so great is this weapon's power of intimidation that the mere act of 'painting' alone by the low-power marking beams you see now should cause hostile forces to quit the field rather than face instant annihilation. What we have developed here at Systems Technologies is the perfect defensive weapon, a satellite that will provide not only an impenetrable nuclear shield but also an overwhelming tactical advantage on the battlefield for generations to come: a weapon designed to make other weapons systems and, indeed, war itself obsolete. Ladies and gentlemen, I give you Bright Star."

PART I

4 August

They were pulling themselves down the anchor line, their bodies extended like flags in the cold, dark current. Philip Drake glanced up at Jack Henderson, his best friend, wondering if they were going to make it to the wreck, wondering if they *should* make it. They were diving to the SS *Andrea Doria*, the famed Italian luxury liner that sank fifty miles south of Nantucket Island in 254 feet of water, and they were descending straight into a bottom current.

On the surface the ocean had been calm and dully reflective, as though bearing the matted sheen of oil. Gearing up for the dive aboard the research vessel *Wahoo*, they had gazed out at the orange buoy that marked the end of the 300-foot trail line. The buoy had fluttered back and forth in a lazy S, the rollers having flattened hours before under the hot August sun. Now, a hundred and fifty feet below the surface of the Atlantic, the current surged against them like a freight train.

The dive had been Drake's idea. Over the years he had logged close to two hundred dives to the Italian luxury liner, but this year he hadn't visited the *Andrea Doria* once. For a man accustomed to an adventurous life—he had run a charter dive operation out of the Bimini after leaving the SEALs—Drake had adjusted to married life with surprising ease.

Through the grapevine he had heard that Steve Bielenda was running a *Doria* expedition at the end of the season, so he had called Jack and they had signed on. One of the top wreck divers in the United States, Bielenda owned and operated the *Wahoo* out of Captree Boat Basin on Long Island. The *Wahoo* was the premier dive boat in the Northeast.

It was Jack's first trip to the *Doria,* though he had been familiar with the story of the *Andrea Doria*'s sinking since the day he had met Drake at the Navy's Basic Underwater Demolition SEAL training facility in Coronado.

Now crooking the thick line with his right arm, Drake hit the power-inflator button on his dry suit, jetting argon gas inside to offset the ambient water pressure that squeezed his body like a fist. He glanced at his depth gauge, then directed the powerful beam of his light down, illuminating a blizzard of tiny organisms.

An empty window frame appeared in the darkness. Drake moved closer, pulling himself down against the current. Other window frames appeared. They were over the promenade deck. Suddenly he could see the port hull, speckled with anemones. The *Andrea Doria* lay intact on her starboard side, slowly disintegrating on the ocean floor. The anemones were flesh-colored in the penumbra of his dive light, a welcome burst of color had they not reminded Drake of the pallor of the dead.

Surrounded by darkness, Drake descended to the hull and gripped the edge of a giant window frame, the current billowing up over the superstructure and pushing against his mask. Henderson moved in beside him to his right, and together they pulled themselves down into the sheltered canyon of the promenade deck.

In the stillness, Drake could feel the weight of the cold water above him. With each breath he could hear trimix—mixed gas—slipstreaming through the first stage of his regulator, gas molecules traveling at nearly supersonic speeds. With each exhalation he could hear the silvery eruption of exhaust bubbles venting into the cold sea. These were the telltale signs of deep diving.

Like everything else in the world, trimix had its advantages and disadvantages, the primary advantage being that it allowed a diver to venture to extreme depths without experiencing the narcotic effects of nitrogen narcosis, the fabled "rapture of the deep." It also eliminated the danger of oxygen toxicity, the primary drawback of deep air.

Oxygen toxicity occurred without warning. One minute a diver would be happily swimming along at an extreme depth, the next minute he'd convulse and black out, sinking to the bottom, his regulator falling out of his mouth. Oxygen toxicity had been Drake's main concern in recovering the gold from the USS *Norfolk* the previous year during Operation Torchlight. On those dives, he and Jack had had no choice but to breathe compressed air.

The disadvantage of breathing trimix is that divers have to carry a tank of nitrox and a tank of oxygen for decompression. Humping two extra tanks, called stage bottles, in addition to the twin OMS cylinders mounted to a backpack, was a genuine pain in the ass—especially when a diver was deep inside a cave or a shipwreck and trying to slide through a constriction. In this respect, diving with compressed air was simpler. But Drake wasn't in the habit of taking unnecessary chances. Compressed air might be easier to use, but breathe it at extreme depths and you could easily wind up dead.

Together Drake and Henderson headed forward, sweeping their lights from side to side, the magnificent teak planking of the promenade deck rising like a wall to their left, the large window frames passing above them, receding into the distance like railroad ties. Straight ahead, the promenade deck became enclosed, leading to an area known as the Winter Garden, where the *Andrea Doria's* wealthy first-class passengers had once looked across the bow to the glittering Atlantic.

The collision had occurred on the foggy night of July 25, 1956. How two great ocean liners managed to collide on the open seas was never resolved, the Italian and the Swedish-American lines having settled out of court rather than face months of continuing bad publicity. It seems likely, however, that someone, aboard either the *Andrea Doria* or the *Stockholm,* misread a radar screen.

Aboard the *Andrea Doria,* forty-six passengers had died, most crushed to death instantly while they slept as the steel bow of the *Stockholm* cut a gigantic V-shaped hole in the *Andrea Doria's* starboard side seven decks high just forward of the bridge. Six crewmen had died inside the *Stockholm.*

Despite heavy damage to her bow, the *Stockholm* retained her watertight integrity and remained at the scene, taking on many of the *Andrea Doria's* passengers. She would eventually reach New York Harbor under her own power. The *Andrea Doria* was not as lucky. Listing heavily to starboard as tons of seawater poured through the gaping hole in her side, the *Andrea Doria* remained afloat for eleven hours, a near miracle that would allow for the rescue of 1,660 passengers and crew in what would become the greatest maritime rescue operation in history.

Now, as he swam to a double doorway and dropped down into an open area between the Grande Bar and the first-class lounge, Drake felt surrounded by the presence of history as well as by darkness. Taking point, he drifted down between rotted bulkheads, once a corridor. Electrical cables dangled to his left, the thick strands a dull orange in the penumbra of his dive light. Drake checked his depth, leveling off at 210 feet as Henderson dropped down beside him. He directed the beam of light to the fingers of his left hand and flashed the OK sign, making sure that Jack was comfortable with the dive. Henderson returned the signal, nodding, the exhaust bubbles streaming up past his forehead, eyes sparkling behind the mask. *Same old Jack, raring to go.*

Drake recalled the nights they had practiced landing IBSs— small inflatable rafts—on the jagged rocks fronting the Hotel Del in Coronado during Basic Underwater Demolition SEAL training. Fearless, Jack would leap onto the rocks, wrapping the bowline around his waist and wedging himself between two boulders, "taking a bite," before the five-foot surf came crashing down. Then Drake recalled moving up the tarmac at Paitilla Airfield fifteen minutes before H-hour Operation Just Cause, the U.S. invasion of Panama. His squad had been the lead element, tasked with disabling Noriega's jet: a fucked-up mission from the start. The planners had sent forty men up the center of a brightly lit runway instead of placing a sniper team on one of the high-rises overlooking the airfield as Drake and other SEALs had recommended. One exploding round from a sound-suppressed 50-caliber sniper rifle and Noriega's jet would have been history. A classic SEAL mission: maximum effect with minimum risk to the few men involved. But the planners hadn't seen it that way. So Drake and his men had moved up the runway as ordered, scanning the darkening buildings to either side with a growing sense of trepidation and doom. A hundred feet from the hangar where Noriega's jet was stored, they had been ambushed.

The Panamanians had exercised fire control, skipping rounds off the tarmac as his squad—or what was left of his squad—had fought for their lives. Four of his men had been killed and nine had been wounded. He had been wounded twice. Bleeding on the tarmac, struggling under the weight of his pack, he had directed fire at the muzzle flashes flickering inside the dark hangar. Jack had dragged him to safety.

Depth gauge in hand, Drake moved slowly aft until he encountered the fractured railing of a stairwell. Quickly locating the hollow center of the stairwell, Drake burrowed in, his tanks clanging on the steel above, the silt billowing around him. The center of the stairwell was what tactical units called the "hell hole." In building takedowns, the hell hole was a hot zone—a good place to avoid peeking into unless you wanted to get your head shot off. Now Drake was swimming through one in 210 feet of water. The experience was like crawling through a drainpipe.

He pulled himself along, the silt curling around his mask as he carefully examined the muddy space ahead for entanglements. He kept his legs motionless in case Jack crept too close behind him in the silt-blackened water.

Because the *Andrea Doria* rested on her starboard side, Drake and Henderson were moving horizontally through the wreck, pulling themselves through the narrow center of the stairwell from the promenade deck, past the upper, foyer, and the A decks, to the B deck, where the lower staircase bottomed out.

Rust flakes, dislodged by their exhaust bubbles, rained down everywhere. Reaching the end of the stairwell, Drake tied the end of his penetration line to a flattened pipe of rusted steel and headed aft, entering a region that had once contained staterooms, an area so vast, dark, and intimidating that whenever he directed his light up it seemed as though he were staring at a universe devoid of stars. Everything that hadn't been bolted to the floor had collapsed into an enormous debris field. Twisted wreckage lay scattered in heaps: bed frames, bulkheads, pipes, cables, shattered wood—and five feet away, a typewriter rusted down to the stainless-steel keys.

They crossed over the wreckage, Drake unreeling line, Henderson carefully checking its placement, making sure that the line would not become entangled in wreckage when they groped their way out in silt-blackened water.

A dark, jagged hole loomed straight ahead at the base of the debris field where a bulkhead had partially rotted away. Drake checked his air and signaled to Henderson, then carefully pulled himself through, taking care not to snag the wreckage or sever the line. Inside the room, Drake knelt beside the hole's jagged edge, the silt swirling around him, the brightness of his light vanishing in the murky water. He waited a minute longer in the darkness, beads of sweat trickling down his backbone, listening to the magnified sound of steel striking steel as Jack worked his way through the hole. Then Drake felt a bump in the darkness. He reached out and touched his friend, invisible only a foot away.

They moved aft, the beams of their powerful lights extending once more into the dark, clear water. They were inside a steel compartment twenty feet square, the walls dark orange with rust. Hovering above the wreckage, Drake tapped Henderson on the shoulder and directed a beam of light to the statue at the far end of the room.

Four feet tall, an angel with golden wings leaned against a shattered crate. Hewn of green Italian marble, the angel was intact, its delicate eyes gazing heavenward in an expression of gratitude and everlasting hope. Jack could sense the enormous power of the faith it represented, his own eyes sparkling with wonder and joy at the delicate sculpture. *So that's why we are here. We're here because the angel is irrecoverable.* He thought of his wife, Mary, and their son, Andrew. *If only you could be with me now, to see this . . .*

But that was impossible. They were too deep, too far inside a wreck that was beyond the reach of all but the most highly skilled divers in the world. Even now, hovering inside the secret room, they had only one sublime minute before the rust flakes darkened the water. Within the next few decades the angel would vanish completely, crushed by enormous plates of steel as the *Andrea Doria* slowly collapsed on the ocean floor. Already a veil of silt was swirling around them. They ignored it, lingering for as long as they could, breathing quietly as the exquisite angel faded fast, its beauty, like life itself, a fleeting moment in the course of time.

5 August

Darkness surrounded him, the clear vault of the heavens spinning as he plummeted through the sky. Thorne ignored the cold, concentrating on the lighted buildings in the distance below. The digital altimeter inside the visor of his helmet was a blur of cycling red numbers. To the right, a miniature screen displayed four green dots in proximity to one another, the position of his team free-falling through the night sky around him. They had exited the aircraft at thirty thousand feet, executing a technique called HAHO—high altitude high opening. The wind rushed past his helmet in a muted hiss. Thorne smiled at his omniscience. He was like a god soaring through the night sky, invisible to the world below.

At 29,000 feet the altimeter numbers turned green. Thorne pulled the rip cord and felt the sudden shock as the parasail filled with air, breaking his fall. The numbers slowed. Above the altimeter, a digital compass read 274 degrees. He looked up and checked the guides and foils of his parasail, then rechecked the position of his team. They were swinging on line, their parasails deployed. He banked left and swung on course, looking out at the distant lights, catching sight of one of his team gliding past him like an angel of death, the silhouette of a sound-suppressed Heckler and Koch MP5 clearly visible against the lighted base ahead.

They glided thirty miles in silence, the Naval Research Test Facility at Bristol, Maine, growing larger as they approached unseen over the Atlantic. Angling down through the warm night air, Thorne could see the target clearly now, a tall concrete structure about the size of a football field bordering the sea. Like an aircraft hangar, the facility had massive doors that stood three stories tall. The doors were shut.

Below the entrance, a flooded dry dock led out to the Atlantic. A mile from target, Thorne aligned himself with the lighted channel like a plane heading toward a runway. He glanced at the digital screen as his men took up their positions behind him, four dots forming a single line. They were headed for the lighted building, gliding down toward the doorway.

A tall chain-link fence surrounded the perimeter. They angled down to eight hundred feet, gliding over the shallows. Thorne could see waves breaking against the sand. Then the lights went out and the submarine base was engulfed in darkness.

Thorne switched to night vision and brought his MP5 up as the gigantic doors rolled apart with the lumbering grace of dinosaurs. Immediately he spotted three men inside the facility, standing transfixed or groping in the darkness. The air was warmer now, thick with humidity. The entranceway loomed before him like a cave, and he fired at a man in coveralls, then shot two technicians, reloading his MP5 as the men crumpled to the concrete. Then he sailed through the open entrance and felt the sudden chill of air-conditioning. A flashlight beam skittered across his chest and he fired in its direction as he swooped down inside the vast structure, past rows of computers and heavy machinery. He could see rounds sparking off the catwalks above as his number two cleared the high ground, just as they had rehearsed. Concentrating on his field of fire, Thorne shot another technician and two Marine guards on the main platform straight ahead while the last two members of his team fired right and left, respectively. He sailed over the miniature submarine docked below and dropped a CS canister through an open hatch. A burst of fire came from a catwalk to the left. Thorne tossed another CS grenade onto the concrete apron, then glided in for a landing, hitting the floor with a jolt. The concrete facility echoed with the screams of dying men.

Slipping out of his harness, he scanned a 180-degree arc, peering down through the center of the vast building. There was an office high up on the second story. The glass wall had been shot out and a body lay in front of a desk. Thorne raised his weapon, then spotted a Marine guard crouching beside a forklift. Thorne shot the man where he stood, the Marine guard clutching his face and screaming as he tumbled to the floor. Thorne pumped a round into the body for good measure, laying down several short bursts of covering fire as the rest of the team touched down, their parasails collapsing around them in a silken rush.

Commander Skip Jenkins sipped his coffee and stared out through the glass enclosure of his office at the Naval Research Test Facility in Bristol, Maine. He was thinking about the springer spaniel puppy that he had brought home to his two sons the day before. They had named the dog Lily because as soon as they released her in the front yard, she had wobbled over to one of his wife's prized daylilies and gripped the slender stalk between her teeth, gnawing it like a bone.

It was well past midnight and he was working late, trying to get everything in order so that he wouldn't feel guilty about taking a couple of days off. He would drive down to Cape Cod in the morning with the wife and kids. His brother lived in Chatham and had invited them to spend the weekend. The boys had insisted on bringing the dog, and one of the computer technicians had offered to lend them a cage for the drive south. He glanced at his watch, deciding to call it quits. He would log off the computer, pick up the cage at the lab, and head home. But as he began logging off, the monitor blinked. Then the lights went out.

He waited a few seconds, expecting the auxiliary generators to restore power. Nothing. Then he heard the rumbling of the facility's doors, and as he gazed out his office window down the length of the building's dark interior, he saw the shadowy figures of four men gliding through the vast opening. Black as Valkyries against the starry sky, the men sailed over the submarine *Trident* and, for a moment, Jenkins thought with growing anger that someone had arranged for a SEAL exercise without informing him. He picked up the phone, prepared to raise hell. No dial tone. Then he saw muzzle flashes, the glass enclosure shattering around him as he hit the deck, the screams of wounded and dying men filling the void.

Lying on his belly, shards of glass digging into his forearms, Jenkins cursed more in anger than in pain, wishing he were armed with an M-60 machine gun as the terrorists swooped down, killing technicians and Marine guards alike. The terrorists moved with the cohesion of a well-trained unit, landing with efficient grace on the concrete apron that overlooked the *Trident's* berth. They moved quickly down the gangway, two men climbing down the main hatch of the submarine while another freed the lines as the lead terrorist picked off resistance. Jenkins squinted in the darkness, tear gas searing his eyes, already sensing from his unique vantage point that he would become the chief witness to a terrorist act that would set the world on the brink of nuclear war. Then the lead terrorist brought his weapon up and Jenkins squeezed his eyes shut. But the rounds went elsewhere.

He could hear engine noise. Motionless on the office floor, he opened his eyes a crack and looked down again as the *Trident* began to back out of her mooring, the remaining terrorists hopping aboard and disappearing down the conning tower hatch. The *Trident* descended several feet and entered the flooded dry dock, open now to the sea. And a moment later, the most highly classified submarine in the U.S. fleet slipped beneath the dark Atlantic and was gone.

6 August

Summoned to the Oval Office by the president of the United States, CIA Director Charles Francis Adams strode through the West Wing with a singleness of purpose that belied his seventy-three years. His right leg ached, an old war wound from his days of jumping out of Lancasters into Nazi-occupied France. If he had remained at Harvard teaching law, he'd still be in bed, reading the *New York Times* and anticipating the sunrise. But like his mentor, Wild Bill Donovan, Adams had divided his career between law and government service. Passing the Roosevelt Room, he glanced at his watch. It was 5 A.M.

He greeted the two Secret Service agents stationed outside the Oval Office and entered the inner sanctum. McKendrick and Elliot were seated on the two white couches flanking the fireplace. Standing in the middle of the room, National Security Advisor Bud McGuire and Chief of Naval Operations David Archer chatted in hushed tones. An unsmiling President Thomas Young glanced up at Adams and nodded as he stood at his desk, concluding a telephone conversation. Through the thick windows behind the president's high-backed bulletproof chair, Adams could make out the colorful blossoms of the Rose Garden.

McKendrick took Adams aside and quickly filled him in on the latest from Bristol. As far as McKendrick was concerned, Adams belonged right up there in the pantheon with his illustrious forebears. A direct descendant of two American presidents, John Adams and John Quincy Adams, and the great-grandnephew of Henry Adams, one of America's finest historians, Adams had not only served in the OSS, he had also become a law professor at Harvard and a foremost authority on constitutional law in the United States. Only a year before, as director of Central Intelligence, Adams had guided the United States through the severest test of its Constitution, a crisis that had led to the resignation of President Jefferson Marshall.

Adams took a seat and poured himself a cup of coffee from the silver service. President Young crossed the Oval Office and pulled up an armchair, his features haggard and grim. McGuire and Archer did the same. It seemed to Adams that the men had aged a decade overnight.

"Eighteen Americans dead, murdered in cold blood. Thirty wounded," the president remarked in a tone of rueful anger. "Walt, where do we stand?"

McKendrick leaned forward, his back straight, gazing directly into the president's eyes. "Sir, an FBI forensic team is flying up to Bristol now. DIA ought to be arriving as we speak. Whoever the perpetrators are, they're professionals. The lights went out and the auxiliary generators failed to operate, yet the facility's doors opened. These people may have penetrated the Navy's computer network. The base commander saw the whole thing go down from his office. The man's lucky to be alive."

"What about the *Trident?*" the president asked.

Admiral Archer fielded the question. "The *Trident* is designed to sneak into harbors undetected. We use her to tap phone lines. She's fast, quiet, sonar-proof, and virtually undetectable. We were about to deploy her to North Korea."

"You're saying the *Trident's* lost?" the president asked.

"In a nutshell—yes," Admiral Archer explained. "Unless these people decide to surface. They may have no other choice. The *Trident's* not an easy vessel to operate. These terrorists obviously know enough about running a nuclear-powered submarine to get her under way. The question is, Do they know enough to keep her operational?"

Secretary of Defense Richard Elliot set his coffee cup on the table. "How long can she stay submerged?"

"With her nuclear reactor—indefinitely. She can go pretty much wherever she pleases—provided, of course, that she is adequately provisioned. Food, not fuel, is the limiting factor here. Unfortunately, we had her up at Bristol for just that reason—for resupply. She's been ready to deploy for a week."

President Young pressed his lips together, staring up at the Remington bronze gracing the mantelpiece.

Bud McGuire cast a significant look at the men around him. "Mr. President, perhaps we should consider retasking our reconnaissance satellites. We don't know if these terrorists are foreign or domestic, but if we don't recover the *Trident* soon, this situation is going to magnify and we're going to get blindsided. Who knows what these people are up to? Full coverage of the Atlantic could give us an early edge."

The president nodded in agreement. "Charles?"

"Consider it done, Mr. President."

"Good. Walt, David, I want your people ready to go the minute we spot that submarine. SEALs, Delta—whatever it takes."

"Yes, sir," the two men answered in unison.

A woman's voice came over the intercom: "Mr. President?"

Thomas Young looked at the group and crossed the room, pressing a button on his desk console. "Yes?"

"Sir, I have the telephone numbers you asked for—the families of the men who were killed."

The president looked up, contemplating the grim task before him. "Gentlemen, this meeting is adjourned."

"Daddy!"

Still in his pajamas, Andrew Henderson rushed down the front steps of Drake's farmhouse in Greenwich, Connecticut, and straight into his father's arms. Smiling broadly, Jack lifted the boy high in the air, then held him close. Gazing at the stone house, Drake could see Jennifer and Mary Henderson crossing in front of the bay window in the dining room as they rushed to the front door.

Andrew looked excitedly at the dive gear filling the back of Drake's Explorer. "Daddy, did you bring me anything?" Locked in each other's arms, they were in a world of their own. Jack carried his son over to the trunk, popped open the rear window, reached deep into the open pocket of a gear bag, and withdrew a chambered nautilus. The shell was creamy, spiral-shaped, and encrusted with salt.

The boy gazed at the shell in wonder.

Drake lifted a set of scuba tanks out of the trunk. "Your dad found that at the bottom of the sea."

"Dad, when are you going to take me diving?"

"As soon as you learn how to swim," Jack answered.

"Next year?"

Jack smiled at Drake as he lowered his four-year-old son to the ground. "Maybe."

"Hey, Mom! Dad's going to take me diving next year!"

"Honey—"

Mary Henderson turned to Jennifer, laughing as she picked Andrew up, her wheat-colored hair matching her son's. "The man who can't say no."

Jack wrapped his arms around his family and Drake did the same with Jennifer, closing his eyes, smelling the jasmine in her hair, feeling the earth sway beneath his feet, his body still acclimated to the sea. He kissed her on the mouth. He was glad to be home.

"You need a shower," she said, holding him close.

"So do you."

They were sitting at the kitchen table, enjoying each other's company, ignoring the breakfast dishes spread before them. It was almost noon. Drake and Henderson had unloaded the Explorer and had cleaned their gear while Andrew ran around the yard with the hose, spraying everything in sight, including his black cocker spaniel, Becky. Jennifer and Mary had watched from the porch. The cocker had leaped at the sparkling water, the mist casting a rainbow around boy and dog as the sun edged above the trees.

Now as he sat at the breakfast table, glancing at Andrew cutting out a pair of scuba tanks that Jack had drawn on a poster board, Drake looked at his wife and friends and thought about how much his life had changed for the better since his days of guiding and living in self-imposed exile following the ill-fated assault on Paitilla Airfield.

They had met and fallen in love aboard the *Avatar* during Operation Torchlight the previous year. Jennifer was the adopted daughter of international arms dealer Erich Wilhelm Gerhardt, whom the CIA had been after for years. Turning his luxurious yacht, *Avatar,* into a salvage platform in an attempt to raise a billion dollars of gold from the USS *Norfolk,* an armored cruiser torpedoed off the Rhode Island coast during World War I, Gerhardt had planned to use the gold as a means to finance a tactical nuclear weapons deal between Saddam Hussein and a band of renegade Russians. Once Jennifer discovered the true nature of her father's business, she had contacted the CIA, who sent Henderson to infiltrate the salvage operation. But the *Norfolk* had been even more dangerous to explore than Jack had expected. Needing a diver who was adept at exploring deep-water shipwrecks, Jack had tracked down Drake in Bimini. So Jack was responsible for their meeting. They hadn't liked each other at first. Now as he sat in the kitchen watching Jennifer chat with Mary about Andrew's school, he couldn't imagine living without her. Her chestnut hair, now damp, fell to her shoulders. Earlier that morning, while Mary and Jack had prepared breakfast for Andrew, he had made love to her in the shower as the warm water sprinkled down on their faces like rain.

Jack held up the pair of cardboard scuba tanks that his son had handed him. "These look great!"

"Thanks, Dad."

"Phil, remember the time we went skiing in Tahoe?"

"You mean the time we blew all our money gambling?"

Jennifer and Mary laughed.

"Sad but true," Jack explained. "We walked into Harrah's with five hundred dollars and an hour later walked out with barely enough gas money for the trip home. And we didn't even get a free drink!"

Jennifer looked at Jack in mock reproval. "A very wise decision on the part of the management, I'm sure."

"Yeah, well, we could have used it at the time. We had driven all the way up to Tahoe to go skiing and wound up flat broke."

"Is that when you guys decided to take up diving?" Mary teased.

"We drove up to the Desolation Wilderness area instead. We had our cross-country skis in the back of the truck. It was snowing. So we parked on the side of the road and headed into the backcountry. In three hours we had skied to a terraced slope overlooking Emerald Bay. At the end of the slope, a cliff dropped off about five hundred feet. The bay was turquoise around the shallows and cobalt farther out. All around the lake, snow was stacked up on the branches of the pines. The peaks of the Sierra Nevadas were rocky and glazed with ice. Remember the avalanches, Phil? We could hear them echoing across the basin. They exploded like sonic booms; we could see the snow tumbling down the chutes, sweeping away the pines."

Drake sipped his orange juice, savoring the memory. They had skied for hours, the snow up to their knees. At night, exhausted, they had headed back to the truck using a topographical map and a compass to keep themselves from skiing over a cliff.

"We should do that again," Jack suggested. "See if we can't get out there next spring—all of us."

"Avalanches?" Mary inquired with raised eyebrows. "You're not getting me out there." She looked at her son. "Or Andrew." Then she said, "Do you think the angel was early Renaissance?"

The phone rang. Jennifer wandered over to the counter and picked it up. Drake could hear her answer "yes" a couple of times. Then she was gazing at him, concerned. Their eyes met. "Phil, it's for you."

"The *Trident* is approaching, sir."

Geoffrey Clayton turned from the bank of computers that filled his underground command center and peered down through the glass enclosure to the rocky subterranean pool that dominated the cavern. Under the halogen lights, the clear water appeared as crystalline as a block of ice.

The pool formed the culmination of an elaborate underwater cave system stretching a half mile to the Atlantic, the primary reason Clayton had selected the finger-shaped island on the northern coast of Maine for his base of operations. The other reason he had selected the site was the island's remote location. Capped by a granite bluff amid a forest of dense pine and surrounded on three sides by a mile of shallow boulder-strewn water, the island was inaccessible to all but a handful of chopper pilots who transported equipment and supplies to the remote facility twice each week. In addition to the vast array of state-of-the-art computer equipment, the underground complex housed luxurious living quarters, including a theater, bar, gymnasium, swimming pool, and library. By special arrangement with a Park Avenue agency, Clayton also provided his men with a steady supply of the most beautiful women in the world, making sure that they had little reason to venture forth to seek the varied comforts of civilized society. In those rare cases when a man did stray, he quickly vanished from the earth—thanks to Thorne, whom Clayton sent to hunt him down.

But Clayton could take such minor difficulties in stride. His men were specialists, graduates of the top technical schools or products of the most highly touted special-operations units in the United States. They were the elite, and like himself, they deserved the perquisites that all too often accrued to the scum of society: the lawyers, bankers, and congressmen who had gleefully expedited his downfall.

Five years earlier he had been a rising star in the defense industry. His picture had appeared on the cover of *Forbes,* his accomplishments had been lauded in *Fortune,* and his opinions had appeared on the editorial pages of the *Wall Street Journal.* Having built Clayton Industries from the ground up, he had been on the inside track for the Defense Department's billion-dollar top-secret laser research project, code-named Bright Star. He knew how the game was played and he had played it well, creating over fifty political-action committees, making sure that money got to the men who could make a difference. In Congress, money not only opened doors, it also brought power and influence, and he marveled at what it could accomplish. In 1996, he had watched in amazement as the Senate delayed its adjournment for two full days to grant a regulatory exemption to a large corporation in the express-delivery business. That the beneficiary ran one of the top five corporate PACs in the nation was a lesson in financial efficacy that Clayton took to heart. Within a year, he was a frequent guest in the dark warren of new Senate hideaways that populated the upper floors of the Russell Building, an area that in previous years had housed a library. He had entered the inner sanctum and had talked turkey, noting the abundant custom-made, silk-covered chairs that the leadership had ordered for themselves at $20,000 a pop, courtesy of the U.S. taxpayer.

Not that it had bothered Clayton any. Every time he had strolled up to the Hill to schmooze with a committee chairman, he could envision the FOR SALE sign hanging on the Capitol door. In seeking influence, he had leveraged Clayton Industries to the hilt, but it hadn't mattered—the twenty-billion-dollar research project had been in the bag. Pressure had been applied to men who awarded contracts. Chits had been called in. Appropriations had been pushed through. Then the bottom had dropped out.

The saga of President Jefferson Marshall's demise had reverberated throughout the nation, but no more so than within the corridors of Clayton Industries. The president of the United States had resigned in disgrace, implicated in a diversion and cover-up that had spiraled out of control. The president's national security advisor, Martin Vaughan, was now serving two consecutive life terms at the federal penitentiary at Marion, Illinois. Vaughan had been Clayton's chief advocate within the Marshall administration. Clayton had spent a fortune keeping Vaughan happy, even going so far as to rent a villa on the Chesapeake for a party billed as the social event of the year. The former national security advisor had enjoyed himself immensely, bedding the gorgeous wife of a real estate tycoon.

Overnight, the stench arising from Clayton's close association with Vaughan had transformed Clayton from golden boy to outcast. Desperate, Clayton had redoubled his efforts, hiring the most expensive lobbying firm in Washington, but to no avail. All the money in the world couldn't rehabilitate Clayton's reputation, and the senators and congressmen who had once been his closest friends and advisors now made a point of distancing themselves at every opportunity, awarding the coveted laser research contract to Systems Technologies, an up-and-coming firm and Clayton's main competitor.

By then loans were coming due. And the big New York banks, having squandered millions in bad loans to the Third World, were in no mood to renegotiate. Faced with bankruptcy, and desperate to save his corporation, Clayton had contacted a friend in the import business.

He recalled with acute embarrassment and shame the day the FBI had broken down the door to the room he had rented at the Crazy 8 Motel. He had inadvertently wandered into the largest sting operation in U.S. history, and the hundred kilos of pure cocaine he was selling in a desperate attempt to refinance his corporation soon became Exhibit A in the most publicized criminal trial of the year. He had lost everything: his friends, his house, his corporation, his pride. He had spent three years pulling crab grass and scrubbing toilets while his wife did the horizontal bop with the next-door neighbor.

Now primed for revenge, Clayton watched with rapt attention as three commandos moved out onto the dock. The clear water began to shimmer, the fine tremors sparkling under the lights. Gazing down through the clear depths, he could see a miniature submarine, dark as a sorcerer's tongue, emerging from the mouth of the cave. Then the water began to tremble violently as the submarine broke to the surface, saltwater cascading off her decks in a boiling rush. Poised on the surface, her black hull gleaming under the lights, the *Trident* looked as deadly as a bayonet. The conning tower was painted red, the color of fire streaking from the midnight sky.

This looks like a safe spot. Julia walked inside the Rite Aid pharmacy in downtown Titusville at 9:00 A.M., heading toward the pay phone. The air-conditioning felt wonderful against the Florida heat. As she walked down the center aisle, past the deodorant and toothpaste displays, she noticed a well-groomed young man of college age glancing furtively at the multitude of wrapped condoms that hung from the revolving rack like ornaments on a Christmas tree. The youth looked up at Julia and blushed. The bashful girlfriend hovered a short distance away.

Stiff with tension, she slipped a quarter into the pay phone and dialed a number. A man's voice came on the line.

"For a moment I thought you had forsaken us," Clayton said with wry amusement. "How's the project coming?"

"We're set to launch."

"When?"

"August tenth."

"That's my girl," Clayton chimed by way of congratulations. She quietly hung up the phone and headed outdoors. The traffic sprang in the heat.

8 August

The sun edged up over the horizon, warming the leathery backs of the alligators milling about the brackish ponds of the Kennedy Space Center. Gerry Elkins gazed up at the mammoth Vehicle Assembly Building, his brain awash in dreams of dusky women and Caribbean isles. A senior computer technician with a sagging belly and a balding pate, Elkins was getting to work early, a dismal prelaunch routine that he had resented for years. Now as he crossed the vast parking lot, his mood brightened with each buoyant step.

He entered the mountainous building and headed for the low bay area where the orbiter was housed. The polished concrete floor gleamed under the floodlights, the only place in the world where you could flick a marble from one corner of the building and watch it roll thousands of feet to the other side. Soaring 525 feet into the Florida sky and enveloping eight acres of Merritt Island along the Banana River, the Vehicle Assembly Building—VAB, for short—was the size of four Empire State Buildings. Within its vast interior, the separate components of the space shuttle—the orbiter, the external tank, and the twin solid rocket boosters—would be mated by two gigantic bridge cranes capable of lifting 250 tons each. Within a week the assembled components known as the space shuttle would lie in a vertical position atop the mobile launch platform. From the VAB, the space shuttle would be rolled out to Launch Pad 39A and prepared for liftoff.

Inside the low bay area, a complex series of mobile work platforms enveloped the orbiter *Atlantis* like a cocoon. Through the maze of yellow scaffolding, Elkins could see a technician peering into one of the orbiter's funnel-shaped main combustion chambers.

Elkins slipped inside an office, changed into his work clothes, and gripping the soft nylon briefcase that held his laptop computer, mounted the metal staircase that led to the crew compartment hatch on the left side of *Atlantis*. As he looked up at the orbiter's tiled surface, he could hear the whine of a power screwdriver in the distance and the muted conversation of two men on the upper platform. They were discussing avionics. The VAB was air-conditioned, and in his light technician's outfit, Elkins felt his perspiration cool against his skin.

As he reached the upper platform, one of the avionics teks looked at him with a jocular smile and said, "A hundred bucks says that the Dolphins go all the way this year."

The other man nodded thoughtfully and looked at Elkins: "I'd take that bet."

Elkins couldn't have cared less. "Two hundred and it's a deal."

The two men glanced at each other, momentarily startled. Then the first man laughed. "You want it, you got it. Shit. Since when did *you* become such a big spender?"

Elkins slapped the man good-naturedly on the shoulder and said in a winning tone, "I'm not planning to spend a dime."

The circular hatch leading to the mid-deck was open and Elkins crawled through, the agreeable odor of new plastic filling his nostrils. The interior of the *Atlantis* was spotlessly clean and brightly lit. Across the small compartment lay a stack of three bunks, and to his immediate right stood the waste-management compartment—the toilet. The obiter's five general-purpose computers and one backup flight system were also distributed throughout the mid-deck area. It was Elkins's responsibility to see that the multiple redundant computer system ran without a hitch. So without delay, he removed his laptop from its case, and dreaming of the new life that awaited him, began a series of final diagnostic checks, downloading the program until the damage was done.

"I'll have the Beef Wellington, please."

"Sir?"

Julia looked up at Lawrence as if to say: Is he always like this?

McKendrick was having fun. "Sorry, kid. Two cheeseburgers, fries, and a Coke. And supersize it!"

McDonald's was busy that Friday afternoon. Outside, in the shimmering Florida heat, a pretty blonde in a tank top cussed out a truck driver for stealing her parking space. Inside, customers homed in on the excitement.

"Betcha five bucks the guy moves his truck," Lawrence quipped. "Look, there he goes!"

McKendrick had arrived at the Kennedy Space Center the previous morning to meet with a comptroller over some funding problems: a dry duty that he nearly postponed, given the *Trident* emergency. But there was little he could do in Washington at this stage of the investigation. Reconnaissance satellites were scouring the Atlantic in case the terrorists mishandled the *Trident* and were forced to surface. The Navy was on full alert, ready to pounce. The National Security Agency was intercepting military and government communications from a host of suspect nations and allied terror groups. Eventually something would turn up. The only question was when.

In the meantime, the Bright Star project was coming to a head. For the past three weeks Julia and Lawrence had been working diligently inside the Defense Department's classified facility at the Kennedy Space Center, where the laser satellite had been fitted to the booster that would propel it from the orbiter's cargo bay into high orbit, out into the 34,000-mile geosynchronous range away from the prying eyes of foreign reconnaissance satellites. McKendrick had stopped by the facility after his meeting just as Julia and Lawrence were heading out to lunch. The Florida humidity, reminiscent of Vietnam, was drenching. Within minutes, his uniform clung to his body like a wet sleeping bag. Moving quickly from one air-conditioned building to another, McKendrick felt as though he were crossing a stream, hopping from stone to stone. The Florida shuffle.

They sat near a window. Across from them, a high-school couple dressed in shorts and T-shirts grooved to a Stevie Wonder tune blaring from a boom box.

Lawrence was enjoying the music, nostalgic. He took a bite of his Big Mac, bobbing his head in pleasure as Stevie Wonder wailed on the harmonica. "Man, it doesn't get any better than this!"

Lawrence was in his element. McKendrick glanced at the people eating lunch around them: high-school kids; young mothers with children; businessmen on the fly—not one of these people would have guessed that the amiable, boyish, and casually dressed black man across from him had donated close to a billion dollars to the CEL Foundation and other charitable causes.

McKendrick glanced out the window at the thermals shimmering off the blacktop. "I don't know if I could live here. In the winter the weather's great, but this—"

"I grew up here," said Julia.

"You're kidding."

"Miami Beach."

"Do you come here often?"

"Twice a year. I've become fond of Michigan; the change of seasons, especially. Florida's a nice place to visit, though. My father lives in Key West. That's what brings me back."

"Do you dive?"

"I did when I was a teenager. Comes with a Florida upbringing. Why?"

"That means you're certified."

"Certifiable, maybe," Lawrence interjected with a grin.

Julia made a face. "My boss, the comedian."

"Would you like to dive the *Nuestra Señora?*" McKendrick asked with as much nonchalance as he could muster. Truth was, he was as nervous as a school boy.

"When? *Today?*"

"Tomorrow. I'm serious. You, too, Billy."

"No thanks, man. No C-card. Besides, I prefer to take my chances above water. A Spanish galleon, huh?"

"A *capitana.* Similar to a galleon, but smaller. Galleons were top-heavy and difficult to sail. By the early 1700s the Spanish had taken them out of service."

Lawrence turned to Julia. "Wow. You've won a free trip, lady!"

McKendrick laughed. "Only if you accept the offer. And it's a good one. A lot of history behind that ship. The *Nuestra Señora de la Regla* was the flagship of General Juan Esteban de Ubilla, a commander of the treasure fleet of eleven ships that sailed from Havana on July 24, 1715. She was carrying the bulk of the treasure that the fleet was transporting to Spain."

"Ill-gotten gains . . ." Lawrence observed.

"Undeniably. The conquest of another people is never a pretty sight. The treasure, the gold, silver, and gems—all the stuff that holds us in thrall—cannot be valued in dollars or pesos merely. You have to look at the other dimensions these artifacts contain . . . the history, the bloodshed. . . ."

Julia looked at him intently.

McKendrick glanced to the right as the couple across from them finished their burgers, still bopping to the Stevie Wonder tune. "Six days after the 1715 fleet set sail from Havana, a hurricane struck. Ten ships were swept to their destruction against the jagged reefs just a few miles south of here. Seven hundred souls and over fourteen million pesos in gold, silver, and jewels were lost. Only a handful of people survived. The Spanish salvaged what treasure they could. Pirates got some. It wasn't until the early sixties that the wrecks were rediscovered—most lying in water less than thirty feet deep, only a stone's throw from shore. For years people had been walking those beaches after a storm and finding Spanish coins washed ashore. A couple of enterprising fellows from NASA did some research, then ventured out to see what they could find beneath the sand. That's how the Florida treasure boom got started. You may have read about it in *National Geographic.* What they did not find, however, was the treasure from Ubilla's flagship. During the storm, the entire bottom of the *Nuestra* let go, spilling treasure miles from where she finally broke up on the reefs.

The treasure was discovered only a couple of months ago. A local fisherman snagged his line and, instead of breaking it off, decided to free it. What he found in sixty feet of water was silver bullion stacked like cordwood six feet high, covered with fishing nets. A friend arranged for me to take an underwater tour of the site." He looked straight at Julia. "It's a great opportunity. History right at your fingertips. I couldn't pass it up. Neither should you."

"It does sound exciting."

"Come on. I'll take you to dinner afterward."

"Are you asking me on a date?"

"Yes," McKendrick said evenly, a smile breaking across his face. "I am."

9 August

The wind was kicking up the ocean to a nasty four-foot chop as the *Voyager* cruised out of Fort Pierce beneath a sweltering midday sun. Seated inside the *Voyager's* spartan wheelhouse, Julia and McKendrick chatted with their host, marine archaeologist David Sanders.

"You're getting out here just in time," Sanders shouted over the engine noise. Sporting a handlebar mustache and the stooped shoulders of the perennial academic, Sanders looked more like a poet than a diver. "We're just about finished mapping the site," he explained. "Everything is still down there the way we found it. There're over a hundred artifacts, including the stack of silver bullion and fingerbars of gold. We found a lot of stuff not listed on the manifest."

"Sloppy bookkeeping?" Julia asked.

Sanders shook his head. "Contraband. The Spanish crown levied a twenty percent tax on gold and silver; if you got caught cheating, you spent the next ten years of your life rowing on a Spanish galley. Not exactly the way to enjoy your retirement. You'll see the royal tax seal stamped on some of the gold bars. Hey, are you okay?"

Suddenly pale, Julia swallowed hard a couple of times and stared across the cabin. "Touch of seasickness. I go years without even a trace of a symptom, then out of the blue it strikes. Ever since I was a little girl. I never get sick, though. Just a twinge of nausea. Then it disappears. I'm fine, really."

"You sure?" McKendrick asked.

With a reassuring smile, she patted him on the shoulder. "Walt, I'm so glad we're doing this," she said brightly.

McKendrick nodded with concern.

"How do you know Drake?" Sanders asked. Through the windshield they could see a large Grady White tied to a buoy.

"His father and I were roommates at West Point," McKendrick said, not caring to elaborate. His emotions were still too raw, his memories of the day Drake's father died too vivid for him to want to get into it more than that.

"Is he the friend who arranged the tour?" Julia asked, slipping on a pair of Ray-Bans. She swiveled in the padded chair to face him.

McKendrick reached for the forward edge of the open skylight to steady himself as the *Voyager* bucked against the waves. Sunlight poured through the windows beneath a china blue sky. "He's the one. Great diver. Ex-SEAL. Used to run a charter diving operation out of Bimini—Blue Water Adventures."

"I've heard of it. Is he still in the dive business?"

"Got married, last year. Lives in Greenwich, Connecticut, these days."

"He must have done well."

McKendrick chuckled. "He did—his wife's one of the nicest people you ever want to meet. Smart, like you. Her father was the arms dealer involved in the Marshall scandal."

"That's the Drake you're talking about, the ex–Navy SEAL who recovered the gold?"

"That's the one."

"I'm impressed."

McKendrick peered out the windshield, wondering how Drake and Henderson were doing in Bristol. He had brought a SAT COM on board; he would phone the Pentagon after the dive. "What about you? Were you living in Michigan before you started at Systems Technologies?"

"I was teaching at MIT." She paused for a moment, then smiled, her natural ebullience lighting up her features as though she were back at the cocktail party the day they had unveiled Bright Star. "I bought a sailboat the day Billy hired me—a Meadow Lark, A kind of celebration gift, if you will. Have you ever seen one?"

"I don't think so," McKendrick said, noting with happiness the pleasure she took in describing the event.

"They look like catamarans. The wonderful thing about them is that they have a draft of only fifteen inches, a remarkable feature in a thirty-three-foot sailboat. You can sail them anywhere. They have oil lamps instead of electricity and a huge cabin that has a bowed roof. In the summer I sail in my spare time. Last summer I took a group of my college friends to Isle Royale. It's lovely there. Completely wild."

McKendrick looked at her, captivated. He was thinking that he would have to wrangle an invitation from Drake. Julia would love the *Lady Ann,* the schooner that Drake had restored during his years in Bimini.

Then she said, "There's a touch of the wanderer in us all, don't you think?"

The water was as clear as the Florida sky and nearly as warm. Even through the surface chop, McKendrick could see divers hovering near the sandy bottom. He helped Julia with her tank as she slipped her arms through the buoyancy compensator, the inflatable vest that divers wear to keep themselves neutrally buoyant so that they can hover in the water, a condition very much like weightlessness. With a trace of self-consciousness she had slipped out of her khaki shorts and white button-down shirt to a black nylon tank suit, revealing a supple fullness of breasts and hips that McKendrick did his level best to ignore for fear of "popping a rod," as his school chums had called it during his teenage years. Nevertheless, the sight of Julia's body had made him as giddy as a kid on Christmas morning.

"OK, folks," Sanders lectured as they sat on the starboard gunwale in their diving gear. "You're on your own, so be careful and dive safely."

McKendrick looked at Julia, not quite believing that at the age of fifty-five he was about to jump into the water with a beautiful brunette. They wore standard recreational dive gear: single tanks and wetsuits. Julia's excitement was palpable. She looked at him in gratitude. "This is really great, Walt. I can't wait to see what's down there."

They tumbled backward into the blue water, momentarily dazzled by the evanescent folds of white bubbles shimmering around them. The water cleared, and directly below they could see small white ridges of sand. The bottom of the ocean resembled a washboard. Then, looking to their right they saw the grid, a hundred feet square and raised two feet over the sand. Constructed of narrow gauge plastic piping, the grid reminded McKendrick of a *Goban,* the board of nineteen intersecting lines used to play Go, the world's oldest and most difficult game of strategy. Six divers were spread out across the grid. A diver using a small handheld blower and partially obscured by a cloud of silt looked up, spotted them, and waved. McKendrick could see piles of ballast stones and sections of the *Nuestra's* planked hull that had lain beneath the ballast, protected for centuries, all other traces of wood having disappeared into the flux of time and the elements. To the right, a cannon crossed a grid like a hash mark, and beside it a gold disk the size of a Frisbee glimmered under a light dusting of sand. But the dominant spectacle by far was the tarnished stack of silver bullion. Strewn with fishing nets that rose below them like buildings of an ancient city, the bullion beckoned them as though harboring the spirits of the dead. Over the grid, bars of sunlight penetrated the clear blue depths, angled and as bright as lasers. Glints of gold ignited the ocean floor.

Enthralled, they descended.

To Julia it seemed as though they were descending to the ruins of Byzantium, this ship pounded apart by a hurricane. She touched McKendrick on the arm, and together they swam over the grid, gazing at uncut emeralds the size of thimbles, elaborate money chains of twisted gold, blackened pieces of eight welded together in the shape of the sacks that had carried them, silver patens and chalices lined in gold for the bread and wine of the Eucharist, and—Julia's favorite—a gold scallop-shaped locket that opened to thirteen tiny gold stars set in blue enamel. Near the cannon an oval silver box held egg-shaped bezoar stones, the organic concretions formed in the stomachs of goats and llamas that alchemists believed would absorb arsenic, death by poisoning having been a preferred method of surreptitious murder in the days of the Spanish Empire. Then there were the many emerald rings marking the final resting places of the dead.

Following the laminated chart that Sanders had given them, McKendrick and Julia swam from square to square as schools of bonita and pompano cruised overhead. There was too much to take in, yet they wanted to see it all—the experience akin to stepping inside the British Museum for the first time. They felt overwhelmed. Toward the end of their dive McKendrick stopped to watch Julia hovering close to a rosary, a silvery plume of bubbles rising above her head. He longed to take her hand as she gazed at the coral beads and crucifix; he longed to follow her thoughts as she leaped across the rough stones of memory.

They swam to the stack of silver bullion, a reef in microcosm, strewn with fishing nets and coral while hundreds of feeding grunts and porkfish gathered about. People had been fishing these banks for centuries, mistaking the stack of silver for a rock. McKendrick wondered how many nets had rotted away over the years, vanished like the thoughts of the men and women who had created them and the stack of silver they concealed. Like the gold fingerbars, the silver bore markings as well: tax stamps, shippers' marks, and roman numerals denoting the fineness of the metal. Then before they knew it, their time was up. McKendrick tapped Julia on the shoulder and pointed to the white hull of the *Voyager* bobbing on the surface. They angled up through the clear water, taking their time, enjoying themselves, rising no faster than their slowest bubbles. After a two-minute safety stop they broke through to the surface, the sun warming their faces. McKendrick climbed aboard the *Voyager* first, then helped Julia up the ladder, the corners of her eyes wrinkling with delight as she said, "Did you see the locket, the one with the stars inside?"

McKendrick recited a few lines of poetry:

> *Give me my Scallop shell of quiet,*
> *My staff of faith to walke upon,*
> *My scrip of Joy, Immortall diet,*
> *My bottle of salvation:*
> *My Gowne of Glory, hopes true gage,*
> *And thus Ile take my pilgrimage.*

"That's lovely," Julia said. "Who wrote that?"

"Sir Walter Raleigh. He detested the Spanish."

Julia regarded him with an appreciative look. Then she looked out at the strip of sand lining the Florida coast. "I can almost see them—the survivors, huddling together on that strip of sand against the wind and rain."

DIA agent Dick Jackson gave them a tour as the FBI forensic team huddled over the bloodstained concrete. "The lights went out, the doors opened, and the bastards glided in, shooting everyone in sight," Johnson explained, disgusted.

Drake and Henderson gazed out at the gray Atlantic. Four Boston Whalers, equipped with side-scan sonar and GPS receivers, were slowly cruising back and forth, performing a search pattern, looking for any paraphernalia that the terrorists might have dropped on the way in. Drake could see divers on the stern of each boat. "No possibility that they had help from the inside?" Henderson asked.

Johnson scratched his gray beard stubble and looked at the two men standing before him inside the facility. He had never met Drake and Henderson before, but he knew them by reputation as the ex-SEALs who had recovered the gold from the *Norfolk*, uncovering a scandal that had led to the downfall of an American president. Though their quiet and watchful manner suggested equanimity, Drake and Henderson were relentless, and Johnson wondered if the terrorists had any idea what kind of trouble was headed their way. After interviewing the wounded, some of whom would never walk again, he longed to be in on the action himself. He looked at Henderson with respect and shook his head.

"Not during the raid. Too many things happened at once, too many people would have been involved. The doors, the lights, and the dry-dock gates are controlled by separate computers. The only way to override those systems is through a series of passwords that have to be logged into the computer in Jenkins's office. And at the time that the attack went down, Jenkins was on the SIPR-NET—the secret Internet protocol network—talking to a guy in Guam. We figure the intruder slipped in that way. How he managed to do this, we don't know. He's good, that's for sure. So were the shooters." He reached down and pointed to three chips at the base of a concrete wall. Drake saw that the chips were tightly grouped. "One of the few times they missed."

Drake recalled McKendrick's instructions two days before: "You and Jack go up there, take a look at how the terrorists carried out the attack, and tell me what kind of training these people had and where they may have gotten it. Are their techniques identical to ours? Or do they suggest foreign involvement? I want your gut reactions."

Drake looked out at the boats again, then at Jackson. "What kind of bottom do they have out there? Sand or mud?"

"Sand, I think," Jackson said.

"Has the dry dock been checked?"

"Not yet. Normally we could shut the gates and drain it, but the computer that controls the gate got shot to shit. Same with Jenkins's computer. Those computers are off-limits anyway; the folks at the National Security Agency want to pull them apart— electronically. We strung a net across the opening to keep any evidence from washing away in the tide. We want to cover the deep water first before anything that might be out there gets covered with sand. Saves time in the long run. We've got the dry dock scheduled for tomorrow morning."

Drake was thinking. Then he said, "Between the time the doors opened and the time the terrorists sailed inside the building, they were firing their weapons, right?"

"The point man was. Jenkins wasn't sure about the others."

Henderson looked out at the flooded dry dock, then back at Drake. "I'll get the gear."

Jackson looked momentarily startled. "You guys on to something?" he asked.

They were skimming along the smooth surface of the dry-dock floor in a hundred feet of water, moving past giant intake pipes and other steel structures as they followed the lines they had strung like guitar strings along the length of the pool three hours before. The water was cold, dark, and tranquil. Sweeping their lights back and forth, they carefully searched the concrete, moving in tandem, Drake on one line, Henderson on the other. After swimming the length of the dry dock along one set of lines, they moved to the next set of lines and repeated the process, continuing their search. Eventually they would cover every square inch of the concrete floor.

It was tedious work, but if Drake's hunch proved correct, they were bound to hit pay dirt. In conducting a search-and-recovery pattern, it helps to know what you're looking for, and Drake and Henderson had a damn good idea of what they expected to find. As the lead terrorist had glided toward the open facility, he had been firing his weapon, according to Jenkins, killing people and keeping heads down. Then he had stopped, preparing to land. The second he touched down, he would be exposed and vulnerable. Not the time to be standing there with a half-empty weapon. If the terrorist knew what he was doing, he would have slapped a fresh magazine into the receiver just before he landed, ensuring maximum firepower at the moment of maximum exposure, even if he still had rounds left in the original magazine. His number two would provide cover, but the point man would want to have a fully loaded weapon at the ready. Which meant that somewhere at the bottom of the dry dock lay an empty or a partially empty magazine.

They searched for a half hour and found nothing. In the dark stillness of the water Drake felt as though he were searching a flooded basement, the unfamiliar stanchions and retracted scaffolding providing an aura of disturbing incompleteness, as though he were trying to decipher a soul by the possessions it had cast away.

Swimming along the middle set of lines, they continued to

sweep their lights across the concrete floor. They came to the net blocking the passage to the open sea and checked its base, running their gloved fingers through the furrow of sand that the tide had deposited along the net's bottom edge. Drake could feel the gentle pull of running water and hugged the floor so as not to become entangled in the net as the tide receded. The flow of water was nearly imperceptible, but even a whisper of tide could draw him forward, a lesson he learned years before when he had drifted into a net draped over the pool verandah windows of the *Andrea Doria*. One second he had been checking his air in the darkness; the next second he was entangled with no corresponding awareness of having moved an inch. It was as though he had been swept along in the palm of the Devil's hand. The net had ensnared his tank valves, and as he turned to cut himself free, the net had snagged other equipment, the difficulty of extricating himself compounded instantly. By the time he had finally reached the surface, reveling in the air and light, glad to be alive, he had maybe five minutes of air left in his tanks.

Now, as he sifted through the sand, Drake felt a spider crab nip his index finger before striding away in a huff, its carriage erect beneath its spindly legs. *Well, so much for that.* He waved his light in front of Jack to get his attention, and together they swam to the next set of lines.

Suddenly the water turned brilliant with light. Drake blinked a couple of times and looked at Jack. The power had been restored. Then he spotted the magazine to his right, ten feet away.

He quickly grabbed it, noting the tiny arrowhead stamped on one side. *That shouldn't be there.* There were rounds inside; he could tell by the weight of the magazine the instant he picked it up. He stuffed it into the utility pocket of his dry suit. He turned to give Jack the thumbs-up sign, pausing as a rising hum filled the water around them. For a moment Drake thought one of the search craft had entered the dry dock but realized that he would have heard the craft coming long before, as water magnifies sound. He isolated the source of the hum the instant he began to be drawn back toward the right side of the pool.

Impeller blades. The huge intake pipes were disgorging water from the pool into the ocean.

Had the gates been shut, the pool would have drained in seconds, leaving Drake and Henderson in a world of decompression trouble, flopping around the concrete floor like dying fish. The open gates had saved them—at least for the moment. For as they gripped the net, hanging on for dear life as the ocean roared past them, they could feel the net slowly giving way.

His stomach churning with fear, Drake pulled himself to the right, his body whipping in the strong current. He could see Jack in the periphery of his vision, moving hand over hand in his direction. He could not look directly at Jack without the current dislodging his mask.

The right side of the net broke free, and Drake and Henderson swung in a rapid arc, slamming into the wall on what was now, as they faced the ocean, the left side of the dry dock. His mask flooded, his body aching from the blow, Drake was now completely entangled, wrapped like a mummy. Jack was somewhere below. Gripping the net with his left hand, he slipped his right hand down to his thigh and drew a knife, knowing that if something didn't happen fast they were going to die. Choking down the panic, not thinking of Jennifer or Jack, but concentrating on the task at hand, he began to cut himself free. And suddenly he was falling, drifting down to the concrete floor in darkness again. The impellers had stopped. His heart raced in the surrounding quiet. Then he could feel Jack's hands touching his face, making sure that he wasn't drowning, that his second stage hadn't been ripped from his mouth. Looking up at his friend, he vowed that as soon as they got done tearing someone a new asshole, he was going to treat himself to a stiff Maker's Mark. Jack, too. Neither Drake nor Henderson drank much these days—Henderson mainly because he was a family man, Drake because he considered drinking to be a piss-poor way of blowing off steam. God had granted him only a certain number of days on earth, an allotment that could easily be curtailed, given his profession, and he didn't want to spend them getting wasted. Incidents like this, however, were exceptions to the rule.

It took Henderson ten minutes to cut through the net before Drake was free. Midway through their decompression, Drake and Henderson were greeted by a team of rescue divers called in from the search boats. Expecting the worst, the divers were astonished to find Drake and Henderson OK. So were DIA agent Dick Jackson and other members of the forensic team. "Sorry, guys," Jackson said, relieved that Drake and Henderson had climbed out of the pool without assistance. "The power guys fucked up."

10 August

The four astronauts lay strapped to their seats, staring up at the elaborate controls and display panels that crowded the flight deck of the *Atlantis,* ignoring the clear blue Florida sky that filled the forward windows. They were T-minus three minutes forty-five seconds to liftoff. Commander Pete Miller glanced at pilot Jeremy Sanchez, then scanned the controls and displays once more, making sure that the switches were set to their proper positions.

"Control, this is *Atlantis.* Prestart complete. Powering up APUs, over."

"Roger, over."

Miller flipped the switches. "APUs look good, out."

So much for the auxiliary power units. Now check the hydraulic pressure 1 indicator. Hi green? Yep. Next. . . .

He was following a routine that was the culmination of years of hard work and training. A graduate of the United States Air Force Academy in Colorado Springs, Miller had majored in astronautical engineering, dreaming of the day when he would be admitted into the elite fraternity of astronauts. By the time he had been selected by NASA, he had accumulated over five thousand hours' flying time, having done an exchange tour at the U.S. Naval Test Pilot School at Patuxent River, Maryland, before being assigned to Elgin Air Force Base in Florida to conduct weapons and electronic systems testing on F111s and F15s. Now with four space flights under his belt, he was NASA's most experienced commander. But despite his high-level security clearance, not even Miller knew much about the satellite that they carried on board *Atlantis*. Loaded aboard at the special facility run by the Defense Department, the "package," as they called it, carried a Sensitive Compartmented Information, or SCI, classification, an even "blacker" classification than Top Secret. As far as the public knew, the crew of the *Atlantis* would conduct microgravity experiments during their six-day mission.

"*Atlantis,* this is Control. H-two tank pressurization OK. You are go for launch, over."

"Roger. Go for launch. Out."

Miller ran through the last of the procedures, enjoying these final minutes talking with Ground Control at the Kennedy Space Center. Eight minutes into the flight, communication with *Atlantis* would be handed over to Mission Control in Houston for the duration.

"*Atlantis,* this is Control. APU start is go. You are on your onboard computer, over."

"Roger, out."

Miller checked the computer display. It looked A-OK. He glanced at Sanchez, winked, and nestled deep into the padded seat as the final seconds ticked away. With nervous anticipation, Sanchez gazed up at the clear Florida sky. A graduate of the United

States Naval Academy, he had majored in aerospace engineering and, like Miller, had gone on to test-pilot school. Born and raised in El Paso, Texas, he was slated to command the next shuttle mission in January.

Behind Sanchez sat Payload Specialist Dave Cameron and Mission Specialist Dennis Franks. Both men looked straight ahead, listening to Miller talk in a clipped monotone with Ground Control in the remaining seconds before liftoff. Then with T-minus 3.8 seconds and counting, the orbiter's three main engines ignited, the shuttle lurching forty degrees forward in what astronauts call the "twang." An instant later the solid rocket boosters ignited, and looking out the port window Sanchez could see the launch tower drop from view as the shuttle rose trembling off the platform.

Liftoff!

They cleared the pad and rolled 120 degrees to the right, arcing over the ocean, each booster creating close to three million pounds of thrust. The astronauts were now upside down, g-forces squeezing their bodies like grapes in a wine press as they reached the speed of sound. Inside *Atlantis,* the roar was deafening. Miller kept his mind focused on the tasks at hand, checking gauges and relaying information.

T-plus two minutes and counting, the solid rocket boosters broke away from the shuttle, their drogue parachutes popping open as the twin boosters drifted back to Earth. Seven minutes into the flight, the astronauts were traveling at fifteen times the speed of sound. When they reached an altitude of eighty miles, the shuttle began a long shallow dive as the external tank dropped away, the shuttle maneuvering down and to the left to avoid collision. Then *Atlantis* angled up again toward space.

It doesn't get any smoother than this, Commander Pete Miller thought. "How you guys doin' back there?"

"Happier than a couple of squirrels in a peanut factory, Commander. The voice was Cameron's. "Whoa, look at that!"

The sky was changing—blue to purple to black. Suddenly, it was night and they could see the sun and the moon and the stars.

From the pilot's seat Jeremy Sanchez chuckled, imagining the astounded look on Cameron's face. "Welcome to the universe, boys."

11 August

With a tense smile, Lieutenant Commander Frank Donnally quietly shut his office door deep inside the Pentagon and got to work. A liaison officer assigned to Special Operations Command, Donnally had his hands full these days. The search for the *Trident* and the terrorists who had engineered the attack continued full force, which meant that there would be no golf for Donnally this weekend. But what the fuck. Golf could wait. He was sick and tired of playing at those shit-ass public golf courses anyway, waiting behind kikes and niggers just to tee off.

But that was about to change. In a few short months he'd be rich enough to join a country club. He smiled just thinking about it: eighteen holes in the morning, a leisurely swim before lunch, then back to his place for a shower and an hour of slipping hog to one of the luscious babes he had charmed by the pool while the kids got swimming lessons and the husband plowed the back nine. What else were country clubs for? Hell, the men were secretly bored with their wives, anyway. Apart from the prestige, that's why men joined country clubs in the first place. After five days working in the city, they needed a place to dump the wife and kids each weekend so that they could run off to play golf. Men who enjoyed hanging out with their wives and children took up family sports like hiking or skiing. After all, how often had Donnally seen a husband, wife, and two small children playing golf together as a foursome? Miniature golf, maybe. But golf at a country club? Never. Which made country clubs target-rich environments, as far as Donnally was concerned.

But not on Army pay. Golf and pussy didn't come cheap, at least not the kind of golf and pussy that he hankered for. You had to be on the gravy train to lay your hands on that.

He recalled the political fund-raiser to which Clayton had invited him when Systems Technologies had been hot and his career prospects cold. Cocktail in hand, Clayton had strolled about the fancy French restaurant, fashionably located within walking distance of Capitol Hill, explaining how the legislative process worked. Donnally remembered the event vividly for the revelations it contained. Historians would remember the event vividly, too, as the day the Republican-controlled Senate killed campaign finance reform after spending millions raking the Democrats over the coals for accepting campaign contributions from Johnny Huang.

Clayton had lifted his drink in the direction of a stunning blonde in a black cocktail dress as the fund-raiser swirled around them. "See that little lady over there? Sally Mitchell. Works for the liquor lobby. The fella drooling over her tits is Warren Fowler, Senator Armstrong's chief of staff. Ah, here comes the good senator now!"

Donnally had watched the proceedings, transfixed. Silver-haired, tanned, and dressed to the nines in the pinstriped navy suit that he had bought on a congressional delegation trip to London, Senator Richard Armstrong had smiled warmly at the comely blonde while offering up a few choice anecdotes regarding the opposition that had had Sally and Fowler giggling like children. Then it had been Sally's turn. Gathering herself with racy aplomb, her breasts rising in earnest, Sally had launched into conversation. Armstrong had moved in, his head tilted to catch her every word as he nodded in agreement, a sympathetic hand encircling her waist. Then, when he thought no one was looking, Armstrong had slid his hand down to hers and given it a quick squeeze.

"Remember when Congress wanted to crack down on drunk drivers by passing a law that would have lowered the legal blood/alcohol level in many states? Virtually every police organization in the country agreed that such legislation would save thousands of lives each year." Clayton sipped his Jim Beam, obviously relishing the moment. "Sally Mitchell's the reason it didn't happen."

Clayton surveyed the room like a big-game hunter on safari. "That guy over there? The big bald-headed fuck with the envelope? That's Fred Lockhart. The guy he's handing it to is Billy Santori, another one of Armstrong's gang. Lockhart represents the telecommunications industry. Rumor is, they're looking for a big tax break this year. And judging from the size of that envelope, it looks like they're going to get it. Of course, you and I and every other average Joe out there will be picking up the tab. Tax revenue's got to come from someplace, right? But that's our Congress, the best that money can buy!"

"They're not actually exchanging money. . . . Are they?"

Clayton had looked at him as though he were dumber than a cinder block.

"It's called bundling: PAC money in the form of checks bundled together to evade the contribution limits. And it looks like Armstrong's just garnered himself another seventy-five thousand dollars for his reelection campaign—or whatever. And that's just the tip of the iceberg."

"I can't believe this."

"Why, sure you can. It's the gravy train! You tell me, what congressman or senator is going to look out for the common good when an industry can direct hundreds of thousands of dollars in PAC contributions to his opponent's reelection campaign? Don't tell me that you're naive enough to think that we still live in a democracy? Look out the window. That building you see over there—the Capitol? It's an illusion; it's a fairy tale we tell ourselves so that we can sleep at night." Clayton laughed. "Look, here comes another one!"

Donnally had watched incredulously as a fetching redhead strolled up to Santori and started chatting away. A few minutes later she had handed him an envelope, too.

"Hear that cash register ringing? That's the sound of legislation being enacted right before your very eyes. The gravy train . . ."

Donnally had shaken his head.

"It's your life, commander. But if I were you, I'd hop aboard. Because this restaurant *is* the reality—Sally Mitchell, Fred Lockhart, Senator Armstrong, and people like me doing deals in this restaurant and a thousand other places like it where legislation gets bought and sold every day. Republicans, Democrats; it doesn't matter who's in charge. Think I'm kidding? Next time you're on the Internet, check out Web sites like Common Cause or Vote Smart—you know, the public-interest organizations that tell you which senator or congressman has 'Property of Citibank' tattooed

on his ass. Then take a good look at how these senators and congressmen vote. Want to know why nothing ever gets done in
Washington? Check it out. The president doesn't make the laws,
Congress does. And don't think that Congress is about to clean up
its act anytime soon. All this talk about campaign finance reform's
a bunch of happy horseshit. In the end, they'll pass some Swiss
cheese legislation and go back to business as usual. Just as they did
the last time. So you might as well hop aboard, commander, because Geoffrey Clayton's gotta way of making your wildest dreams
come true. Think about it."

Donnally had thought about it, all right. With frustration and
rage he had thought about all the times he'd been passed over for
promotion, about all the tony country clubs he had never joined,
and above all, about all the luscious babes like Sally Mitchell to
whom he had never slipped the wild Hibernian hog. And it made
him want to tear someone's heart out.

Now, as he hunched over his computer terminal with vindic-
tive glee, he thought about all the money Clayton had stuffed into
his secret bank account in the Antilles. Geoffrey Clayton had risen
from the ashes with a fistful of dollars. And all Donnally had to do
to earn the money was type a few short paragraphs into his computer and then delete them. That's all it took.

To his closest friends at Hillside Manor in Rye, New York, he was
known as the Gatemaster. To law enforcement agencies throughout the world, he was known by a series of case numbers, his iden-
tity unknown. The product of too much money and too little
love, and a wayward private school that had jettisoned traditional

education in favor of an experiment, the Gatemaster was the world's most elusive criminal mastermind, a virtuoso of cyberspace.

His sobriquet derived from the college admissions that he had engineered for his friends the year of their graduation. To the administration at Hillside, the acceptance of three students by Harvard, Columbia, and Yale was a cause for uncommon celebration, for despite its lovely brick buildings and a tuition that ran into the tens of thousands of dollars each year, Hillside had a long tradition of sending the bulk of its students to ivy-draped colleges of last resort, colleges whose administrations, like Hillside's, favored wealth over brains. Recently, the Hillside tradition had grown worse.

His obsession with computers had begun in kindergarten but hadn't reached full flower until the sixth grade, when the Hillside administration, in its considerable folly, embarked upon a laptop computer program, proclaiming it the way of the future. Every student was required to buy a laptop computer and bring it to class, as the portable computer became the centerpiece of the educational process. That these computers performed functions that the children were supposed to be learning for themselves—spelling, grammar, and mathematics—was a glitch that the administration could easily ignore. Other private schools were doing it. So just as the Gatemaster was entering the sixth grade, and over the objections of a few outraged parents and an elderly English teacher who quit in disgust, Hillside flung itself—or rather its impressionable young charges—headlong into an educational experiment predicated on wishful thinking.

For the Gatemaster, owning a laptop computer at such an early age was an opportunity of ever-yielding richness, and by the time he had reached his freshmen year, his mastery of cyberspace far exceeded the veneer of computer knowledge possessed by the

Hillside faculty. In class, while his fellow students surreptitiously exchanged E-mail while supposedly taking notes, the Gatemaster quietly delved into school records, his mind awhirl with possibilities. By his senior year he had devised a computer program that would instantly transform C's into A's. With overworked secretaries handling the crush of transcript requests, the Gatemaster could selectively alter grades without anyone's noticing, giving his friends the competitive edge needed to gain admission to the Ivy League.

From Hillside, the Gatemaster went to MIT, but after two years he was sick of school and ready to move on. By then, he was cracking Defense Department computer networks at will, bouncing past firewalls—computer programs designed to prevent break-ins—and rewriting programs to allow him entry anytime he wished. It was child's play. Still there were places beyond his reach, computer networks containing top-secret information that were walled off from the outside world. To get at those, you had to be on the inside, which is what brought the Gatemaster to Geoffrey Clayton's door. As one of the nation's top defense research facilities, Clayton Industries had access to classified information beyond the reach of even the Gatemaster's superlative abilities.

Almost immediately, Clayton had become appreciative of the Gatemaster's unique talents. If Clayton needed information about a competitor's recent discovery, or the direction in which certain senators or Pentagon officials might be leaning, the Gatemaster had a way of providing exceptionally accurate analysis. Within a year, the Gatemaster had become Clayton's exclusive personal advisor. He was a thin twenty-five-year-old tousle-haired kid with a goofy expression concealing a very shrewd mind—a kid who loved baseball caps. They had become his standard attire.

Now, typing away at the keyboard, the Gatemaster thought

about the man who had recruited him. Clayton could read people like a book; he could play to their hidden desires. He would have made a perfect case officer for the CIA, building agent networks in foreign lands. Newly paroled, Clayton had stopped by his office at Rockwell International. An hour later, over lunch, his former boss offered him the opportunity of a lifetime—a computer-cracking scheme of unparalleled dimensions. The only catch was money.

Clayton had broached the subject before, prior to Clayton Industries having gone bankrupt. But the theft of money ran contrary to his ethics. This time, however, Clayton had persisted: money brought access, and access brought power. Clayton had called it the gravy train. Money was merely a means to an end, like using a computer terminal to acquire information.

It had taken nearly two years to devise the method that would allow them to plunder the big New York banks that had denied Clayton credit. In computer cracking, the trick is to get in and out unseen. Once you start stealing millions, government agencies get involved. Secret Service. FBI. What Clayton had asked for was perfection. And perfection didn't happen overnight.

In the end, they had acquired all the money they needed. It was a game, really. You siphoned off a few million here, a few million there, laundered it electronically through a half dozen banks around the globe, and presto! The money was yours, no strings attached. And the banks? Well, they had been robbing people for years. Hard to feel sorry for them, especially when they made damn sure Congress got enough PAC money each year to look the other way while they charged their credit-card customers interest rates that up until the 1970s had been outlawed as loan-sharking.

Yes, Clayton had it right: It was all a means to an end. And the end—the most elaborate computer-cracking feat ever—was only hours away.

Hmmm. What's this? The Gatemaster examined the information that he had picked up on his little Pentagon shopping spree. *Julia and McKendrick? Wait until the boss sees this!*

12 August

Strapped snugly into their bunks, arms rising above their chests in weightless repose, the astronauts slept with little difficulty after a sixteen-hour workday. All was quiet aboard the *Atlantis*. They were flying upside down, facing the earth two hundred miles below, traveling at speeds in excess of seventeen thousand miles per hour. Against the black void of space, the stars glistened in all their splendor, the gravitational fields of a billion suns bending the universe in a space/time continuum, the Earth a jeweled globe.

Commander Pete Miller shifted in his sleep but did not awaken. He was dreaming of the Alps, of rocky escarpments threaded with snow clinging to the fracture lines. He was skiing with his wife and three boys, watching anxiously as his wife and children hurtled down the mountainside into a blizzard.

Inside *Atlantis* the clock struck midnight. And inside the orbiter's five general-purpose computers, Elkins's electronic mice began to play.

It was the sudden closing of the cargo bay doors that woke Miller up. He remained motionless for several seconds, not daring to breathe, listening to dozens of latches clicking shut. Sliding weightless out of his sleeping bag, Miller floated over to Jeremy Sanchez and gently nudged the pilot awake, taking care not to wake the others. "Something's wrong."

Together they bounded up to the flight deck and scanned the displays, the Earth sliding past the forward windows as the orbiter pivoted in space.

In a tone of mild inquiry that belied the growing panic inside his heart, Miller said: "They can't do this from the ground, can they?" It was a rhetorical question, and without waiting for an answer Miller slid into the commander's seat and stared at the computer displays. The auxiliary power light flashed on. They were flying tail first, positioned for retrofire. Payload Specialist Dave Cameron floated up through the hatch, a smile breaking across his handsome face. "Say, you guys are up early!" Then he noticed Miller's blanched expression and muttered, "Oh, Jesus," just as the orbiter's three engines ignited.

Miller looked at Cameron and said, "Get Dennis up, quick! Then he got on the horn: "Houston, this is *Atlantis*. We have a problem. Houston, do you copy?"

At Mission Control at the Johnson Space Center in Houston a thousand events cascaded at once, driving fear into the hearts of the flight controllers trying to figure out what was going on. It was like nothing they had seen before, primary and backup computer systems crashing around them in an electronic avalanche, transforming their famous resolve into hopeless despair as their ability to monitor *Atlantis* vanished before their eyes. Flight Director James Kirkwell, whose close-cropped white beard and bushy eyebrows lent him the jovial appearance of Santa Claus, quickly surveyed the rows of flight controllers working at their consoles, nausea filling his gut. He turned to his ground controller, George Davis, hoping to hear the right words: that the Emergency Control Center at the Kennedy Space Center had gone on-line. Instead, what he saw was Davis's blue eyes widening in helpless appeal: "Sir, the Emergency Control Center reports that they are nonfunctional."

Praying for a miracle, Kirkwell looked up at the huge projection displays that filled the front wall of the Control Room. They were as black as an open grave. Flinging his headset to the ground, Kirkwell reached for the hot line, a direct link to the Pentagon. Fear rocked his gut like an earthquake. "This is James Kirkwell at JSC. All systems are down. I repeat: All systems are down. We've lost *Atlantis*. Condition Red."

Seventy miles above the Earth, *Atlantis* plunged through the atmosphere. Strapped to their seats, the four astronauts prayed. Buffeted by the thick air, the orbiter shook violently as its exterior became incandescent, reaching a temperature of 1,540 degrees centigrade. Sparks gusted up over the windows. To the astronauts, it seemed as though they were passing through the gates of Hell.

All Pete Miller could do was to try to remain calm. *Atlantis* was flying itself, performing flawlessly. But it was obvious that the computer system had been sabotaged. There was no other explanation for what was happening. And it had to have been an inside job. *God help the son-of-a-bitch who did this.* He thought about his wife and kids, wondering if he would ever see them again. Then he thought about the pandemonium breaking loose at Mission Control.

He glanced at the clock. Within minutes *Atlantis* would be making its final approach. Soon he would have to steer the orbiter through several S-turns to reduce speed—if *Atlantis* responded to the controls, a long shot at best. But if they could land safely—it didn't matter in what country—they would be OK. He knew that. The government of the United States would expend every resource to bring them back safe and sound. And once home, he would find the saboteur and rip his fucking throat out.

Outside *Atlantis,* the heat subsided. Miller followed the descent trajectory on the computer display. He tried working the control stick. No dice. He felt something plummet inside him and thought for a second that he might vomit. Then he felt the g-forces increasing as the *Atlantis* banked through a series of S-turns. *Sweet mother of Mary.* They were slowing down. He could have cheered.

They were plummeting through the darkness. *Atlantis* banked again, then angled down on a twenty-two-degree glide slope. *So far, so good,* Miller thought as he watched the altitude/vertical velocity indicator. At two thousand feet they were thirty seconds to touchdown. Sanchez extended an anxious hand and Miller grasped it as the orbiter's nose flared up. Then with the other astronauts joining in, Commander Miller began reciting the Lord's Prayer aloud.

Flanked by Chief of Staff Margaret Abrams and Vice President David Kendall, President Thomas Young gazed about the White

House Situation Room with a sense of urgency he had not known since the precipitous events that had led to Jefferson Marshall's resignation. National Security Advisor Bud McGuire conducted the briefing.

"Mr. President. Twenty minutes ago both the Johnson and Kennedy Space Centers sustained massive computer failures, effectively shutting down their primary and secondary systems. We've just received word from the Tracking and Data network that *Atlantis* reentered the Earth's atmosphere. She'll be landing in minutes."

"Where?" the president asked, paling at the news.

"The Atlantic Ocean, sir. Off the coast of Maine. Fifty miles north of Bristol . . ."

At the stern of his lobster boat, *Sunshine*, Frederick O'Reilly was smoking some of Mother Nature's finest when suddenly he heard a muffled boom. He looked up at the midnight sky and spotted a black triangle slipping across the coppery moon. Astonished, he gazed at the joint in wonder, then took another hit, closing his eyes and holding his breath in a tight-lipped grin.

Man, I gotta get me another bag of this shit!

He exhaled a bluish cloud of marijuana smoke, examined the moonlit sky for another minute, then inhaled again, eyes shut, the fragrant smoke wreathing his head like a dream. He thought about the cold six-pack of Schlitz in the cooler. Time to fire one down. Then he felt a hot gust of wind at his back. Startled, he turned, the half-smoked joint tumbling from his astounded lips. He dove into the pilothouse, grabbed his camera, and raced outside again snapping pictures, his lower jaw gaping a country mile as the orbiter *Atlantis* soared past him fifteen feet above the tranquil sea.

The landing gear. It wasn't deploying. *Jesus, Lord. Why this? Why now?* Close to tears, Commander Pete Miller flicked the toggle switch. No response. Nothing. In desperation he glanced at Sanchez, then looked out the port window, his heart recoiling in shock. They were gliding over the ocean, and it wasn't the Florida ocean, either, judging by the rocky coastline. *Oh, my God . . .*

He slammed against the restraints, the magnificent harvest moon vanishing from the port window as the orbiter skipped across the hard surface of the Atlantic. The lights went out. He heard a cry of pain. Then he, too, vanished into the darkness, slipping back into the universe of dreams. He was skiing down a mountainside in a blizzard, calling out for his wife and children lost amid the whirling snow.

The phone rang. Drake looked up from his copy of *Immersed* and glanced at the clock. Couldn't be Jennifer—or could it? Worried, he reached across the hotel room bed and picked up the receiver.

"Your tanks filled?"

McKendrick.

Drake straightened. "Why? What's up?"

"The shuttle crashed fifty miles north of Bristol. In the ocean. We're flying you and Jack there now. And Phil?"

"Yeah?"

"Watch your back."

———

At the Johnson Space Center in Houston, Public Affairs Officer Timothy Kindregan paced the anteroom floor, beads of sweat pebbling his furrowed brow like sandpaper. In T-minus fifteen seconds and counting, he would march out into the press room and deliver the briefing of a lifetime—or else. His boss had told him in no uncertain terms: "You'd better go out there and kick ass, Timbo, because the future of NASA is at stake." Already, the rumors were flying: *Atlantis* had incinerated upon reentry, a massive computer failure had sent the orbiter veering toward the sun, the astronauts had been asphyxiated by toxic fumes . . . An accident worse than *Challenger,* people were saying. Kindregan peeked out at the reporters packing the room and shuddered, thinking how good a cool Finlandia-and-soda would taste right now, the anxiety rolling down his gut like a bowling ball.

Commander Pete Miller awoke. Darkness. He was still alive. The right side of his rib cage hurt. He could hear moaning coming from the pilot's seat to his right.

"Jeremy?"

No answer.

"Dennis? Dave? You guys OK?"

"I think so." The voice was Cameron's. Feeble. Unsure.

"Shit, where are we?" Dennis asked.

Wincing, Miller tried reaching down to his right thigh for a penlight, but the pain searing his ribs became too intense. "Jeremy's hurt."

"Just a sec," Dennis said.

In the darkness Miller heard the unfastening of a restraint system. A penlight snapped on, the thin beam sweeping across the controls, then up, illuminating the forward windows.

"Oh, God," Cameron moaned.

A steady stream of bubbles rose from the cracked fuselage.

They were underwater.

Inside the cabin of the Seahawk, Drake and Henderson slipped their arms through their tank straps as the crew chief briefed them on the operation. Invisible in the darkness save for its running lights, another Seahawk hovered over the ocean a quarter of a mile away, casting a wide circle of light down to the textured surface where two men sat inside a zodiac. Beyond the bright circle, in the penumbra, the ocean was pale green and glimmering.

"She's in two hundred fifty feet of water," the crew chief explained, handing Drake a light.

"How long have they been down there.?" Henderson asked.

"Forty minutes, maybe longer." He shook his head in frustration. "We haven't been able to make contact. We assume they're alive. The bottom is sand, thank God. No current. That's the good news. The bad news is that they're going to need air. They've got enough to last awhile, but not enough for the time it's going to take to get them out. There's a compressor aboard the zodiac. We need you guys to open this access panel on the orbiter's starboard side and connect the hose." He pointed to the fax that he had received from Houston showing *Atlantis* in profile. "Think you guys can do that?"

Drake studied the fax, then handed it to Jack. He wasn't thinking about the hose; he was thinking about McKendrick's warning.

Were the *Trident* highjacking and the shuttle crash related? Staring down at the water, he felt as though he were being watched, a mere mortal, a plaything of the gods. The sensation filled him with the same foreboding that he had experienced moving up the tarmac at Paitilla Airfield during Operation Just Cause, the darkened buildings looming to either side. They had strolled into Ambush City. Now, they were going into the water unarmed. He knew the unspoken reason he and Jack had gotten the call in the first place, and not the dozen search-and-recovery divers at Bristol. Because he and Jack had been tested in combat. Because the authorities knew that when push came to shove, they wouldn't back off.

Squeezed between the commander's seat and the pilot's seat, Payload Specialist Dave Cameron knelt beside Sanchez, checking his vital signs.

"How's he look?" Miller asked.

"I think he's punctured a lung. Dennis, hand me the O_2."

Franks unfastened the survival pack clipped to the back of the pilot's seat, opened it, and handed off the cylinder. Then he felt a faint tapping on his left shoulder. Miller. "How're you feeling, sir?"

"I need you to check the spacecraft."

Franks nodded. Damage control. He had also seen the silvery stream of bubbles rising from the cracked fuselage.

With growing anxiety, he grabbed a flashlight and opened the flight-deck hatch, shining the light down to the mid-deck floor. What had been familiar territory only an hour before was now as dark and forbidding as the inside of a burial chamber. He climbed down the ladder, doing his best to keep the anxiety at bay. The floor was dry—a good sign. He could hear the reassuring hum of the circulation systems. The auxiliary power supply was functioning. He swept his light along the surrounding bulkheads. Intact. Then he switched off the light and listened for other sounds, unfamiliar sounds, as he had been trained to do.

His parents had been so proud of his accomplishments. They had retired to South Carolina the previous year. Two days prior to launch, his father had called, promising to keep the TV tuned to CNN twenty-four hours a day. Now if he and his fellow astronauts didn't get out of here soon, some fucking Navy chaplain was going to be knocking at their door. He concentrated against the fear swelling inside his heart. A faint hissing noise came from below.

Shit. He quickly opened the lower-deck hatch and climbed down, sweeping his light over the life-support systems. They were dry. Switching off the light, he held his breath and listened again, praying for silence; a leak in this compartment would be fatal. A steady hiss came from somewhere aft. He moved toward the sound, his heart filling with dread, crossing a garden of battery packs. The hissing grew louder. He moved toward the sound, his reluctant body trembling as he swept his light across the aft bulkhead, then down along the auxiliary power supply.

A thin stream of water jetted across the deck in a gap between two battery packs. Dennis Franks stared in horror at the puddle collecting at his feet. He stood in the aftermost section of the equipment bay, trying to calculate its flow, trying to calculate how much time they had, wishing he were someplace else. Despondent, he retreated to the mid-deck, shut the hatch, then climbed up to the flight deck to inform the others.

———

The other chopper moved off as the Seahawk positioned itself in front of the zodiac. Drake glanced at Henderson and slipped a mask over his face. Neither man spoke. They didn't have to. They had known each other for years, knew each other's habits by rote.

The crew chief hunkered down near the right side of the door. "Good luck. And for God's sake, be careful."

Hunched under the weight of their twin steel 120s and aluminum stage bottles, Drake and Henderson moved to the door and stepped off the helicopter, dropping thirty feet into the cold Atlantic, the Seahawk roaring above them.

They bobbed to the surface and swam to the zodiac, cold water slapping against their faces. Two sailors in Navy windbreakers sat to either side of the compressor. Drake could see that they carried radios with headsets. The guy to starboard was talking to the chopper pilot. The sailor on the port side tapped Drake on the head and hollered: "We're directly over the shuttle. You should be right on it when you get down there." Drake hoped so. The air hose was already in the water, its heavily weighted end resting on the bottom. The compressor was bright and compact, a design neither Drake nor Henderson had seen before. They switched on their lights and submerged feet first into the lighted water along the hose. Jack took point.

"How're we doing?" Miller asked. He was still strapped to his seat. Kneeling over Sanchez, Dave Cameron looked up with hopeful expectation.

Franks struggled for composure. "Not good, sir. We're taking in water on the lower deck."

Cameron halted his ministrations. "Damn it," he said.

Miller calmly looked at Franks. "You done good," he said by way of reassurance. He reached out with a weak smile and touched Franks's arm. "How long before the battery packs are submerged?"

"Ten minutes . . . maybe fifteen."

Miller nodded, expressionless. They had maybe an hour before they would slowly asphyxiate on their own carbon dioxide. "Don't worry, kid. They'll find us."

With a halfhearted nod, Franks turned to Cameron. "How's Jeremy?"

"He'll make it. We'll all make it," Cameron said with determination. "I need your help, Dennis. We need to lay him flat."

Franks squeezed forward. Something dripped on the back of his neck. He flashed his light up and moaned as the water dripped again.

Together they stared at the cracked skylight with fading hope, not daring to touch the broken glass or water collecting around its sides.

Cold water surrounded them. Drake looked down, watching the beam of Jack's light stretching into the darkness as they descended along the hose. The water was clear, and Drake could see strands of seaweed floating up toward the surface. He swung his light around. Twenty feet away a thin stream of bubbles shimmered toward the surface.

Picking up speed as he descended, he jetted air into his dry suit to offset the increased water pressure. The air seemed to wrap itself around his skin. He felt warm. He sailed past a school of baitfish, their opalescent scales gleaming in the light. He could hear the hammering din of the compressor. He thought about lying at the bottom of the dry dock, entangled in the nylon net after having nearly gotten sucked into the intake pipe. At least here they were safe from the power company.

He wondered what he would find once they located the shuttle. The rising bubbles could be coming from any of a thousand places, not all of them potentially fatal to the astronauts. But *Atlantis* must have taken a terrific beating when she landed. *What if the crew compartment had broken away? The compartment would still be intact; even the* Challenger's *crew compartment had remained intact after the explosion and its long tumble back to Earth.*

At 160 feet Drake could feel a mild tingling sensation in his brain—nitrogen narcosis, the famed rapture of the deep, the mild delirium that divers experience at extreme depths. He slowed his descent, hoping to minimize its effects. Jack slowed his descent as well.

Because they were breathing compressed air instead of trimix, they would have to work slowly and carefully, making sure that they didn't overexert themselves and black out from oxygen toxicity. Overexertion wouldn't be a problem if *Atlantis* lay directly beneath them. But if the crew compartment had separated, they would have to drag 250 feet of hose behind them as they kicked through the water. Drake dreaded the possibility.

The water was colder now. They had passed a thermocline. Drake could feel cold water pushing against his face. A bottom current? Drake checked his depth gauge: 200 feet. They were almost there.

They continued their descent, sweeping their lights down in a circle around the hose. A school of cod swam past. Drake concentrated against the narcosis. *Come on, baby. Show me where you are.* He concentrated on the beam of Jack's light as it reached out into the darkness below. They would hit bottom soon. Then, out of the corner of his eye, he saw a flash of white. Drake swung his light to the left as the beam of Jack's light swept over the fuselage once more. *Atlantis* lay upright on the sandy ocean floor less than twenty feet away.

He could see the flight-deck windows; the crew compartment hadn't separated as he had feared. The orbiter itself was mammoth. Coming upon it after having drifted down through the watery darkness, he felt as though he had journeyed through the desert at night and wandered into the Valley of Tombs. Dark, quiet, mysterious, tragic, *Atlantis* seemed to be a modern Icarus fallen from the sky. Were the astronauts still alive?

Hovering, he swept his light over the port cockpit window, then pressed his light to his chest, darkening the ocean. He stared into the void, a universe bereft of stars, hoping to catch a glimmer of light, a sign of life. *Atlantis* was invisible now, swallowed once more by darkness and black water. Then a faint beam of light darted inside the flight-deck windows. His heart soared.

He looked below at Jack, who had dropped down to the sand to free the hose from the lead weight. The hose lay only ten feet from the orbiter; the guys in the zodiac had done a fantastic job. The heat-deflecting tiles of the port wing were black and smudged with carbon from reentry. Swimming down to the hose, Drake swept his light over the emblazoned words: UNITED STATES. Then he spotted the red, white, and blue of the American flag that graced the orbiter's side.

In tandem, they dragged the hose to the access panel, using the crew hatch as a point of orientation. Jack inserted a knife blade into the panel release and pried open the bar, the panel, and heat-resistant tile that protected it, levering out and to the side. He quickly fitted the hose into its coupling, feeling it snap into place, water venting out another port.

Gripping the hose with his left hand, Drake could feel the rhythmic contractions of air pumping through. He looked at Jack with cautious optimism. Jack flashed the OK sign and pointed toward the cockpit. Swimming up along the orbiter's port side, they could see a faint beam of light emanating from the cockpit windows. Mission accomplished. They would signal the astronauts and head toward the surface.

Inside the situation room, President Young and his advisors sat nervously around the conference table, listening to the open communications line as they watched the rescue operation in real time, courtesy of a KH-24 surveillance satellite that had been retasked to cover the Eastern Seaboard. From its geosynchronous orbit thirty thousand miles above the earth, the KH-24 projected back to Earth magnified images of such fine resolution that they could read the dials through the cockpit windows of the Seahawk helicopters hovering over the crash site.

Secretary of Defense Richard Elliot glanced at his watch and tapped his fingers on the table as the chopper pilots exchanged information with the zodiac crew. President Young looked at McKendrick, pressed his lips together, raised his eyebrows, and shook his head in helpless despair. So far there had been no word from Drake and Henderson. McKendrick felt raw, tense.

"How long have they been down there?" the president asked.

McKendrick looked at his watch. "Fifteen minutes, sir."

"How much longer can they stay down?"

"Depends on how much air they're carrying. Knowing Drake and Henderson, they're packing a shitload, if you'll excuse the vernacular, sir."

A ghost of a smile flitted across the president's face.

McKendrick glanced at Elliot, who was shaking his head at McKendrick's choice of the word *shitload,* trying to conceal the smirk creasing his lips. *Good. Keep their spirits up. Don't let the tension grind them down.* "The problem is depth," McKendrick explained. "At two hundred fifty feet they're going through their air supply eight times faster than if they were swimming near the surface. At extreme depth, water pressure squeezes the volume of air to a very small size. They end up sucking a lot of air from their tanks just to fill their lungs with each breath."

The president nodded.

But deep inside, McKendrick was worried, too. He thought about Julia, wondering what she must be thinking. News of the shuttle accident filled the airwaves. After the dive they had returned to their hotel rooms, changed, and had met for dinner. To her delight, McKendrick had ordered Beef Wellington for two. Afterward they had strolled on the beach. She had promised to come to Washington soon, flattered by the attention, suddenly interested in the man who was obviously interested in her. Now it appeared that she would be making that trip sooner than expected. Lawrence, too. Could Bright Star be what the terrorists were after? How could they have learned the launch date? Only a handful of people knew. Or was the shuttle crash a diversion? Was it related to the *Trident* highjacking at all?

In the background, McKendrick could hear the CNN coverage on one of the monitors. Recently updated, the computer and communications equipment inside the compact Situation Room was the most sophisticated in the world. With the touch of a button, the president could talk to anyone, anywhere. If the person stood outdoors, thanks to the imaging magic of the KH-24, the president could see that individual as clear as day, even if that day were fogbound and overcast. If the individual stood inside the Kremlin or deep inside an Iraqi bunker, he could isolate his or her body shape and the shapes of the other bodies and the furniture around them. From its geosynchronous perch, the KH-24 could magnify a fifty-foot area in stunning detail. If it wanted to, it could even measure the shortness of Saddam Hussein's dick. You simply had to tell it where to look. But it couldn't see the *Trident.* Technology had come back and bitten them in the ass.

President Young looked up at the young technical expert from the National Reconnaissance Office. "Can you take us underwater?"

"We can try." The aide quickly typed a command into a computer, and suddenly they could see the pale white image of the orbiter lying upright on the ocean floor. The men and women inside the Situation Room fell silent as they stared at the monitor in wonder. Two divers were swimming up toward the cockpit windows—the divers, like *Atlantis* itself, ghost images beneath the sea.

They were angling up toward the flight-deck windows, sweeping their lights up along the orbiter's mammoth white fuselage. Drake glanced back into the darkness, then at Henderson, who was moving up on his right. They could hear the compressor, but no other sounds, no prop or engine noise. The silence was reassuring.

Drake gazed at the flight-deck windows. A light flickered against the glass. A signal? He glanced again at Henderson and closed in. Fifteen feet from the port window he saw bubbles gushing out of the skylight, so many that he was shocked that he hadn't heard them above the din of the compressor. He quickly moved to the windows.

The flight deck resembled a shower.

Henderson by his side, Drake directed his light into the dark interior, illuminated by only a single flashlight taped to a storage compartment. Three astronauts stared back in desperation as they struggled to keep an injured man sheltered from the water. The injured astronaut wore an oxygen mask.

Drake swam back to the access panel and disconnected the hose—it was only making the leak worse. He wasn't thinking about the *Trident* now. He was thinking about the astronauts, how to get them out in the next ten minutes before they drowned.

He hurried back to the flight-deck windows, tapped Jack on the shoulder, and jotted a note on an underwater slate. He pressed it to the windshield.

> Egress in pairs via airlock. Use scuba rig.
> 1st pair: strongest with injured.
> At surface keep scuba rig clipped to hose;
> we'll pull it down for next pair.
> Take injured man off oxygen now.

"Hang on, Jeremy," Cameron whooped, ignoring the cold water spraying down. "We're getting the fuck out of here!"

Commander Pete Miller gazed out the cockpit windows at the two divers pressing the underwater slate against the window, not daring to believe that he might live to see his wife and children again.

"SEALs?" Franks asked.

"Angels," Commander Miller said. "Come on, let's get that hatch open."

With no time to spare, Drake and Henderson swam to a hatch atop the cargo bay and popped it open. Shining his light down into the wide bay, he could see a large piece of equipment wrapped in a protective sheet of Mylar; equipment for the International Space Station, probably. The bay was so large that a bus could fit inside. In front of the package, attached to the bulkhead separating the crew compartment from the cargo bay, Drake spotted the boiler-shaped airlock. When he looked up, Jack was hovering beside him, air hose in hand.

Drake descended through the open hatch, his brain pounding from the narcosis, Jack's light shining down like a beacon. Reaching the airlock controls inside the cargo bay, he could feel the tension building inside his chest. He had fifteen minutes to retrieve the astronauts, no longer. Even with his side-mounted tanks, his air supply was rapidly dwindling. Within minutes, he would be breathing air he needed for decompression.

He could not enter the flight deck. The air pressure inside *Atlantis* corresponded to the air pressure at the Earth's surface. Entering the flight deck would be tantamount to shooting to the surface without decompressing; millions of microscopic nitrogen bubbles in his tissues would come rushing out of solution. He would be dead in minutes—if he was lucky.

He would hand off his main tanks and hope for the best. There was no other option. Mounted to a backpack, the twin OMS 120s carried enough air to allow two astronauts at a time to swim safely to the surface. They would only need five minutes to decompress, if that. Drake could remain inside the cargo bay waiting for the next pair, using his side-mounted tanks as his principal air supply. Although handing over his main tanks to the astronauts wouldn't leave him enough air to complete his lengthy decompression, he could rely on the extra air that Jack carried.

But would the airlock work?

In the darkness of the cargo bay, he directed the beam of his light to the controls. He knew how to lock out of a submarine. He could do that blindfolded. But the orbiter was designed for space. And judging from what he had seen of the flight deck through the cockpit windows, the auxiliary power supply had shorted out.

He carefully examined the controls, then turned what he hoped was a flood valve, shining his light through the thick observation window. Water filled the chamber. Elated, he looked up at Jack, pointed to the airlock, and flashed the OK sign. He quickly opened the hatch, unclipped his side-mounted tanks from his backpack, and clipped them to a D-ring on his wreck harness. Then, having drained air from his dry suit to compensate for the sudden weight loss, he carefully slipped out of his main diving rig, attuning his senses to any change of buoyancy. He glanced up at Jack leaning through the cargo bay hatch ten feet above and shoved his tanks and backpack and two spare masks inside the airlock. The astronauts now had an emergency egress system. Not the most efficient system in the world, but feasible. He shut the hatch and drained the water. The airlock worked like a charm, evidently designed to operate on an independent power source.

Peering through the observation window, Drake watched an astronaut pull the scuba rig from the chamber, his face taut with concentration. He donned the tanks, stepped inside the chamber, then gathered the injured man with the help of another astronaut. A minute later, two men were equalizing the pressure in their ears as the water slowly rose around them.

The airlock flooded. Drake opened the hatch and pulled the astronauts out. The injured man was conscious. Barely. Drake wrapped the backpack waistband around both men, using an extra piece of line. The alert astronaut jetted air into the buoyancy compensator until they slowly began to attain neutral buoyancy. Drake mimed the procedure they would have to follow to ascend to the surface safely, showing them how to purge air from the BC as it expanded to ensure that they made a safe and slow ascent. The astronauts were certified divers; they knew the drill—diving had been an integral part of their training. The alert astronaut nodded. He jetted another burst of air into the buoyancy compensator and rose toward the open cargo hatch.

Outside *Atlantis,* Jack clipped them to the hose and attached a line to a D-ring on the backpack so that he could retrieve the scuba rig once the astronauts had risen to the surface. Then the alert astronaut jetted another burst of air into his BC and off they went. Tense, but breathing at an easy rhythm, Jack checked his air, looked down at Drake, and flashed the OK sign. Now it was a waiting game. Jack settled down against the cargo hatch, listening to the sound of the compressor's rattling hum.

"Dallas One, this is Zodiac. We have recovered astronauts Cameron and Sanchez. They are alive. I repeat: They are alive. An emergency egress of the other two astronauts is under way at this time. Cameron reports that *Atlantis* is taking on water fast. Diver in the red dry suit accessed the airlock. Astronauts are using his tanks. Diver will need additional air to decompress. Over."

Hovering overhead, pilot Todd Benjamin looked down at the two astronauts in the zodiac. "Dallas One, copy. Two Seahawks with support divers are inbound. Stand by for ETA."

"Jesus Christ, they're doing it!" President Thomas Young exclaimed to McKendrick, his eyes welling with hope. The men occupying the Situation Room looked at one another, not daring to believe that Drake and Henderson could pull this off, that the astronauts might emerge from this catastrophe alive and relatively unscathed. With a solemn expression, McKendrick returned the president's gaze and nodded. He could hear cheering coming through the open communication line; the chopper crew, no doubt. He was thinking about what it must take to hand off your primary scuba rig deep inside the cargo bay of the space shuttle in 250 feet of cold, dark water.

Drake had yet to emerge from the orbiter with the other two astronauts.

President Young looked at the technician eagerly. "Can we see inside the orbiter?"

The technician shook his head. "Not even the KH-24 can take us that far. I'm sorry, sir."

Fraught with anxiety and hope, they stared intently at the screen, praying that Drake, Henderson, and the remaining astronauts would survive. Time seemed to slow to an agonizing halt. The men and women gathered around the monitor in silence. Suddenly the president said, "What's that?" McKendrick bent forward. To the right of *Atlantis* a dozen pale images appeared, hovering over the sunken spacecraft like fireflies. *Rescue divers? No, they couldn't be, they're not descending. . . .*

"Walt?"

"Oh my God, no," Elliot whispered.

The tension on the line went slack. Then the hose softened. The men in the zodiac had shut off the compressor as a signal—the astronauts had made it to the surface alive. Elated, Henderson quickly reeled up the line, pulling the scuba rig down even faster along the hose. Gathering the rig, he looked down at Drake, then tossed him the line reel.

There was little time. Drake stuffed the tanks into the open airlock, closed the hatch, and completed the transfer. A minute later the last two astronauts were standing inside the narrow airlock as the water rose above them. One of the astronauts held his rib cage. Drake cranked open the hatch, helped the astronauts exit, and tied the waistband around both men as he had with the first buddy team, reminding them to purge air from their buoyancy compensator during their ascent. Then the astronauts ascended through the hatch. Holding them with one hand, Henderson clipped them to the hose. The stronger of the two astronauts jetted air into the BC, and they rose to the surface.

Hovering beside the open cargo hatch Henderson checked his air, then looked down at Drake, who was arranging his side-mounted tanks, preparing to ascend. He was relieved and happy. He thought of the astronauts, how ecstatic they would feel when the warm night air rushed against their faces. His dive computer showed a bottom time of thirty-three minutes and a decompression schedule that was daunting. They would be okay, but they couldn't afford to linger.

He signaled Drake and looked up, suddenly illuminated by two powerful lights. Intense. Blinding. A Navy rescue team? The *Trident?* He could see swimmers in the water, black against the brilliant curtain of light. They were armed with spearguns. He swung his light down to warn Drake and felt the pointed barb of a spear enter his shoulder. Then another spear entered his chest, and he couldn't breathe. The pain was searing. He tried to scream, but there was blood in his throat, the water around him turning bright red as another bank of lights switched on, illuminating the cargo bay. A long mechanical arm reached out of the darkness as the divers popped open the cargo bay doors. He moved away from the hatch, drawing his attackers away from Drake.

A man with a speargun was swimming toward him. In agony, he stripped the light from his arm, letting it fall to the ocean floor as a decoy. He reached for the power inflator button on his BC but felt the cold shaft of another spear rip through his stomach. He curled up in a ball, gritting his teeth, squeezing his eyes shut against the pain. *I love you, Mary. Take care of our son.*

He was sinking, drifting down to the ocean floor. Forcing his eyes open, he looked for Drake. The light that held him in its glare was fading fast. Then he felt himself being grappled from behind. He fought with all his ebbing strength, then saw that it was Drake pulling him up and away into the dark. He looked up into Drake's eyes and saw that agony lived there, too. He felt Drake's arms around his body, Drake his friend. The arms were warm. He was cold. Darkness filled his vision in bursts. The lighted water felt like a dull razor scraping against his face, a razor of frozen steel. *Did Drake feel it too? Oh, God, take me away from this place.* He looked into the light again. The man with a long ragged scar on his cheek reared up and aimed again and Henderson saw another flash of silver. He gritted his teeth against the searing blow. It never came. And Jack Henderson never saw again. He was dead.

PART II

20 August

The generous shade from the magnolia trees provided no surcease from the heat that August day at Arlington National Cemetery, and even if it had, it could not have assuaged the searing pain that welled inside young Andrew Henderson's heart as he squeezed his mother's hand, staring in disbelief at his father's flag-draped coffin.

Gathered on the hillside, more than a thousand people stood in grieving silence as the minister recited the "Burial of the Dead" from the *Book of Common Prayer*.

With his arms around his wife and children, Commander Pete Miller gazed solemnly at the coffin. Nearby, Dave Cameron, Dennis Franks, and Jeremy Sanchez stood with their families. Also present at Arlington were former members of SEAL Team 4 who had fought beside Jack and Drake in Panama. Still others were close family friends.

The president and the first lady consoled Jack's elderly parents, who had arrived that morning to bury their son. Drake and Jennifer stood to Mary Henderson's right, Drake placing a comforting hand on young Andrew's shoulder, remembering his own time here, the hours standing over his father's grave, trying to recall the proud Army captain who had died when he was two. His soul was aching for the boy in front of him now. Turn on the six o'clock news on any given night and one might easily conclude that the heart of the United States lies at 1600 Pennsylvania Avenue or on Capitol Hill. It doesn't. The heart of the country lies here among the verdant hills and white tombstones of Arlington.

At the National Cathedral twenty minutes before, President Young had read a passage from Ecclesiastes. Drake had delivered the eulogy, quoting a passage from Thucydides that he had memorized in his youth. The cathedral had been filled to capacity. As he looked out over the gathering of high-ranking military officers, cabinet members, congressional leaders, friends, and family, Drake had twice lost his composure, turning to wipe tears from his cheeks as he gathered himself, struggling to come to terms with the undeniable fact that his best friend—the man who had saved his life—was gone.

He had been inside the cargo bay when the light appeared. Startled, he had looked up to see the spear entering Jack's shoulder. By the time he had reached the hatch, Jack was sinking toward the bottom, the man with the ragged scar reloading the speargun. Desperate, panicked, his heart pounding with sickness and rage, Drake had jettisoned his lights and side-mounted tanks and had raced toward his dying friend. Jack's light had tumbled to the ocean floor, and for an awful minute Drake had lost him in the darkness. In desperation Drake had angled down to locate Jack before the man could fire again. But he was too late. The third spear had found its mark, piercing Jack's stomach. Reaching Jack an instant later, he had pulled the long hose from one of the side-mounted tanks that Jack carried and gulped lungfuls of air, feeling his brain surge with renewed hostility and fear. He had wrapped his arms around his dying friend and had hauled him up into the darkness, twisting as the fourth spear streaked toward them. With a sharp ping, the spear had glanced off Jack's main tanks. Drake had kept his eyes on the man with the speargun, waiting for the next shot. It never came. Backlit against the orbiter, the *Trident's* mechanical arm lifted the Mylar package from the cargo bay. If the man with the scar had known what Drake was thinking, he would have fled to the ends of the earth. Drake kicked toward the surface, feeling his best friend and the man who had once saved his life grow weak and still in the dark water.

He had called Jennifer from Maine Medical where they had flown Jack. Jennifer and McKendrick had broken the news to Mary Henderson while Drake remained at his friend's side, escorting the body home to Concord, Massachusetts. Mary had collapsed to the floor, Andrew running into the room to find out what was wrong.

Now as he listened to the resounding crack of the honor guard firing a twenty-one-gun salute, Drake swept his gaze over the crowd. Occupying a nearby hillside, a bank of television cameras broadcast the funeral live, for the United States was burying a hero that day, a man who had given his life to save the astronauts. The story of the orbiter's sabotage and astronauts' dramatic rescue had captivated the world. O'Reilly's photographs of *Atlantis* skimming the ocean had become some of the most-sought-after photographs in the history of twentieth-century journalism. According to the newspapers, terrorists had sabotaged the orbiter and had stolen a top-secret reconnaissance satellite. Only a few people in the crowd knew of Bright Star's lethal capabilities. And those who did, had fear—as well as grief—inside their hearts.

He had never seen a night so clear. The stars glistening against the cobalt sky, the crescent moon casting shadows among the palms, the trade winds filling his nostrils with the odor of sage—yes, at long last Gerry Elkins had reaped his reward. Clayton had provided all the amenities, just as he had promised—everything from the three-million-dollar bank account to the lavish 75-foot Tom Fexas–design motor yacht in which Elkins had regally transported himself to the British West Indies. Seacliff, his new four-bedroom oceanfront villa on the island of Providenciales in the Turks and Caicos, stood atop a limestone crest at the tip of Ocean Point, an exclusive compound dotted with the homes of wealthy individuals not often in residence. Not that Elkins was planning to leave his newly acquired villa anytime soon, even to buy groceries. He had someone else to do that. And that golden-haired someone was now slipping off the straps of her white muslin dress, her nipples hardening in the faint chill of the evening air.

Her name was Catherine. Elkins had hired her from a Paris agency as a gift to himself, a bon voyage present. She was tall and slender with blue almond-shaped eyes. As they sailed the Caribbean, she had wrapped her supple body around his ample flesh for ten lustrous days and nights. Elkins couldn't get enough. Every night he had held her close, the salt air infused with the damp musk of her vagina.

Smiling, he watched her step into the pool, descending the concrete staircase like a gazelle and wading close until her nipples touched his chest. Without speaking, she took the daiquiri from his hand and set it on the concrete. He kissed her on the mouth, his dick as hard as a baseball bat. Then, gripping her slender bottom, he lifted her up, still captivated by her beauty, and buried himself inside her, certain that all the world was his.

With a contentment that he had not known in years, Geoffrey Clayton clicked off the three television monitors to the right of his desk and activated the walnut panel that hid them from view. Funerals bored him.

He stood and stretched. The night had been long, but profitable, and though he hadn't slept, his fatigue had been assuaged by a gratifying sense of accomplishment. He had pulled it off, he had turned the tables on the men who had betrayed him, he had fulfilled the dream he had nurtured since the day of his incarceration at Allentown.

He had greeted Thorne and the others on the concrete platform overlooking the subterranean pool the day before. As the *Trident* slid into its pen, the big mercenary had climbed out of the conning tower dressed in a black nomex flightsuit and had leaped onto the dock, grinning. That was Clayton's first indication that the mission had been a success—a grin so wide that the ragged scar cutting across Thorne's left cheek had tightened like a noose, pulling the mercenary's face askew. Only after he had peeled the Mylar wrapper from the gleaming satellite had Thorne mentioned that he had killed a Navy diver.

Earlier that morning two federal investigators had stopped by the island. Routine questions. Clayton had sent one of the girls upstairs to the mansion to act as lady of the house, explaining that her husband was away. The FBI had eventually written off the island along with other millionaire island compounds that flourished along the Maine coast. The ruse had worked like a charm.

Now arrangements had to be made and a few loose ends cleared up. He thought of Julia. Complicity ought to guarantee her silence, but who could plumb the mysteries of a woman's heart, especially that woman's heart? And McKendrick's interest in her was disconcerting, to say the least. She would have to be watched. Good thing he had a source within the Pentagon; Donnally had proven to be a valuable asset after all.

Summoning Thorne, Clayton shut the door to his paneled office and brought up Elkins and his girlfriend on the computer; as a precaution, he had had the villa at Ocean Point wired for pictures and sound. *Let's see, where is Gerald cavorting today? The bedroom? No. The living-room floor? No. The dining-room table? That was yesterday. The swimming pool? Ah, yes . . .*

Elkins's ardor was impressive; for a fat man, the former NASA tech could really shake and bake. Who could blame him? The girl was superb.

Clayton had known Elkins for a decade. Resentment was the defining mood of the age, and Clayton, like his former cronies in Congress, had milked it for all it was worth. The soldiers and technicians he had quietly recruited throughout the United States loved their work but had struggled to make ends meet. After years of graduate school or elite combat training, they had worked in quiet anonymity while the cash and glory went elsewhere, the quiet acceptance turning into rage every time they switched on the TV. If it wasn't a smooth-talking millionaire talk-show host dishing up one outrage after another, you had some foul-mouthed professional athlete with a third-grade reading ability and a cocaine habit telling the world that fifteen million dollars a year wasn't good enough. America was trading cash for trash. Who could remain loyal to that?

Not Elkins. When Clayton Industries had been in its heyday, Elkins had given Clayton a VIP tour of the Kennedy Space Center. When Clayton reappeared in his life years later, the NASA computer tech was drowning in a sea of debt. The rest, as they say, was history.

Clayton gazed at the desktop monitor. Water sloshed about the pool like the inside of a washing machine. With a yawn, he handed Thorne an envelope containing a half dozen plane tickets and an address.

"He's with a girl," Clayton instructed. "Make them disappear."

They were seated inside the cramped quarters of the White House Situation Room, Henderson's funeral having ended only an hour before. General Walt McKendrick looked across the conference table at Julia and Billy Lawrence, with whom he had shared a limousine from Arlington. Their expressions, like his, were somber, if not grim. They had talked little during the ride to the White House, still shaken by the sight of young Andrew standing over his father's grave. As they pulled out of Arlington, Julia had wept silently, tears rolling down her cheeks beneath her sunglasses.

For Lawrence, the image of a boy standing over an open grave had resurrected memories of his own childhood. His father had been a talented sax player and had bought him a tenor saxophone for his fifth birthday. Lawrence still had the sax, which he had played all through high school in the hours when he wasn't wrestling or doing homework. The saxophone was what Lawrence had had instead of TV. With all his heart, he wished he had the power to restore the special happiness born of a father's relationship with his son, now gone from that boy's life forever.

For McKendrick, the awful symmetry of Jack's death loomed over his soul like a curse—déjà vu and Gödel's boomerang rolled into one. Shot in both legs, he had watched Drake's father die in the tall elephant grass of the Ia Drang Valley in '65 as the North Vietnamese had moved in after the ambush, executing American wounded. He had held Drake's father in his arms urging him to lie still and had been present at Arlington when they had lowered him into the ground. He had placed his hand on Drake's shoulder. Then at Jack's funeral he had watched Drake do the same: place a comforting hand on the shoulder of *his* best friend's grieving son.

Now, seated around the conference table, they looked up as CIA Director Charles Francis Adams arrived, followed by Secretary of Defense Richard Elliot, National Security Advisor Bud McGuire, and other high-ranking officials. President Young was the last to arrive. He nodded by way of greeting and took his seat at the head of the table, his eyes leaden with fatigue. A stocky, even-tempered man, President Young had owned a desktop computer company before entering politics. Had circumstances been otherwise, he might have invited Julia and Lawrence up to the Oval Office for coffee; he had admired their work for years. But now, as he settled into his chair, the strained smile disappearing from his lips, he looked at Julia and Lawrence and got straight to the point.

"I'm setting up an emergency task force headed by CIA Director Adams. I'd like you people on it."

"We'll help in any way we can," Lawrence said in a firm voice. The computer genius looked at the president and his advisors: "Any news on Bright Star?"

The president glanced at Adams.

"None, unfortunately," Adams remarked, jumping in. "The orbiter was brought down by a Trojan horse, a computer program that looks identical to the original but has been altered in some way. According to the National Security Agency and NASA, there's no other explanation. Had the orbiter's computers merely failed,

Atlantis would still be in orbit. Reentry is an exceedingly difficult procedure to pull off. To reenter the Earth's atmosphere safely, *Atlantis* has to follow a very narrow corridor, approaching the Earth at an inclination no shallower than five point three degrees and no steeper than seven point seven degrees. If the approach is too shallow, the orbiter skips off the Earth's atmosphere and enters a deadly orbit around the sun. Too steep, and she plunges through the Earth's atmosphere at speeds at which astronauts are crushed by g-forces long before they strike the Earth. *Atlantis* not only reentered the Earth's atmosphere but also landed flawlessly on the ocean. Her computers were programmed prior to launch, we believe, by this man."

Adams quickly opened a folder and held up an eleven-by-twelve glossy photograph. "His name is Gerald Elkins. He's a senior computer technician at the Kennedy Space Center, or at least he was until two days prior to liftoff—he's missing."

"God help the son-of-a-bitch if he's responsible for this," grumbled Secretary of Defense Richard Elliot.

Adams looked at the group with a mirthless smile. "A couple of months ago, Elkins purchased a custom-designed yacht under an assumed name. The FBI uncovered the information this morning, after finding a parking ticket that had slipped behind the rear seat of his Skylark. The ticket was issued at a marina outside of Miami. According to the dockmaster, Elkins boarded the boat two weeks ago. Neither he nor the yacht has been seen since. Walt is coordinating the various search elements."

"Mr. President, if he's on that boat, we'll find him," McKendrick said with determination. "We're sweeping the Eastern Seaboard and the Caribbean now with everything we've got. We'll track this guy."

"What about the *Trident?*"

Adams went straight to the issue. "We're still searching. According to Drake, the terrorists used a submarine to steal Bright Star. That submarine did not appear in the images provided by the KH-24. Therefore, it had to be the *Trident.* Obviously, the people behind these attacks are not only well financed but also extremely sophisticated in their use of technology. The massive shutdown at the Johnson Space Center wasn't mere happenstance, either. We must assume that these people have penetrated our most secure computer networks. We still don't know whether they are foreign or domestic. They could have brought *Atlantis* down anywhere. They chose Maine. Could be a ruse. At this point, we just don't know. It's crucial not to make assumptions. We're checking for unusual activity along the Eastern Seaboard and elsewhere. But Elkins is the key. Finding him must be our first priority."

"Good."

Adams was pleased. "Our second priority must be to locate the leak of sensitive information and shut it off. Information regarding Bright Star came from the Pentagon. No other federal entity possessed the spectrum and quality of information that these people required." Adams looked at Lawrence. "That is where we need your help. We need you to comb through the Pentagon's computer network. Quietly. We have to be careful not to arouse the intruder's suspicions. Until he can be tracked, we don't want him—or her—closing up shop prematurely. The people who've had access to the Bright Star project are few in number. The Bureau has been running security checks on these people for the past couple of years. None has shown any signs of unusual activity. No dead-letter drops. No million-dollar yachts like Elkins's. Therefore, given the terrorists' cybernetic expertise, the exchange of information is most likely taking place electronically. We need you to isolate the source of the leak."

Lawrence flashed an easy grin, flattered to have been asked, eager to bring these terrorists down. He looked at Julia, who smiled faintly. Still stricken by Jack's funeral the hour before, Julia seemed to be barely listening. Lawrence placed a reassuring hand on her shoulder. "I can start immediately," he said.

President Young looked at Lawrence in gratitude. "I'm placing the entire resources of the United States Government at your disposal. All you have to do is ask."

"Thank you, sir."

Adams looked at Julia. "We also need to know if Bright Star can be adapted to foreign weapons systems. Can a nation such as Iran or Iraq bring her on-line?"

"It's possible," Julia admitted, her face clouding, "if they were to gather the right experts, the right equipment and software. Technology is like language; it's eminently transferable. The Russians and Chinese could have Bright Star operational in a matter of weeks."

For a long minute nobody spoke. The implications of Bright Star's falling into the wrong hands were patent; the president would be under tremendous pressure to order a preemptive strike. Bombing Iran or Iraq would pose serious diplomatic problems and might incite terrorist attacks, though the United States would probably receive at least the tacit support of most nations. But bombing China? The United States would be faced with a scenario worse than the Cuban missile crisis; the world shoved once again to the brink of nuclear war.

With relentless precision, Adams pursued another line of questioning: "Let's say that Bright Star does fall into foreign hands. Could we disarm it?"

This time, Lawrence fielded the question. "The satellite's acquisition, tracking, pointing, and laser systems are classified and would represent a technological windfall to whatever nation acquired them. Julia can provide a more detailed explanation with regard to that aspect. But to answer your question, yes—Bright Star can be disarmed. But you need someone to crawl inside the satellite and pull the software disks. There's an access panel on the right side. By entering this panel, a technician can actually stand inside Bright Star to accomplish whatever work is required."

"You can't disarm the satellite by remote command?" the president asked.

"Yes. But it may not work. We have to assume that these people have obtained a copy of the software that allows us to operate Bright Star from the ground. That software has been installed into several computer networks, including one at White Sands, which I assume is linked to the Pentagon network. The terrorists could have suborned someone who has access to it—someone like Elkins. Or they could have lifted it electronically. And it makes sense that once they had obtained a clean copy, they would infect our software with viruses.

"The key to disarming Bright Star, therefore, is the software inside the satellite itself that allows Julia's high-tech gadgetry to mesh, if you will. Without that software, Bright Star is defunct. And the operating program cannot be rewritten, either. I have the source code."

"I'm not sure I understand," the president said.

Lawrence looked around the room. It was obvious that the president wasn't the only person confused. "Source code is programming code in its raw state. It's human readable; in other words, its computer language is written in words. We test the source code to weed out the bugs, then put it through a compiler, converting it to a numerical binary form so that it can operate on one or more platforms. What's important here is that you can't take the binaries and reverse the process to reveal the source code. That's how Microsoft protects its Windows software; it keeps the Windows source code locked up. And I mean tight. You can copy Windows software but you can't change it in any fundamental way. At Systems Technologies we do the same, but with ten times the security. Not even Julia has access to the source code. I have access, Howard Collins at the National Security Agency has access, that's it. But with Bright Star, we've built in an additional safeguard. The minute the disks are pulled from the system, they self-destruct. Unlike the software that allows us to control Bright Star from the ground, the disks can't be copied. We designed the disks to have this capability in case Bright Star fell out of orbit and wound up in foreign hands. The disks resemble CDs and are easily identifiable; no other piece of equipment inside Bright Star is similar in appearance."

"Would you provide us with a diagram showing exactly where these disks are located?" the president asked.

"The schematics are in Michigan."

"A sketch should be sufficient," Adams remarked. "As long as these disks are in plain view."

"They are. Anyone entering Bright Star will spot them immediately."

"Good," Adams remarked. "The next item we have to consider is getting our people ready in Florida in the event that we discover Elkins's yacht. Reason suggests that he is headed for the Caribbean. We doubt he would attempt a transatlantic voyage. Once we locate that yacht, we have to move very quickly indeed."

McKendrick gazed at Adams. "Send Drake."

President Young looked at McKendrick, startled. "Do you think that's wise? These people just killed his best friend."

McKendrick was adamant. "That's exactly why we should send

him, sir. Drake wants in. And things could get sticky if we have to assault that yacht, or whatever building Elkins is holed up in, especially if he is on an island and the host country is less than receptive to our operating on their soil. As Charles said, we have to move quickly. Drake has proven himself in the past. And no one wants to apprehend these people as badly as he does. Drake will go the extra mile to make sure that Elkins stays alive."

"You sold me," said the president.

Bud McGuire looked at the group, his silver hair gleaming beneath the fluorescent lights. "Might be prudent to offer a reward—two million dollars, say, for information leading to the arrest and conviction of the terrorists who brought down *Atlantis.*"

The president nodded. "Good idea. Let's do it." He looked at the men surrounding him. "Anything else?"

Nobody spoke.

"Okay, people, let's get to work."

21 August

The ghosts of SR-71 Blackbirds soared over Moffett Field as Dennis Chang emerged from the corporate headquarters of Digitek and strode across the sun-baked parking lot to his Ford Explorer. Located along the southwestern banks of San Francisco Bay, near NASA's Ames Research Center, Digitek provided state-of-the-art microprocessors to the aerospace industry. Chang had been with Digitek for twenty-five years. The previous autumn he had been promoted to CEO by Digitek's board of trustees, a cause for celebration in a place worlds away from Sunnyvale, California. Dennis Chang was a *chen diyu,* or a "deep-sinking fish," the name the Chinese Ministry of State Security conferred upon its dormant agents, the men and women it sent to the United States as college students to become naturalized citizens and rise in the corporate world. Dormant no longer, Chang had been activated the previous year.

Approaching the blue Explorer, Chang palmed the car keys

and pressed the remote lock button on the key fob. He was late for the parent-teacher conference at his son's private school. In a rush, he climbed into the Explorer, switched on the ignition, and powered down the windows, allowing the fresh air to cool the Explorer's superheated interior. Then he noticed the package.

It was a padded mailer, placed on the passenger-seat floor so that it would not lie directly in the sun. The mailer bore the designation: EYES ONLY. Inside was a videocassette wrapped in a protective layer of thermal plastic.

Chang called his wife on the car phone, made an excuse, and drove directly to their cedar home set in the foothills of Santa Cruz, knowing that his wife would not return for at least an hour. He snapped the video in the VCR, locked his office door, and for the next twenty minutes sat spellbound in front of the television monitor as a thousand needles of light exploded from the satellite, punctuating the darkness.

The voice in the background minced few words: "What you see before you is the reconnaissance satellite removed from the orbiter *Atlantis* several days ago. It is in fact the most advanced compact laser weapons system devised by man, code-named Bright Star. This system will not only provide your nation with an impenetrable nuclear umbrella, but will also allow you to pinpoint up to a thousand targets and carry out a multiple-beam, high-energy laser attack to eliminate your opponents from the battlefield. The nation possessing this weapon will be invincible, a fact your nation should consider most carefully. You are invited to bid on this weapons systems over the Internet address below, sealed bids only. Interference or tampering of any sort will not be tolerated. The auction will take place on August twenty-fourth at eight P.M. The nations invited to participate are as follows: China, Libya, France,

Iran, Iraq, India, Pakistan, Syria, and Israel. The bids will start at four billion dollars. If that amount seems excessive, we suggest that you dwell on one fundamental question: What price do you place on your nation's survival?"

His clothes laid out on the bed, Drake looked up from his packing and cast a small smile of encouragement at Jennifer, who sat in one of the plush armchairs that occupied their bedroom suite at the Hay-Adams. She didn't buy it. The North Portico of the White House in all its evening radiance filled the mullioned windows to their right. The splendid view didn't matter, either. She was fraught with anxiety. The people who killed Jack knew too much and were too well organized.

Even her father, international arms dealer Erich Gerhardt, could not have put together an organization like this, even with his genius for manipulating people, even with the vast fortune at his disposal. She had worked as his assistant; she knew firsthand the depth of his relationship with foreign intelligence services, who had marveled at his ability to get things done. In the eighties he had assisted the Iraqis in putting together their elaborate procurement networks, a ramified string of European shell companies that existed for the sole purpose of circumventing the arms-export restrictions emplaced by the United States and other nations against Saddam Hussein's murderous regime. If Iraq needed a special phosphate for the manufacture of Tabun, a nerve gas, for example, a Swiss corporation would place the order with a German chemical manufacturer, who would truck the product to a French pesticide corporation in Marseilles, who would in turn ship the contraband to an export company in Venice, where it would be transferred to another ship headed for Turkey. From Turkey, the phosphate would be trucked via Jordan to Iraq.

Deals of this nature often had the tacit approval if not the outright blessing of governments more interested in the bottom line than the use to which these dual-use chemicals might be put. And Jennifer was certain that a foreign government that to be behind the downing of *Atlantis,* a government that would use its considerable resources to kill anyone who stood in its way.

And Drake would stand in their way. She knew Drake well, loved him more than anything. He had saved her life. He was as mysterious as the ocean to which he returned time and again. She knew implicitly that she would love him for the rest of her life, but never quite grasp the depth of his soul or the breadth of his imagination. Gerhardt had possessed those qualities also, but cruelty and cynicism had dominated. In Drake it was love that dominated: love of family, friends, love of her.

He hadn't talked much about Jack's death. He'd told her what had happened but hadn't delved into his feelings. A part of him seemed to be elsewhere. Yet beneath his distant demeanor, she knew that he was grieving, struggling to find a way of making things right. Still, it was as though Jack's death had thrown up a wall between them.

So in silence she watched her husband pack. McKendrick had sent a driver over to take him to Nellis Air Base.

"I'll call when I can," Drake said when he'd finished.

"Okay." She forced a smile, not wanting him to feel burdened by her anxiety.

Drake looked at her closely. "You should go ahead with the addition. Gives you something to do while I'm gone. The architect called the other day and said that the plans were ready. Why not start now?" Drake had kept over five thousand books in storage, a fact she had discovered following their marriage. Most of these books had belonged to his father, who had been valedictorian of his class at West Point. They had decided to build a library, as their family room with its floor-to-ceiling bookshelves was already filled to capacity.

"OK."

He put his arms around her waist and for a long time held her close. Then he kissed her. "I love you, Jen."

She looked deeply into his eyes, then rested her head against his chest, listening to the rhythmic pounding of his heart.

Deep within the labyrinthine confines of the Pentagon, Billy Lawrence flipped up the screen of his laptop computer and went to work. McKendrick had supplied him with the passwords he would need to take control of the Pentagon's computer system. It would be up to Lawrence to gain access without alerting the Pentagon's systems administrators that someone was snooping around.

The information McKendrick supplied had helped, giving him a detailed description of the firewalls in place. Lawrence found them to be woefully inadequate. Firewalls were the cybernetic equivalent of the Maginot Line. Lawrence hadn't found one yet that he couldn't "spoof" within minutes or circumvent completely with a set of cracking tools that had been recently devised.

The same bitter truth applied to encryption. Sending encrypted information from computer to computer—missile specifications from a research lab in California to a testing facility in New Mexico, say, a common practice within the military—was like transferring gold by armored car from one cardboard box to another. If you wanted access to that information, you simply lifted it and the encryption key from the recipient's computer.

And breaking into Defense Department networks was easier than people imagined. Many of the tools an aspiring criminal hacker needed were available for downloading on the Internet. Contrary to popular belief, criminal computer hackers were not errant geniuses. For the most part, they were individuals of limited imagination, even in cases where their technical abilities were quite good. To a startling degree, their bulletin boards and Web sites displayed a mind-numbing uniformity: screen names like Master of Doom and Web sites filled with the same quasi-medieval sci-fi hokum abounded. Even the legitimate hacking community rarely rose above the dreck. Lawrence called these people the Dungeons & Dragons crowd. He hadn't seen such conformity masquerading as freedom of expression since the New Left politics of the late 1960s.

The only way to prevent intruders from stealing classified information was to take all the computers containing such information off-line. If a computer isn't plugged in to a modem, then information can't be accessed from the outside. Sadly, either through misplaced faith in firewalls or sheer laziness, the folks in charge of computer security at the Pentagon and at other Defense Department organizations had not taken the obvious step to prevent computer break-ins.

And you'd think they might have learned. During the Gulf War, a group of criminal hackers operating from the Netherlands had broken into the Pentagon's computer system, stolen classified logistical information about U.S. troop deployments in the Gulf region, and sold the information to the Iraqis. And now someone had accessed classified information to steal Bright Star. Lives had been lost.

Lawrence was angry. His personal stake in the Bright Star project had no bearing on the middling pride he took in developing such a weapons system. He had devoted his life to creating Bright Star as a way of not only ensuring the security of the United States and her allies but also as a means of cutting defense spending in half. Once operational, Bright Star would render other defense platforms obsolete and in the process save taxpayers a hundred billion dollars a year, if not more—the only justification for building such a weapons system in the first place. A great deal of good could be accomplished with the money. Lower taxes meant more families could afford to send their children to college. Some of the money no longer needed for defense could be used for raising teachers' salaries, attracting the best and the brightest to help shepherd America's children into the future.

During the eighties, Lawrence had watched with increasing dismay as defense spending had skyrocketed, sending the national debt to the moon. Having violated the fiduciary trust that bound them to future generations, the men in charge in Washington, the supply-siders, had turned the United States into the world's largest debtor nation, a gilded Easter egg—strong on the outside, hollow in the middle. By 1997, the *interest* on the national debt alone amounted to 238.5 billion dollars, making it the third-largest expense of the federal government, nearly equal to the defense budget and more than twice the cost of welfare. The CEL Foundation and the stunning breakthroughs at Systems Technologies had been Lawrence's way of fighting back.

Now, at best, it was a dream deferred. And as he scanned the Pentagon's operating system, looking for security holes and signs of tampering, his competitive instincts tuned and ready to rock and roll, Lawrence slipped a Stevie Wonder tape into his Walkman, vowing to search all of cyberspace, if necessary, to track these people down.

Israeli Defense and Armed Forces Attaché Major General Ben Yanov quietly removed the videotape from the VCR and sat down at his desk. He was alone and clearly shaken. After discovering the video in the front seat of his red Nissan Pulsar, he had retreated to his spare but comfortable Washington embassy office, telling the curious that he had forgotten something in his office. Whoever had placed the unwrapped cassette on the driver's seat of his locked Pulsar had taken great pains to assure him of its safety. The cassette had been constructed of clear plastic, and Yanov had seen at once that it contained no explosives. The label had been plainly visible, marked EYES ONLY.

Now, as he sat at his desk contemplating the dilemma before him, the temptation that the satellite Bright Star presented dazzled his senses. For Israel, bordered on one side by water and on three sides by hostile nations, such a defensive weapon would be the answer to its prayers. But as much as he marveled at America's ingenuity in creating such a weapon, he feared the destructive power that it would place in the hands of the men possessing it; the temptation to use Bright Star as an offensive weapon would greatly exceed the temptation to use nuclear weapons. Its selective targeting ensured that there would be few moral qualms about pressing the button, especially among hard-liners for whom moral qualms were nothing more than liberal weakness. And in Israel, hard-liners were in vogue these days. The Hamas terror bombings had gone a long way toward achieving the classic objective of all terror groups: to foment revolution by forcing a state to adopt repressive policies that would incite the underclass. Hamas had planted the bombs; Israelis had elected the "Serial Bungler," to use the *Econo-*

mist's salubrious phrase; and the peace process, despised by Hamas, had withered. Overnight.

No, given the state of the Israeli government, there was only one responsible course of action: He had to do everything in his power to assist the United States in recovering this weapon. He flipped through his Rolodex, an ancient artifact in this cybernetic age. Then, having memorized the number, Yanov stuffed the tape into his briefcase and drove to a diner on the outskirts of Washington to use a pay phone.

22 August

His men were in position, concealed among the limestone outcroppings that formed the tip of Ocean Point. Thorne glanced at his watch: 0200 hours. The trade winds had increased, stirring the brush that surrounded the villa fifty yards above. Elkins and the girl had turned the lights out several hours before and had gone to bed.

The limestone appeared white and luminous under the stars. Wearing black-and-gray camouflage pants and a T-shirt, and armed only with a sound-suppressed Browning .45, Thorne signaled his men and carefully moved up the rocky slope, never taking his eyes off the wide porch straight ahead. He moved slowly, halting every ten feet to watch and listen. When he reached the porch, he crouched beside the lattice and signaled for the next man. Forty minutes later, three comrades knelt by his side.

The villa was dark and quiet. No sound except for the rattling palms and the waves slapping against the rocks below. They slowly worked their way around to the right until they encountered an open deck off the dining room. Like the porch, the deck was five feet off the ground, but instead of lattice, it was bounded by conventional posts and rails. Thorne continued moving right until he came to a staircase. He quickly crossed it, moved to the side of the villa, and swung himself up to the deck beneath the bottom rail. One by one, his men followed. Then, crouching beside a screen door, he picked the lock and very slowly pushed the door open, listening for movement. The villa was silent.

Their approach would have been easier had Elkins and the girl kept the air-conditioning on as they had the night before. But tonight, for some reason, they had turned it off. From his lair among the outcroppings below, Thorne had seen the girl open the bedroom windows, her naked body pale in the moonlight.

The bedroom lay on the second floor. Crossing the dining room, they spotted a staircase ten feet beyond and to the right of the living-room entrance. The living room was a beachcomber's paradise: vaulted ceilings, sofas, sliding glass doors, stereo, TV, skylight, and bar. The open staircase led up to a wide balcony. The master bedroom lay at the end of a short corridor to the right.

Thorne signaled and the fourth man broke off, quietly positioning himself near a wall so that he could survey the living room and the sliding glass doors that led to the porch. Then Thorne and the two other men climbed the stairs in silence.

She was wide awake, breathing through her mouth, doing her best to ignore the foul odor issuing from the man beside her. Having satisfied his most urgent lust in the afternoon, Elkins had expended no less energy in satisfying his other desires later that day. Sprawled on the couch watching a Marlins game, he had devoured a plate of mangos and a pineapple while consuming three six-packs of beer. Afterward, he had helped himself to a quart of conch chowder. The eruptions had started the moment he had staggered up to the bedroom to pass out. Now lying beside this drunken wreck of a man in the early hours of the morning, she could hardly breathe. There had been moments when the sheets seemed to rise from the bed.

She had slept with some real pigs in her time, but this was something else. Not even the mild breeze coming through the open windows helped.

Her name was Catherine Durand. A twenty-three-year-old former model with the Estelle Agency in Paris, she had been approached by a woman whose escort business catered to the upper echelons of society. Catherine thought of this work as dating—which, in a sense, it was. Except that it paid exceedingly well, far better than the money she had made from Estelle, a second-tier agency that could not offer her the work she needed. Now, on what she made in a week, she could live comfortably for a year. All the men she dated were wealthy. Most were cultivated. Occasionally, her clients turned out to be undesirable. But none of the men she had slept with in the past two years had revolted her in the manner in which Elkins had.

Disgusted, she climbed out of bed and slipped into her bathrobe. The villa was quiet. She would sleep on one of the sofas downstairs, then leave in the morning. She walked out of the bedroom and padded down the hall, savoring the fresh air. But just before she stepped out onto the balcony overlooking the living room, something caught her eye. She halted, staring down into the dim light, pressing herself to the wall, her heart pounding as four men crossed the living-room floor. The men were armed, their weapons drawn. They were heading for the stairs.

She hurried back to the bedroom, slipped on a pair of shorts and a T-shirt, and rushed to the bathroom. Near the toilet, Elkins's soiled shorts were lying in a heap on the tile floor. She rifled the pockets and found a money clip containing a wad of U.S. currency and a credit card, the same clip from which Elkins had peeled off a hundred-dollar bill the previous morning so that she could go shopping. She stuffed the clip into her pocket and crawled through the bathroom window onto the cedar roof, out over the first story. The shingles felt warm against her feet. She would have to jump. Any second the men would reach the bedroom.

Trembling, Catherine padded to the roof's edge. She was over the driveway. She could see blacktop extending out to the road. Calming herself, she sat down and edged closer until her legs were dangling. She looked down again and braced herself. *If you don't jump, you will die.*

She struck the ground hard, tumbling onto her knees and elbows, too frightened to scream. Scrambling to her feet, she looked around. No movement, no voices; only the wind in the palms and the silent pounding of her heart.

Thorne entered the hallway, moving quickly now toward the master bedroom. The door was open, and he could see a corner of a bed. He paused at the door and listened to the rasp of Elkins's breathing, a foul odor drifting past his nostrils. He winced.

Elkins was lying flat on his back, buck naked, his soft fat white belly rising and falling with each drunken snore. The room stank to high heaven. Now he knew why the girl had turned off the air-conditioning and opened the windows. One of Thorne's men emerged from the bathroom and shook his head. Thorne gestured to the hallway, and the men understood: Check the other bedrooms. Then Thorne rolled the fat computer technician out of bed. Elkins hit the floor with a thud.

"Wake up, you sack of shit!"

Startled, Elkins looked up at the man towering over him.

"No sign of the girl, boss."

Thorne nodded as Elkins drew back in fear.

"Who are you? Hey! What is this? What do you think you're doing? Get out of my house."

"Where's the girl?"

Elkins looked around in confusion, then suddenly realized that Catherine was missing.

"I—"

Thorne holstered his .45 and angrily looked at his men. "Get him into a body bag."

Bound and gagged, zipped inside the stifling body bag, a whimpering Gerry Elkins felt himself being loaded into the trunk of a car. He was going to die. He knew it. He was shivering. *Clayton. Why are you doing this to me?*

The engine started, and he could hear tires crunching the shells scattered about the asphalt driveway. Where were they taking him? His brain throbbed from the beer he'd consumed, and his throat was parched. He curled himself up in the fetal position as the car made a right-hand turn, his head bumping against a taillight. His stomach churned. He moaned again, a hot liquid pressure building inside his intestines.

"Hey, boss, there's something sloshing around inside the bag!"

Thorne watched his men lifting the bag out of the trunk.

"Feels like there's a gallon of water in there. You think this guy ralphed?"

Suddenly Elkins began to thrash about, the men struggling to keep the bag under control. Annoyed, Thorne glanced up at the deserted boathouse, then at Elkins's yacht floating at the end of the dock, and reached for the body bag, lifting Elkins off the ground in such a way that the computer technician's face became submerged in the liquid pool forming at the bottom of the bag. The thrashing stopped. Thorne dropped the bag to the ground and stepped away. The two men picked the bag up again and headed down the dock, giggling with pleasure at the muffled sounds of Elkins moaning.

Julia Reynolds glanced at her watch. It was 3 A.M. She couldn't sleep. She lay in bed at the J. W. Marriott on Pennsylvania Avenue, thinking about the day Geoffrey Clayton had given her the 450,000 check to pay off her father's delinquent taxes. He had also managed to replace the fifty thousand dollars that her father had embezzled in an act of desperation from Cambridge Partners, a global investment firm in Boston before anyone knew that it was missing. Her father's reputation had been saved; he had been spared the horror of going to prison. He had already suffered one heart attack. Julia doubted that he would survive another. Clayton had come through for her at a time when she had thought that all was lost; he had provided her with a way out. Gödel's theorem. It had been one of the happiest days of her life.

She had met Clayton as an honors graduate student at MIT. Clayton Industries had been in its heyday. He had taken her out to lunch and had offered her a job, which she had agreed to accept once she had received her doctorate. Then came the trouble with her father, a quiet and loving man with owlish eyes. She hadn't learned of the problem until he confessed after the IRS had moved in, slapping a tax lien on everything her family had owned. Overwhelmed, burdened with shame and anxiety, her father had suffered the heart attack three months later.

In grief and desperation, she had turned to Clayton, promising to repay the loan when she started work. Clayton had been generous in his commiseration, mentioning how unfair it was that the politicians who enacted the tax laws in the United States penalized hardworking men like her father while allowing wealthy tax exiles with Irish passports or Bahamian citizenship to get away with murder. Why, just the week before, he had had lunch at the Plaza with an American industrialist who'd come to New York for medical treatment. Throughout lunch, the man had boasted that by acquiring Bahamian citizenship and setting up residence on Lyford Cay he was beating the IRS out of twenty-eight million dollars a year. He had urged Clayton to do the same.

As she lay in bed, sick at heart, she saw clearly now that Clayton's generosity was nothing more than an insidious ploy to feed her resentment, that in sympathizing with her family's plight, he had been prying her loose, separating her from her sense of right and wrong. He had portrayed the world as a heap of broken symbols unworthy of her allegiance, and she had made a separate peace.

With the money Clayton had given her, her father had paid his tax bills and had retired from Cambridge Partners after a long and successful career. A year later, Clayton Industries had gone under. With Clayton in jail, she had accepted a teaching position at MIT, then had moved on to Systems Technologies. But she never forgot Clayton's generosity or the debt she owed him.

Then, to her astonishment, Clayton had called her out of the blue. He was doing fine, he had said. He had been thinking about starting another research firm. They had talked about old times. He had inquired about her mother, sorry to hear that she had died. The breakthroughs that she and Billy had engineered at Systems Technologies had made her wealthy and one of the most respected researchers in her field. He had said that she needn't repay the loan. Then, with almost casual indifference, he had begun asking her questions about Bright Star. And when she had balked, he had applied pressure, sending her a sheaf of documents proving her father's malfeasance. In the end, worried about her father's health, she had capitulated to Clayton's demands.

Now people lay dead because of it. *That boy at Arlington standing over his father's grave.* She couldn't forgive herself. She had accepted Clayton's money to cover up her father's embezzlement. Then she had succumbed to blackmail. She had thought Clayton would sell the information to another government. She turned her head toward the window, thinking of Lawrence. Born and raised in the ghetto, his parents killed in a shoot-out between police and snipers, Lawrence could have easily grown up to be a Geoffrey Clayton in spite of his grandmother's loving care. But instead of harboring a galaxy of resentments, he had gone on to lead a contributive life, he had worked within the system to improve the world. Somewhere along the line, he had made that decision. Now she would have to make hers.

They were cruising past Frenchman's Cay, heading south to open water. The small island had once been a pirate's lair, an irony not lost upon Thorne. Now it was little more than an uninhabited bird sanctuary, the perfect spot to get rid of Elkins.

Standing on the flying bridge, Thorne and two of his men relaxed in the warm summer breeze, the phosphorescent wake of the seventy-five-foot motor yacht glowing in the distance. Fifty feet astern, the fourth member of his team trailed in a Boston Whaler.

Thorne slipped the yacht into neutral, then shut down the engines. He looked back at the island. In the dark the surf broke against Frenchman's Cay in a thin white line. The wind felt warm against his skin, and the water shimmered with moonlight. *Too bad they hadn't caught the girl when they had nabbed Elkins. Elkins could have had one last fling before the long good-bye.*

The reef lay a mile astern. Thorne looked down at the clear black sea. According to the yacht's global positioning system, they were drifting over an abyss that plummeted thousands of feet to the bottom of the ocean. They had traveled far enough.

The Boston Whaler swung to starboard, and the two men who had ridden with Thorne climbed down from the flying bridge and hopped aboard. They would wait beside the yacht until Thorne had taken care of business.

Palming a five-pound hammer, Thorne headed below, the scent of varnished oak filling his nostrils as he launched into a snappy rendition of "Mack the Knife."

———

Inside the body bag, a whimpering and begrimed Gerry Elkins rued his existence. His nostrils burned. They had chained him to a bunk up forward and had locked the cabin door, but not before slitting the airtight bag above his feet. Why had they done that? Where were they taking him? He was shivering and perspiring at the same time, marinating in the bag like a bad piece of meat, basting in his own foul juices. He squeezed his eyes shut, wishing he could turn back time, wishing he had never laid eyes on Clayton or the girl. He had been inside the body bag for over an hour. Hadn't he suffered enough?

Suddenly the yacht slowed and someone cut the engines. In the distance he heard another boat approaching. Astern. It bumped against the starboard hull. Then he heard footsteps below and a man's voice singing a Bobby Darin tune: *"Oh, the shark, babe, has such teeth, dear . . ."*

Singing *alto voce* and snapping his fingers, Thorne entered the engine room and looked around for the sea cocks. He was enjoying himself. Killing people before sunrise made his day. Tastier than a bowl of Cheerios. When he had worked for the Russians in Beirut during the eighties, not an evening went by when he wasn't on the prowl, stalking the ruins, honing his lethal skills, piling up the body count before morning. Most of the time he used a knife. Sometimes he opted for a baseball bat. When word got out that the Russians were unhappy with someone and were sending Thorne, even the crazies got out of the way. Thorne tended to make an example of people who interfered. They really pissed him off.

Following the collapse of the Soviet Union, Thorne had em-
igrated to the United States, offering his services to the CIA. As
a part of their effort to collect leftover Stingers from the mujahideen, the agency had sent him to Afghanistan, where he had
first cut his teeth in a Spetznaz unit during the Soviet occupation
in the late 1970s. In the process of collecting Stingers, however,
Thorne had also collected heads, engineering a number of
reprisals against his former enemies. At Langley, his handlers in
the clandestine service tended to overlook such behavior so long
as Thorne came up with the goods. Far from being the noble
freedom fighters depicted by Hollywood, the mujahideen were
heroin-smuggling Islamic fundamentalists about to embark on a
terror campaign against their former ally, the United States. The
World Trade Center bombing had been the outcome. Having a
loose cannon like Thorne rolling around in Afghanistan, killing
whomever he pleased, would only incite the mujahideen to further acts of terror, as they were well aware that Thorne was CIA.
When Adams took over the agency, Thorne got the ax, having
made a bad situation worse.

Unemployed, he drifted into the private sector, where security
companies were springing up overnight. Thorne loathed the do-
mesticated world of executive protection. He wanted to slit
throats. He had been about to join a Serb mercenary outfit when
Clayton had offered him a job.

Opening the sea cocks, and breaking the twin steel handles
with two powerful swings of the hammer, Thorne thought about
the girl. She had slipped the noose. But she couldn't be far. He had
men watching the airport and scanning cell phone traffic. It was
only a matter of time before he'd track her down.

The water rose around the base of the twin Detroit diesels.
That ought to do it. Elkins, the dumbshit, was about to go snorkeling.

Then as Thorne made his way topside, a wicked smile crossed his lips. He got on the intercom. "Attention, all passengers. This is Captain Smith of the SS *Titanic*. We have struck an iceberg. Please report to your lifeboat stations."

Trapped inside the body bag, Elkins was doing the panic dance, thrashing about with even more vigor than he had mustered during his first session with the girl. He flailed against the bag and the chains that held him fast, weeping and wailing to no avail. Suddenly, the door to his stateroom flew open. "Help me," he pleaded.

A mock British accent: "Is that you, Miss Cavendish?"

"Help me."

"Mr. Lightholer, Miss Cavendish is trapped inside her stateroom . . . Wait a minute—"

The voice sniffed. "Good God." The door slammed shut.

Weeping softly, Elkins could hear the receding cackle of Thorne's laughter, then the roar of an outboard as the Boston Whaler sped off. The yacht gurgled and creaked. Thirty minutes later, it listed heavily by the bow, teetering like a stack of rough bricks. Tilted upright in bed, water sloshing inside the bag up to his knees, Elkins felt the yacht shudder, then plunge beneath the sea. A terrible silence engulfed him, draining what little energy he had left, as the yacht spiraled underwater, then scraped to a halt. Elkins blinked in the darkness, then wailed in abject fear, realizing that the quick death that he had prayed for was not to be. A pocket of fetid air had formed inside the body bag around his head. With each breath, he would slowly asphyxiate. In the end, it took Elkins over an hour to die.

"You evil son-of-a bitch. You murderer."

"I don't know what you're talking about, Julia," Clayton remarked, careful to keep his voice steady.

"Don't give me that shit."

"How's your dad doing?" Clayton asked, figuring it would buy him time.

Julia paused. Then she said, "Don't ever call me again, you bastard." She was crying.

The phone rang. Donnally awoke with a start. Annoyed, he glanced at the bedroom clock: 4:45 A.M. *What the fuck?* He picked up the receiver. "Yeah?"

"I need you to go shopping."

Donnally straightened up in bed. It was Clayton. "Now?"

"Get your ass out of bed."

Something was up. Donnally could smell it. He drove to Dulles and headed for one of the pay phones in the vast baggage-claim area on the lower level. As he passed a baggage carousel, a young Spaniard who was being met asked in broken English if he was Mr. Knox. "Fuck you, douche bag," Donnally replied.

He dialed the number, let it ring twice, then hung up. A minute later Clayton called back. "We have a problem."

Donnally listened to Clayton's instructions with rancor. "I didn't sign up for this shit," he remarked by way of response.

It was not the response Clayton expected to hear. Another

voice came over the line. Thorne. The mercenary sounded a long way off, as though overseas. But the rage behind his words came through loud and clear, boring like a deranged worm straight into Donnally's heart.

In the Cabinet Room of the White House, eleven men and women watched the video in gloomy silence. When it was over and the lights came on, General Douglas Creighton said, "This came from the Israelis?"

"Not officially," Adams replied. "It was a gift from a friend—an act of conscience, really."

"Whoever it is, God bless him," remarked Secretary of State Harold Reeves.

"What about the French?" inquired National Security Advisor Bud McGuire. "Have we heard from them?"

"No," replied McKendrick. "We haven't."

"Figures," Creighton exclaimed in disgust. "Hell, if it wasn't for us they'd all be singing 'Deutschland über Alles' instead of the 'Marseillaise'."

President Young gazed at the Army chief of staff. "I appreciate the sentiment, Creighton, but it doesn't get us anywhere."

"Perhaps we should try calling Prime Minister Ganet," suggested Margaret Abrams, President Young's chief of staff. "Nip this thing in the bud. Work from the assumption that we know he's seen the tape. Then offer to underwrite the French bid. Work out a deal."

"And hand over billions of dollars to terrorists?" Creighton exclaimed.

"Consider the alternative."

President Young looked toward Adams. "Charles?"

"Of all the countries invited to place bids, China will most likely win. France doesn't have the resources. Margaret's right. Unless we can locate the terrorists and recover Bright Star, we will have to strike a deal."

A door opened, and a uniformed officer quietly slipped inside. He made his way to McKendrick and whispered a message.

All eyes looked to McKendrick in expectation.

"What is it, Walt?" President Young asked.

"Elkins's boat. We found it. Off the Turks and Caicos. It's in three hundred feet of water, dangling off the edge of a coral wall."

The bell-bottomed juggler tossed a mango high in the air as Dennis Chang strolled past the ornate Conservatory of Flowers in San Francisco's Golden Gate Park. Walking beside him, a young woman of Chinese extraction talked in lighthearted tones as she gazed at the Frisbee players. From her animated features and from the easy familiarity with which she bantered with Chang, most people would have assumed that they were related somehow—father and daughter, perhaps. In fact, they had never met before. The young woman had recently arrived from New York.

They strolled by a eucalyptus tree, the sun filtering through the long, fragrant leaves. The woman continued speaking. "We need the name of someone who can tip the auction in our favor. Someone who will not draw attention to you, but who is exceptionally adept at manipulating the Internet. Someone with a family."

Chang thought for a moment. He knew several such people.

Some were close friends, but the girl wanted a stranger, a man with a wife and children. A twinge of guilt invaded his soul, but he shook it off. Business was business. Then he offered up a name.

"Would you like to go for a walk?"

McKendrick looked up from his desk, delighted that Julia had asked. Only moments before he had been driven back to the Pentagon from the White House.

Julia glanced about his office, admiring the river view. "We could walk along the Potomac."

"I can't, I'm sorry." He rose from his desk, looking at her with genuine regret, and stood beside her, catching the scent of her perfume. He was due in the War Room in fifteen minutes. "Tomorrow?" he asked hopefully.

Julia glanced down at the floor for a moment, considering the proposal. "How about dinner tonight?"

"Great!" McKendrick beamed. "Nine-thirtyish, okay?"

"Perfect." Julia smiled.

McKendrick walked her to the outer door, happy as all get-out, not daring to look at Helen, his secretary, whom he suspected of having overheard the conversation. *Nine-thirtyish? Egad.*

They were soaring five hundred feet above the hard deck, Drake strapped inside the cockpit of an F-14. Looking out through the Plexiglas canopy at the transparent blue Caribbean, Drake could see emerald patterns of coral spread across the sand like an underwater forest. An elegant bone-white sailboat glided across the clear surface of the water as though on ice. Standing near the helm, a couple stared up at the jet in wonder, and Drake sensed that they had heard the F-14 long before it flashed by at nearly twice the speed of sound.

"You ever made a carrier landing in a fighter before?"

"First time."

"You're in for a treat."

The pilot banked right. In the distance, the gray outline of an aircraft carrier appeared, the USS *Theodore Roosevelt*, their destination. The pilot throttled back as he made his approach, the *Roosevelt*'s superstructure a blade of steel, the flight deck a thin black line. Drake sat in the radio intercept officer's seat, feeling like a mouse strapped to a rocket. A few minutes later they were three-quarters of a mile off the *Roosevelt*'s stern and the pilot, Jeffery "Wildchild" McDaniels, was "calling the ball," aligning the F-14 Tomcat to the glide path indicated by the lighted Fresnel lens on the port side of the flight deck. Drake could only imagine what it was like to land at night in heavy seas. Fighters customarily hit the short runway at 135 knots. There was little margin for error. As McDaniels had explained on the way down, drift ten feet to the right or left and you were into the foul lines, parked aircraft, and disaster.

They angled down, McDaniels talking to the LSO, juking the controls to keep the F-14 in the glide path, the stern of the *Roosevelt* filling the windshield.

"Hang on to yer hat, cowboy!" McDaniels cried, feigning an unctuous Texas drawl.

Drake laughed. It was the first time he had laughed in days.

In the life of a man, his time is but a moment, his being an incessant flux, his sense a dim rushlight, his body a prey of worms, his soul an unquiet eddy, his fortune dark, his fame doubtful. In short, all that is body is as coursing waters, all that is of the soul as dreams and vapors.

They landed with a jolt, McDaniels tail hooking the first wire. Looking out through the Plexiglas canopy at the sailors manning the flight deck dressed in their color-coded shirts, then beyond to the green expanse of ocean, Drake felt suddenly isolated and alone. Civilization at his back, he felt as though he were staring across the Danube into the German wilds, anxiety-ridden yet reconciled to his fate, like Marcus Aurelius, whose bleak and cautionary words had burst upon him.

"She's down there, all right," explained the *Roosevelt*'s executive officer, Captain David Karnowski. "Hung up on a coral wall in three hundred fifty-five feet of water. Whoever scuttled the boat expected her to drop in the canyon. Wind must have brought her back. She could slip over the edge at any time."

Captain Tom Weaver, the *Roosevelt*'s commanding officer, looked at Drake with sympathetic concern. He was short but powerfully built. He had been a boxing champion at the academy. "Mind if I say something?"

"Your ship."

"A friend dies in battle, you want to carry on, for his sake, not yours—you want his death to have meaning. I understand the obligation. I respect it. That's why we're here. But what you're about to do is way beyond dangerous. If you get inside that boat and things don't feel right, don't push your luck. Back off and save the fight for another day."

Drake nodded. Captain Weaver was right, of course. Still, no amount of grief seemed commensurate to Drake's sense of loss. His oldest and dearest friend was gone. Many cosmologists believe that the universe originated from a single grain of exceptionally dense matter smaller than an atom—a singularity. The universe began when this singularity detonated in a high-temperature explosion known as the Big Bang. In mourning, Drake seemed to be caught in the reverse of this process, his universe collapsing upon itself until there was nothing left except something he couldn't see. He'd been there before. Only meaning had provided the way out: the sacred joining of word and action undertaken in that dark hour of the soul when hope collides with mortality.

From the door of the Seahawk, Drake could clearly distinguish the stern of Elkins's yacht, *Albatross,* shimmering in the turquoise depths. The slender yacht was pointed down, hanging like a tie on a clothes rack, the stern perched on a coral projection, the hull facing open water. Ten feet beyond the hull, the ocean plunged into a cobalt abyss.

Standing in the open door in full diving gear, Drake had a mild feeling of déjà vu. Had it been night, had they been hovering off the coast of Maine, the sensation would have been complete. He felt haunted. Sick. An orange buoy marked the yacht's location. A squad of SEALs from the *Roosevelt* circled the buoy in a rigid-hulled inflatable. They were well armed. So was the HH-60H chopper hovering nearby. Two Gatling guns protruded from either side. Drake signaled the crew chief and, holding his mask in place, plunged feet first into the tranquil ocean.

An explosion of bubbles. Drake tucked and angled down toward the coral wall, a dazzling community of sea fans, gorgonians, and staghorn coral intermixed with schools of smallmouth grunts and porkfish.

The seventy-five-foot motor yacht looked as incongruous against the coral wall as the livid slash of a vandalized painting. Approaching the hull, Drake could see that the SEALs had secured the sunken vessel as best they could. Cables ran from the blocks up over the edge of the coral wall to a pair of danforth anchors biting into the sand. He swam to the starboard side, slipping through the four-foot gap between the gunwale and the coral wall, and looked up. The yacht was dangling from a giant brain coral that had hooked the transom. Drawing closer, Drake could see that the massive brain coral was uprooting.

Shit.

Surrounded by the yacht and coral wall, he felt as though he had stepped inside an A-frame. Past the gunwales, he could see open water, bright against the colorful wall and stretching two hundred feet to either side before fading in a blur. In front, the coral wall was bathed in blue shadow. Behind him, the main deck of the *Albatross* slanted out toward open water, the flying bridge resting against the wall fifty feet below.

The sliding glass doors were ajar. Looking up once more at the slowly detaching coral, Drake descended through the open door, pushing aside cushions and other debris. He was wearing a black wet suit, two tanks of trimix, and two side-mounted tanks of oxygen and nitrox. Even at a depth of 350 feet the water was warm and clear, a pleasant contrast to the *Andrea Doria* and the water off the New England coast. He dropped down past a well-stocked bar to the galley, where a ladder led up to the pilothouse. Next to the ladder, a short staircase led belowdecks to the staterooms.

Deciding to carry out the most dangerous part of the mission first, Drake ventured down the stateroom corridor, switching on his light. To either side the doors were open, and he peeked inside each room, hoping that something would catch his eye. At the end of the corridor, the door to the master stateroom was locked. He reached back, palmed a small crowbar strapped to his right tank, and bracing his feet against a bulkhead, pried open the door, breaking the lock with a snap.

A Plexiglas skylight filled the room with colorful shadows. In the pale light amid the jumble of wreckage, a wrinkled foot protruding from a body bag. The body had been chained to the bunk. Drake removed a knife from its scabbard and slit the bag open. The man whose face he had memorized from the NASA photograph stared up at him in wide-eyed terror.

Elkins.

Crestfallen, Drake glanced away from the body. Alive, Elkins could have brought them closer to Bright Star and to the people who had murdered Jack. Dead, Elkins was little more than fish food. With glum expectation Drake poked around the damaged suite. Nothing but tables, chairs, lithographs—the usual accoutrements.

Without looking back at Elkins's lined and wrinkled face, Drake left the room, swimming back up the corridor to the galley. Apart from the horror of his discovery, the entire experience of exploring the *Albatross* was surreal: no silt, no skeletons, no rust. No marble angels, either. He headed for the pilothouse.

The electronics were state of the art, vaguely reminiscent of *Atlantis*'s flight deck. Even submerged, the pilothouse had the expensive look of a lavishly appointed office. With a twinge of anxiety, Drake peered down through the wraparound windows.

Tinted green, they offered a bird's-eye view of a coral wall plunging 6,000 feet to the ocean floor.

Best not to think about that.

He glanced at his pressure gauge. Time was running out. He checked a series of drawers in the nav station. No maps, no charts. He checked the large leather pockets to either side of the pilot's seat. *Nada.* No clue as to where Elkins might have traveled. The *Albatross* had been stripped clean. *Son-of-a-bitch.* Maybe Lawrence could get something off the boat's computer. But the Navy was going to have a hell of a time raising the boat. Could take weeks. Drake scrutinized the communications equipment, to no avail. Then, on the dashboard, a foot away from the helm, something caught his eye—a flaw in the cherry paneling. A block of polished wood was separating from the panel. Why? The panel should have been a single long piece of wood like the others.

Drake palmed the crowbar, pried the block loose, and pulled a slender nylon bag from the hole. His spirits rising, he lay the crowbar on the windshield, carefully opened the bag, and withdrew a plastic bag of marijuana.

Hmmm . . .

In the mild suction, fifty transparent rolling papers fluttered up like moths circling a lampshade. But there was something else inside the nylon bag. Drake reached inside and carefully withdrew a six-by-five color snapshot of a blonde sunning herself on the foredeck, a paperback resting in the curled fingers of her right hand. She was naked, her eyes closed as though asleep. Her perfect oval face radiated lassitude and extraordinary beauty.

Elated, Drake carefully slid the snapshot into the pocket of his vest. *So Elkins had a girlfriend. Where was she?* He checked his gauges. Time to skedaddle. He turned toward the door, grasping the frame just as it shifted. *What the fuck?* Then he heard a scraping sound and looked up in horror as the five-foot brain coral burst through the sliding glass doors and smashed through the windshield a foot from his face. The *Albatross* tumbled off the wall, the cables snapping like threads.

Drake slammed against the aft bulkhead, the water channeling through the broken windshield like a jet wash. Momentarily stunned, he could feel his brain tingling. *Narcosis?* His ears hurt. He struggled to gain purchase, to grab something, anything to pull himself through the gaping hole in the aft bulkhead and out through the now-windowless and mangled sliding doors. The mushrooming water kept him pinned. The *Albatross* was sinking fast by the bow. He looked at his depth gauge and shuddered: 526 feet. Suddenly he was tumbling as the heavy stern of the *Albatross* flipped down, the swift flow of water reversing itself. He was being pulled toward the shattered windshield. In the blur of rushing water, he spotted a pilot's seat. He grabbed it, but it slipped from his fingers. The ocean whirled around him like a hurricane. Pinwheeling as the *Albatross* plunged into the ocean depths, Drake burst through the jagged glass of the windshield and out into the open sea.

Lawrence's scanning program had turned up no obvious signs of tampering. Not that Lawrence had expected any. The intruder had easily circumvented the Pentagon's firewalls.

Now Lawrence was at the laptop again, devising a program that would search for unauthorized changes in the code. Like the Internet and the Bell telecommunications system, the Pentagon's operating system ran on Unix, a computer language of exceptional versatility for which the source code was readily available. With Unix at his fingertips, an individual of Lawrence's genius could literally work magic—or disaster. Still, in scanning the Pentagon's operating system, Lawrence faced a daunting task. The operating code that ran the Pentagon's computers numbered in the millions of lines. The telltale alteration Lawrence sought could be minuscule—two or three characters long. To complicate matters, the Pentagon's systems administrators had added or deleted lines of code on a daily basis for years. These changes numbered in the thousands, and Lawrence's program had to account for each and every one.

To isolate any unauthorized changes, he would employ a technique known as stripping. He would take the present code, subtract the authorized changes, and compare the difference to tape backups made in previous years. Starting with last year's tape, he would work back each year until he uncovered an anomaly. The concept was easy enough, but tough to run. The program had to be comprehensive and precise—"elegant," in the parlance of computer jocks. And he needed a big machine to run it.

He headed for Elliot's second-story office, overlooking the Jefferson Memorial and the Washington Monument. The secretary of defense had been meeting with the chairman of the House Armed Services Committee.

Elliot excused himself and walked with Lawrence to a private study. "Hey, Billy. You find something?" Ever since the shuttle crashed, he'd been praying for a miracle. They had to get Bright Star back. Fast. Before somebody put it in orbit.

"The president said that I had the backing of the entire United States Government, right?"

"Yes?"

"I need to borrow a computer."

"Okay . . ."

"Not just any computer."

"You're not talking about the new Cray they just installed at NSA."

Lawrence flashed his best impresario's grin. "That's the one."

"Oh, shit," Richard Elliot said, his smile as broad as Lawrence's. He strode back to the committee chairman, a gravelly voiced octogenarian who was bitching and moaning about a proposed base closing in his district, a tax drain that should have been shut down at the end of World War II. "I'm sorry, Mr. Chairman, but something has come up. Another time? Next Tuesday, perhaps?"

The package arrived by courier that morning. Donnally had called in sick, which wasn't far from the truth, considering the anxiety that had prevented him from falling back to sleep after his trip to Dulles. He took the package, headed down to the basement of his house in Oxon Hills, Maryland, and opened it up. Inside, wound in bubble wrap, lay a sound-suppressed Heckler & Koch MP5K personal defense weapon. Equipped with a folding stock, shoulder harness, and three dual thirty-round magazines, the MP5K-PDW combined the firepower of an assault rifle with the concealability of a big-frame .45. So highly regarded was this weapon that Secret Service agents routinely carried them beneath their windbreakers.

Slipping on an old pair of gloves, Donnally hefted the compact weapon, trying to calm his nerves. *Who in the fuck did Clayton think he was? Abu Nidal? Shit.* In an envelope inside the package Donnally had found a thin plastic card with a magnetic strip on the back, a passkey to the Marriott. Clayton had been precise in his instructions: "We gotta do something about that bitch before she starts running off at the mouth. Go to the hotel, get inside her room, and when she returns, shoot her. I want it done by tonight." *Easy enough for him to say, the fucking cocksucker.*

Donnally glanced at his watch: 3:00 P.M. *Damn.* It was time to move.

The Situation Room staff had put through the call to Prime Minister Ganet in Paris. President Young sat at the head of the conference table, glancing at Adams. *"Bonjour,* Monsieur Prime Minister. Yes, fine, thank you. And Madame Ganet?"

The conversation lasted for ten minutes, President Young's tone never deviating from the cordial as he talked about Bright Star. Midway through the conversation, the president jotted something on a notepad and, with a significant look, slid the pad across the table to Adams.

He doesn't know a thing.

Drake awoke. There was a nurse leaning over him, checking his pulse. It wasn't a dream.

"Where am I?"

"You're on the *Roosevelt.* They brought you in four hours ago. How do you feel?"

"Don't ask."

"You've got forty stitches in your left forearm. And a nasty bump on your head. No concussion, I'm glad to say." She turned to another nurse, a pretty, but quiet brunette. "Marge, notify the CO that Mr. Drake is conscious. And call Dr. Shannon."

"You hit the surface an hour and a half after the boat slipped off the wall," Captain Weaver explained. "The chopper pilot spotted you when you were still beneath the surface, decompressing. Saw the whole thing happen. The SEAL who connected you to the hoist said that you were semiconscious. You told him about Elkins."

"The last thing I remember is getting sucked out the windshield."

"Yes, well, you impressed the shit out of him. And me, too, by the way. You've got guts, kid."

"Yeah . . ."

"Don't kid yourself, you did a hell of a job down there. We found the photograph you recovered, too. We sent a digital copy to Washington."

"Any idea who she is?"

"We found her."

"Dead?"

"Very much alive. While you were diving, we picked up an intercept—a call to Paris. It originated about a mile from here. Woman's voice. Complaining about a guy named Elkins. Guess the computer tech didn't exactly curl her toes." Captain Weaver appeared moderately amused by the revelation. "The girl's name is Catherine Durand."

"Well, what are we waiting for? Let's go get her."

Captain Karnowski looked at Drake. "I'm afraid it's not that simple. She's aboard the *Mirage*," the executive officer explained. "One of the Kuwaiti royal yachts."

"Any chance of getting aboard?"

"Negative. The *Mirage* is Kuwaiti sovereign territory. As long as Miss Durand remains aboard that yacht, we can't touch her."

Jesus Christ. Donnally glanced at his watch. *Where the fuck was she?*

He was sitting on the toilet in Julia's darkened bathroom, where he'd been cooling his heels for the past three hours. The passkey had worked like a charm. Wearing a tan Stetson and a pair of Tony Lama cowboy boots that he had purchased years ago in Lubbock, Texas, he had strolled across the spacious lobby and had taken the elevator to the third floor. Inside a leather briefcase lay the gloves and MP5.

No one had seen him enter the room. The corridor had been empty. Inside her room, the drapes were open. He could see the dome of the Capitol rising in the distance. A copy of the *Washington Post* lay on the bedstand. A small bottle of Chanel stood on the dresser. Donnally didn't touch a thing. He stepped into the bathroom, opened the briefcase, slipped on the gloves, palmed the MP5, flicked the selector to full automatic, and sat down on the toilet seat to wait.

Now his butt was throbbing. *Shit.* He stood and glanced at his watch again, as though he could hurry Julia along. *What if she didn't show up?* He could see the balcony windows in the bathroom mirror. The sun was setting, filling the bedroom with a faint orange glow, reflecting off the mirrors onto the black MP5 he cradled in his arms.

"We might be in luck," Captain Karnowski observed. "Kamal's throwing a party."

"Kamal's whole life is a party," Captain Weaver replied. He looked at Drake. "You sure you want to go through with this?"

Drake wound the elastic bandage around his left forearm and secured the clasp.

"I'm a civilian. I'm the only person here who *can* go through with it."

"If you're caught—"

"I know. My government will disavow any knowledge of my actions," Drake repeated in his best *Mission Impossible* voice. "Tell me about Kamal."

"He's the only son of Kuwaiti oil minister Ali Al Khobar—or rather Ali's only *legitimate* son," Karnowski explained. "Kamal's twenty-nine years old. A playboy, like his father. Loves women and casinos. He spends most of his time in Monte Carlo. He once lost four million dollars in an hour."

"I think I read about that. Playing Chemin de Fer."

"Chemen de what?" Captain Weaver asked.

"A card game like twenty-one," Drake explained.

Captain Karnowski looked at Drake. "When Iraq invaded Kuwait, Kamal headed for the hills like most wealthy Kuwaitis. A reporter who found him in a London nightclub asked him why he wasn't defending his country. Kamal replied: 'Why should I fight Iraqis when I have my American slaves to fight for me?' "

"A prince," Drake remarked.

"Here are the deck plans to the *Mirage*. Al Khobar keeps a security detail on board to watch over his son. The fellow in charge is American, a former Secret Service agent who got fired for beating his wife. A real sweetheart. His name is Derek Teetums. This is what he looks like."

Captain Karnowski handed Drake the photograph. Teetums's head resembled a fire hydrant.

"Their thermal imaging cameras are going to be a whole lot less effective when we start messing around with their electronics. We can do that from a Seahawk. Your SEAL buddies will deploy around the yacht to provide you with some real-time intelligence. That should help you get aboard. After that, you're on your own."

They drove to Galileo in downtown Washington. McKendrick liked the simple elegance of the place. White walls decorated with prints and watercolors. Terra-cotta floor. Private alcoves. Besides, Galileo's northern Italian cuisine was superb.

Despite his anxiety over Bright Star, McKendrick felt happy to be having dinner with Julia. With so much going on, he needed a change of pace, a fresh perspective. Right now he could do little but wait for events to play out: Lawrence was isolating the security hole in the Pentagon computer's operating system, the president and Adams were negotiating with the French, and Drake was going after the girl who might be able to identify the terrorists. So he could either sit around in his Pentagon office and drive himself nuts, or he could get on with his life.

Soon after their arrival, however, McKendrick noticed that Julia seemed distracted. Fatigue, probably. He was feeling a touch of that himself.

"Well, we'll just have to suffer through this." McKendrick beamed hopefully, looking down at their steaming plates of risotto and spinach agnolotti.

She looked at him with a quick, tense smile and tasted the risotto. She didn't have the heart to tell him here. Yet she doubted she could continue her acting performance much longer. She was heartsick. Every time she glimpsed the face of a child, she could see the face of Henderson's son. That afternoon she had written McKendrick a letter, telling him the truth about her complicity, but had tucked it away in her briefcase. She would tell him tonight. In person. But how?

"While you're here, you should visit the Library of Congress," McKendrick suggested. "Or the Kennedy Center. Maybe we could squeeze in a concert Friday night."

She nodded and took a bite of her risotto. Then she said, "Do you ever wonder why childhood affects one's view of life to such an unwarranted degree?"

"When I was a kid, I wanted to be a surfer."

"You?"

"Surprised?"

"Well, yes."

"I grew up in Half Moon Bay. Ever been there?"

"No. California?"

"It was a different place then. Open fields for miles around. Orchards and an occasional artichoke farm. The entire San Francisco Bay was like that. Bucolic. Now it's one vast metropolis, from San Francisco to San Jose. When I was a teenager, my friends and I would drive along the coastal highway to San Gregorio beach with our surfboards sticking out of the back of my Rambler. This was back in the mid-fifties. We'd spend hours on the water, waiting for the sets to roll in, then surfing our asses off. On most days, we would have the beach entirely to ourselves. Sometimes we'd pack burgers and a couple of six-packs of Pabst Blue Ribbon— PBRs, we called them then—and cook dinner out on the beach. Ever seen a driftwood fire? It's full of greens and blues. The alchemy of sand, salt, wood, and flame. It was paradise. I always thought that once I had grown up, after I had become successful in my career, that I could have that again. But adulthood changes you. The last time I lay on the beach, I was bored. Funny the way things work out."

"My father used to take us to the Berkshires," Julia said. "My mother and me. In the summers. This is after we sold the house in Miami Beach and moved to Boston. My father used to love to climb to the top of those mountains, though usually he'd drive halfway up first, saying that he wanted to start out in the wild country and not down below where the houses were. I think he just wanted to get as far away from civilization as possible. For years, I thought my parents would retire there. Life rarely exceeds one's expectations, but you're always so surprised when it falls short. Maybe that's the curse of having a privileged upbringing, or at least the raised expectations that we all came to share in the early sixties. You're left with a kind of Victorian melancholia. Even though nothing's really wrong. It's simply life."

"All's not lost, Julia," McKendrick said, thinking of Bright Star. "A pretty lady told me that once. Gödel's theorem."

"Boomerang, you mean."

McKendrick looked down at her empty plate and smiled. "Speaking of raised expectations, I wonder if they have tiramisù."

In his office at CIA headquarters in Langley, Virginia, Charles Francis Adams sat at his desk, gazing at the photographs on the wall, recalling his year in France prior to D-Day during World War II. He had worked for Donovan then, Wild Bill Donovan, the legendary founder of the OSS.

The grandson of Irish immigrants and a staunch Catholic,

Donovan had gone to Columbia Law School, where his grades had been so poor that he had barely graduated. From Columbia, Donovan had gone on to win five cases before the Supreme Court and to serve as acting attorney general of the United States. Donovan had been fearless. Commander of the "Fighting 69th" in World War I, Donovan had returned home as America's most decorated soldier, having received, among other awards, the Distinguished Service Medal, the Distinguished Service Cross, the Croix de Guerre, and the Medal of Honor. At the outset of World War II, Franklin Delano Roosevelt had tapped him to create America's first spy agency, the Office of Strategic Services, the organization that would lay the groundwork for the CIA. Few men had possessed Donovan's patriotism and restless energy.

In his youth, Adams, like so many other men who would become part of the "Eastern Establishment," had worshiped the very ground that Donovan had walked on. Fresh out of Harvard, Adams had flown to Gravelly Point and had taken a cab to Donovan's headquarters on the outskirts of Georgetown. With penetrating blue eyes Donovan had looked him over, impressed by the young man's intelligence and gift for languages. A year later Adams was parachuting into France, a member of a Jedburgh Team. He would spend a year working alongside the Resistance, blowing up railway lines and dodging the Milice and the Gestapo.

Adams had learned enough about French intelligence agencies over the years to believe that Prime Minister Ganet's profession of ignorance concerning the Bright Star video was probably genuine. A climate of mutual distrust, if not downright hostility, existed between the Direction Générale de la Sécurité Extérieure, better known as the DGSE, and the Prime Ministry. It didn't help matters that Ganet was a socialist. Faced with high unemployment and a sweeping reduction in social services to meet the fiscal requirements for admission to the European Economic Union, the French electorate had panicked, ushering Ganet into power—a mistake as far as Adams was concerned.

As far as socialism went, Ganet's version was mild stuff. Still, Adams wasn't holding his breath. The socialists had transformed France into a nation of high taxes and the thirty-five-hour workweek. Adams couldn't think of a better way to kill productivity.

Unlike their American counterparts, the French intelligence services were a law unto themselves, run by men so conservative that, in the words of one analyst, they would have viewed Richard Nixon as a crypto-communist. Unlike the strict tradition to which Adams adhered, in France there was no demarcation between intelligence and policy. All intelligence was political; in other words, intelligence was slanted to serve partisan causes. Since the DGSE considered Ganet and his socialist cronies to be enemies of the state, they would make no mention of the Bright Star video or any other scrap of information that concerned national security. The only question was: What was the DGSE up to? Adams wasn't waiting to find out. It was time to play hardball.

He pressed a button on his desk console and asked his secretary to put a call through to his counterpart at the DGSE. Fifteen minutes later, he could hear the intelligence chief's querulous and reedy voice coming over the line.

"Jacques? Adams here. Awfully sorry to bother you at this late hour, but we seem to have a minor problem and need your help. We're trying to recover one of our satellites, code-named Bright Star, the one highlighted in the video you received the other day. Yes, that video. We want Bright Star back. Now, Jacques, we have a plan, authorized by the president of the United States. We'd like to underwrite your bid. That's right. We'll provide the money, then reclaim the satellite. We'd be most grateful for your cooperation. As a matter of fact, to ensure your cooperation, the president of the United States has also authorized me to fax you some information regarding the embezzlement of several million francs from a government entity in your control to a private bank account in the Antilles—your bank account, as a matter of fact. We certainly wouldn't want such an alarming coincidence to become headline news, now would we?"

"Walt, I had a wonderful evening tonight." They were standing in the gleaming palatial lobby of the Marriott waiting for her elevator to arrive. Several shops were still open, and a group of college kids were giggling on one of the plush sofas nearby. Julia looked at them for a moment. Then taking his hand, she said, "Would you like to come up?"

In the forty seconds it took them to reach the third floor, neither Julia or McKendrick said a word. Julia held his hand, rubbing her thumb back and forth against his, lost in a refuge toward which she'd been heading since the moment he had asked her out in McDonald's.

The elevator door opened, and McKendrick held it as Julia stepped into the corridor. She reached into her purse and inserted the plastic card into the scanner. The bolt slid back with a snap.

The room was dark when McKendrick followed her inside, and he didn't bother to turn on the lights. The lighted dome of the Capitol seemed to hover over the city like an angel. She turned to him, her face pale in the window light, and suddenly he was kissing her, holding her close as she kissed him back. They never saw the man with the gun. Their eyes were shut when the world tumbled beneath them.

23 August

Three miles from the *Mirage,* Drake slipped over the side of the speeding inflatable, hitting the ocean in a skidding jolt. It was 2·00 A.M. He settled into the water and checked his headset. "Springboard, this is Rainbow, over."

"Rainbow, this is Springboard. You are clear to go."

Dressed in a black wet suit and equipped with a rebreather, Drake began swimming toward the yacht. He stayed low in the water, performing the sidestroke, making sure his fins did not break the surface. He took his time, keeping the phosphorescence to an absolute minimum. In the distance, the white superstructure of the *Mirage* sparkled under the running lights.

Getting aboard the yacht promised to be a tricky affair, and he thought about the possibilities of what he might encounter. Then he thought about Jennifer and how good it would feel to crawl into bed beside her. *Good. Keep thinking that way.*

Drake swam along the surface until he was a quarter of a mile out, still hidden by the darkness beyond the pool of ambient light surrounding the yacht. His left arm was sore, but otherwise he was loose and full of energy. Treading water, he scanned the yacht, noting the layout of the doors. The lights flickered. Three guards appeared topside, peering over the starboard rail and shrugging their shoulders as the lights flickered again. The electronic countermeasures were working; the guards would be alert in the beginning, but then their vigilance would wane. No matter how high-tech and elaborate, security systems were only as good as the people manning them. Given enough time, you could wear anyone down. Drake glanced at his watch. He had been in the water nearly two hours.

He slipped the mouthpiece between his lips and descended to sixty feet, completing the approach underwater. The L-126 rebreather worked like gangbusters. Like the Draeger systems he had used as a SEAL, the recently developed L-126 would leave no bubble trail on the surface. What made this system particularly attractive among closed-circuit rebreathers was its reliability, compactness, and depth rating to five hundred feet. Two small high-pressure tanks inside the unit, which itself was the size of an accordion-style briefcase, provided all the gas needed for extended-range diving. A diver equipped with the L-126 could spend several hours at three hundred feet and decompress with hours to spare.

Using a compass board, Drake swam along the bottom of the harbor until he was beneath the yacht. He ascended to the keel and slowly worked his way forward so that he could surface unseen beneath the curve of the bow. If the *Mirage*'s thermal-imaging cameras were still operational, he was going to be in for an ugly reception. He slipped the MP5 from its scabbard and quietly broke to the surface, scanning the area around him, keeping the barrel of the MP5 aligned to his line of sight. He was clear. He checked in, whispering into the throat mike.

"Springboard, this is Rainbow, over."

"Rainbow, you have two guards fore and aft, and two crew members on the flying bridge starboard. Port amidships clear."

"Copy, Springboard. Rainbow out."

Drake quietly worked his way along the port side of the *Mirage,* feeling the tension pricking his back. When he reached amidships he whispered, "How do I look?"

"Good. Just take her slow and easy."

Drake heard voices.

"Rainbow, be advised two guards approaching from your three. Submerge."

Drake descended under the hull and waited, wondering if the operation was going to pan out at all. He was staring out at bright water. He could see shadows passing along the surface. A school of grunts shimmered fifteen feet away, attracted by the light, their blue and yellow stripes radiant in the clear depths.

"Rainbow, you are clear to board."

Drake surfaced again, extended a telescopic pole, and hooked a ladder of nylon webbing over the gunwale. He removed his fins, slipped them over his left arm, and slowly pulled himself up, allowing the water to roll, instead of trickle, off his body. His muscles burned from the strain of climbing the ladder, a series of loops in the webbing. Thinking of Jack, Drake allowed anger to dominate pain every time he gripped another loop with his lacerated arm. Aboard the *Roosevelt* the doctor had pumped him full of antibiotics and anti-inflammatories to reduce the swelling.

Reaching the main deck, Drake drew his .45-caliber H&K

Mark 23, gripped the rail, and quickly pulled himself over, feeling naked and exposed under the bright lights. He retrieved the webbing, pulled a dry towel out of his pack, and quickly backed through an open door, wiping up traces of water. The last thing he needed was to be spotted. This foray was no ship takedown. He was after the girl, but that was it; he wanted no contact with the other people aboard. The Arabs aboard the *Mirage* weren't terrorists; they were Kuwaiti royalty—vacationers. Given the parameters of the mission, Drake would fire his weapon only to protect the girl or if his own death was imminent, and then only to keep heads down, even if taking fire himself.

Inside the doorway, Drake ascended a staircase to his right, moving quickly and quietly to avoid detection. He was heading for the master bedroom. At the top of the staircase, he encountered a long corridor lined with photographs. According to the deck plans, the master bedroom lay at the end of the corridor to the right. He reached the end of the corridor and listened before rounding the corner. Three distinct voices. Stationary. Nearby. Guards? Drake checked his back, removed a tiny dentist's mirror from his vest pocket and, squatting, carefully maneuvered it around the corner near the floor. One quick glance confirmed his suspicion. Three guards stood outside the bedroom door.

Drake rose, keeping his back near, but not touching the wall, and retreated. He did not wish to become trapped between the guards and anyone entering the corridor from the staircase. Then he heard a low rumble and felt a vibration through his feet as the *Mirage* got under way.

Of all the things to go wrong. Dammit. What the fuck do I do now?

Drake dashed for the staircase, thinking that he had to get off the ship. But there were voices below—male voices growing louder with the sound of approaching footsteps. He was cut off. *Shit.* He twisted the doorknob to his left. Locked. He moved to the next door, twisting the knob, feeling the perspiration pebbling his brow. The door opened. *Sweet mother of Mary.* Drake quickly slipped inside, praying that his luck would hold, that he hadn't backed himself into a corner as the men reached the top of the staircase. He scanned the darkened room for movement, his nostrils detecting the sweet smell of hashish. A naked couple lay sprawled on the bed, an ornate water pipe on the mahogany table to the right. The woman was young and pretty, the man older and a hundred pounds overweight. Not Catherine, not Kamal. The man stirred, caressing the woman's breasts.

Drake dropped down.

"Miranda," the man cooed in an Arab accent.

"Mmmm?"

The man slid his hand across her belly.

"Oh, Abdul . . .

I don't believe this.

Drake crawled under the undulating bed, his earpiece coming alive: "Rainbow, this is Springboard. Rainbow, come in, please. Rainbow. Do you copy?"

"We lost Rainbow, sir."

Captain Weaver paced the floor of the Combat Information Center. "Dammit. Mr. Jackson, any idea where they're headed?"

"Windward passage, sir," the intelligence officer replied, looking up from his console.

With a surge of panic, Captain Weaver examined the radar screen. *Cuba.*

Secretary of Defense Richard Elliot was crossing the Pentagon's River Entrance parking lot at 5 A.M. when Billy Lawrence pulled up beside him in a Ford Taurus. Lawrence was breathless with excitement. "Adams was right. We've had a break-in. I'm not sure how the intruder got in originally. But once he gained entry, he created a series of trapdoors, which allowed him to enter the Pentagon's computer network whenever he wished. Unseen. He also devised a program to cover his tracks, figuring that no one would ever analyze the code line by line. For all practical purposes, this guy could walk right in and help himself to anything he wanted." Then, looking out the windshield, Lawrence noticed the horde of reporters and television crews blocking the River Entrance. "Hey, what's going on?"

The secretary of defense climbed into the passenger seat. "We tried to reach you at the National Security Agency over an hour ago."

"I went out for breakfast. Why?"

Elliot looked sick. "You'd better pull over, Billy."

An hour before dawn, Drake made his move. Slipping out from beneath the bed, he crawled to the door and listened. Silence. He reached up, opened the door a crack, and scanned the corridor with the mirror. The corridor was clear.

He descended the staircase to the bottom-most deck and entered a storage room filled with marine hardware. A workbench stood against the far wall, and above it Drake spotted a wide ventilator shaft. He removed the grate, tossed in his gear bag, and climbed inside. He slid the grate back in place. It was nearly morning. No way he could move around the *Mirage* during the day. He set the vibration alarm on his watch and chewed another antibiotic and an anti-inflammatory pill, sipping water from the camelback hydration system inside his tactical vest. He was exhausted. He slept, dreaming of the day Jennifer had shown him the plans of the farmhouse. The old stone house had dated back to the time of the Revolution but had been razed by a bond trader in his thirties who built a turreted monstrosity three stories high, spread over an acre of land in backcountry Greenwich—a house as large as his ego. To the delight of their neighbors, Drake and Jennifer had torn down the mansion, and using photographs provided by the historical society, had rebuilt the original farmhouse, the restoration being the touchstone of their lives.

She was safe. When the lights had flickered the night before and Teetums had dispatched his security team to check the yacht's perimeter, she had used all her persuasive powers to convince Kamal to sail to another island. First the young Kuwaiti had refused, ordering his technician to run several diagnostic tests, but an hour later when the technician reported that he had found nothing wrong with the security system, Kamal had become suspicious. They had sailed at once.

She enjoyed Kamal's company. He was handsome and cultivated, unlike the unspeakable American with whom she had spent the previous week. She would stay with him for as long as she could, then she would disappear in Europe, joining her younger brother in Munich. Her brother was studying at Oxford, and she was helping to pay for his education. He hoped to become a doctor someday. *Paul.* She couldn't wait to see him again.

Now she left the bedroom, taking care not to wake her lover, and stepped outside, casually tying the belt of her silk bathrobe. She lifted her face to the wind and gazed at the verdant island with its flowering bushes and beaches of white sand. Yes, here she was safe at last.

She recalled the day her parents had taken them to the Louvre. She had been stunned by the proximity of so many beautiful things. Unlike most women who enter her profession, Catherine had come from a happy home. Before he died of cancer, her father had been a successful manager at British Leyland. Her mother still lived in London, where they had been raised.

Perhaps she, too, would settle there one day and find a husband. She had built up a substantial investment portfolio, based on the shrewd advice of men she knew, who tended to be either captains of industry or royalty like Kamal. Another year, and she could retire. She gazed at the island. The beaches were deserted, but they would be going ashore soon and maybe she would have a chance to go swimming. Later they could explore the castle. They could climb to the top and look across the green rolling hills.

Inside the Oval Office, President Young and his advisors listened in shocked silence as FBI Director Dwight Grady described the carnage inside Julia Reynolds's hotel room.

"It was an execution-style slaying," Grady explained, looking at the group, which included National Security Advisor Bud

McGuire and Chief of Staff Margaret Abrams. "Dr. Reynolds was standing between the shooter and General McKendrick and died instantly from multiple gunshot wounds to the head. She took the brunt of the impact, which is the only reason the general's still alive. The shooter used a sound-suppressed MP5 submachine gun equipped with a thirty-round magazine, which he—or she—emptied. Preliminary tests also indicate that the rounds the shooter used are identical to the type recovered at the *Trident* facility in Bristol. We can assume that the same people are involved."

The president shook his head in sorrow and looked at Elliot. "And Walt?"

"Still in a coma, sir," Elliot explained in a leaden voice. "He took two rounds to the head, one through the left eye. He lost a lot of blood. He's not expected to live. Director Adams is with him now."

Lacing her fingers together in a gesture of pensive commiseration, Margaret Abrams looked at Elliot and asked, "Does he have a family?"

"No."

"Dr. Reynolds?"

"She has a father. No brothers or sisters, according to Lawrence."

"Sir?" Elliot asked, turning to the president, who was seated in a wing chair facing the fireplace. "We need to designate an interim chairman. Admiral Archer has my recommendation."

"Permission granted," the president replied in a strained voice. He looked at Grady with an anguished expression. "Why Julia? Why Walt?"

Taking a deep breath, the FBI director glanced at Elliot and said, "Mr. Lawrence recently uncovered evidence of computer tampering at the Pentagon. The terrorists may have wanted to prevent him or Dr. Reynolds from making further discoveries. It's entirely possible that another assassin was waiting in Lawrence's room as well. As it turned out, Lawrence spent the night at the National Security Agency and never returned to his hotel room. The terrorists may also have wanted to put not only Bright Star but also Systems Technologies out of business. My gut feeling is that General McKendrick was not the target of this attack. Killing the chairman of the Joint Chiefs of Staff would serve no purpose. Killing Mr. Lawrence and Dr. Reynolds, however, would strengthen the terrorists' hand in several ways, as I've previously noted. We're examining Lawrence's hotel room, along with Dr. Reynolds's, with extreme care. If the terrorists left a trail of evidence, we'll find it. But it might take some time. Our forensics teams have a set of procedures they must follow. First the rooms have to be photographed—"

"Yes, I know," the president remarked, cutting him off. Then in a calmer tone, he said, "I'm sorry, Dwight. I guess I'm a little on edge."

"We all feel that way, Mr. President."

The president nodded. He looked at his national security advisor. "Bud, have we thoroughly coordinated our efforts with the French? Are we certain that they'll go along with our desire to underwrite their bid?"

"I spoke with Director Adams this morning. We have received assurances from both Prime Minister Ganet and DGSE Chief Jacques Derrière that the French government will cooperate fully. U.S. funds are being transferred to Paris as we speak. After the auction tomorrow night, Bright Star should be in the bag."

Drake awoke. He glanced at his watch: 4:00 P.M. No engine hum. The *Mirage* had anchored. But where?

Sliding the grate to the right, Drake backed out of the ventilator shaft, touched down on the workbench, and hopped down to the linoleum floor. His arm was sore, but OK. He moved across the room in the darkness, taking care not to trip over the stacks of equipment.

Outside the storage room, the corridor was clear. Drake ascended the staircase to the main deck, moving quietly to an outer door.

"Springboard, this is Rainbow."

No answer from the *Roosevelt*. He tried again.

He could see cliffs rising from the turquoise water five hundred meters off the starboard rail. With a growing sense of entrapment, he crossed the weather deck to get a better view. The cliffs rose to a mountain capped by green vegetation and a castle whose gray ramparts Drake had seen from afar during his years of guiding. El Castillo del Morro. No wonder the *Roosevelt* had broken contact.

The *Mirage* had anchored off Santiago de Cuba.

A launch was cruising back from the island. Drake headed up to the master suite, the *Mirage* so quiet that it seemed to have been abandoned. The door to the suite was open. Drake slipped inside and looked around. An enormous circular bed occupied the center of the room. There were closets to either side, and clothes scattered about the floor. Drake crawled beneath the bed and waited, hoping that Kamal didn't own a dog.

With cautious optimism Donnally sat in his cramped Pentagon office, wondering if he could push up his retirement. He glanced at the clock on his desk, where he had been working on a logistics problem. In an hour, he would head out to the driving range to work on his chip placement. Later he would treat himself to a steak dinner at the Occidental Grill and check out the bar scene. Why not? It was Friday night. Hell, he might even get lucky.

In the days following the assassination, Donnally had watched in secret fascination as the mood inside the Pentagon had shifted from horrified shock to a kind of somber concern about what might happen next. At times he had been tempted to toss a grenade into the men's room trash can so he could enjoy the spectacle of his fellow officers freaking out.

Dusting those two cocksuckers had been child's play, and whenever he thought about the events that night at the Marriott, he dwelled on the thrill he had gotten, not on the hours of hand-wringing anxiety that had preceded it. Too bad about McKendrick; the general had been on a pussy hunt and run into Godzilla. Thinking about those electric minutes the night before, sitting on the toilet, his butt burning, he had jumped to his feet as the door unlocked, the bolt sliding back with a snap. By the time Julia and McKendrick had entered the bedroom, he had had the barrel of the MP5 pointed at their heads. In the darkness there had been no screaming, no wild panicky fire. He had simply stepped out from the bathroom and pulled the trigger, emptying the thirty-round magazine into their collapsing bodies, the white dome of the Capitol rising like a cold and indifferent moon at the end of Pennsylvania Avenue. It seemed as though the rounds had come sparking off his hands. Julia had moaned once and he had pumped a final round into her head. Then he had slipped the MP5 into his briefcase, listening to the hum of the air conditioner as blood soaked into the beige carpet. Tugging the cowboy hat low over his forehead, he had exited the room, strolling down the corridor to the elevator, whistling "Dixie." No one had noticed a thing. It had been over in seconds.

Call me Tex.

24 August

Midnight. Dressed in khaki shorts and a photographer's vest containing a two-way radio and a 9mm H&K USP, Derek Teetums gripped the starboard rail and stared up at the lighted castle with a burgeoning sense of pride and vindication. He was loving life, unlike most of his former buddies who were saddled with child-support payments and jobs they hated. His ex-wife had tried to nail him, too; a week before he was fired. Fuck that. The day before he was due in court, he had flown first-class to Mexico City where he had opened up Security International and put out feelers. Two days later the Kuwaitis had made him an offer he couldn't refuse.

Now, basking in the warm night air, listening to the distant sound of a plane overhead, he smiled at the adroit manner in which he had escaped with his nuts intact. Now he was in Cuba. Desperate for cheap oil following the collapse of the Soviet Union, the Cubans had welcomed Kamal with open arms. Teetums had spent the entire day at the beach watching over Kamal and his entourage, meals and drinks compliments of the Cuban government. Tomorrow Castro would join them for lunch; fucking Fido himself would come aboard the *Mirage*. Teetums chuckled softly. Too bad he no longer worked at the White House. His former Secret Service buddies would get a kick out of that.

He stretched, looking up, his eyes suddenly growing wide with curiosity as a constellation of seven T-shaped shadows filled the night sky, blotting out stars as they descended. *What the fuck?* Then he saw the red dots, and his heart catapulted inside his chest. Lasers. He dove behind an open hatch, a silent round puncturing the foredeck where only a microsecond before he had stood. He could hear rounds puncturing the windows of the bridge three decks above. He scrambled for his semiautomatic. Too late. A man with a ragged scar across one cheek flew over him and Teetums felt a red dot on his nose flick up to the center of his forehead as the man took aim. An instant later, Derek Teetums was dead.

Through the deck, Drake heard screaming. Then he heard urgent voices outside the bedroom door. Kamal sat up in bed and spoke in Arabic, calling to the guards outside, his tone anxious, on the verge of panic, a burst from an automatic weapon ending the conversation as the guards fired down the corridor at their assailants. From the sound of the weapons, Drake could tell that the guards were armed with Uzis. Then he could hear a submachine gun clatter to the floor and a guard cry out in pain. Several more shots were fired. Then outside the door there was silence.

The young Kuwaiti dashed for a closet. Dressed in a silk bathrobe, the girl slumped to the floor, shivering, abandoned.

Drake crawled out from underneath the bed, knelt beside her, drew the MP5 from the padded scabbard on his back, and took aim. "Stay down," he whispered to the girl. The door flew off the hinges. Then two men charged through the fatal funnel of the door frame. They were fast, but not fast enough. Drake concentrated, aiming for their heads, avoiding the body armor, and pulled the trigger. The men tumbled into the room, dead before they hit the ground.

"Let's go."

The girl shrank back. "Who are you?"

"A friend. I'm here to get you out."

They edged toward the stairwell. Drake could hear footsteps and the sound of labored breathing, then an overweight Arab rounded the corner, eyes bulging as the sweat poured from his face. It was Abdul. He looked at Drake and screamed, his arms flailing in terror as he barreled down the corridor like a stampeding elephant. A man wearing a balaclava hood charged around the corner in hot pursuit, his eyes popping wide as Drake kicked him in the balls. The man dropped to his knees, howling, his AR-15 clattering on the floor beside him, as Drake slide-kicked the man in the face, knocking him flat. A moment later Drake had the man on his stomach, bound and gagged.

Drake lifted the terrorist to his feet and shoved him forward as they descended the stairs, Catherine sticking close to Drake's side. She had no idea who Drake was, only that he had saved her life and seemed to know what he was doing. He wasn't like any of the men who worked for Teetums or Kamal.

Reaching the main deck, they crouched beside the outer door

while Drake removed two inflatable life jackets from his vest. He handed one to the girl. "Put this on. Don't inflate the jacket until we're away from the boat; we may have to submerge." She was far prettier than her picture. Then, as an afterthought, he added, "You can swim, can't you?"

She wasn't listening. She was staring at the pool of blood pouring from Derek Teetums's skull.

"Can't you?"

Wrapped in her silk bathrobe, the girl nodded, drawing back. Drake slipped the other life jacket over the prisoner's head and cinched the waist strap. Then he clipped the webbing to the man's parachute harness, inflating the jacket with a warning. "The three of us are going over the side. Create a disturbance, and your head will be the thing bobbing on the surface when your buddies shoot. You got that, asshole?"

From high overhead they heard a long, terrified wail.

"Kamal," the girl whispered.

Drake lifted the man to his feet and looked at the girl. "Let's go."

They crossed to the starboard rail. Drake wrapped the nylon webbing once around the cleat and quickly lowered the man to the water, scanning the deck and superstructure, praying that their luck would hold. It didn't. A terrorist walked out on the bridge wing. Drake raised the sound-suppressed MP5 and fired, the round blasting through the man's temple. The man dropped like a gunnysack. They were running out of time. Suddenly he heard footsteps coming from the stairs behind him. He grabbed the girl and ducked into a closet.

Two men rounded the corner and stepped out onto the main deck. Drake thought about the webbing tied to the cleat and the man bobbing in the water below. He prayed the terrorists wouldn't notice. If he got swept up into a firefight now, he was dead. He inserted a fresh magazine into his weapon, opened the closet door a crack, and peeked out. The men were no longer standing on the weather deck where Drake could see them. He motioned for the girl to be still, then quietly moved toward the open hatch. The men were gone.

The girl climbed down the nylon webbing, the wind billowing the silk bathrobe above her knees. She settled into the warm water, clinging to the webbing as Drake climbed down into the water beside her. He raised the telescopic pole, flicking the webbing off the cleat. He grabbed the end to keep the terrorist in tow. The man was shivering—a good sign.

They glided away in the current, the lighted stern of the yacht receding as they drifted into the darkness. They could see men searching the ship. Then a group of men gathered on the bridge wing, looking down at the body of the man Drake had shot. The tallest member of the group broke away and stared out into the darkness for several minutes in their direction. Then he hoisted the dead man to his shoulders and reentered the yacht, his men following behind him.

Edward Coleman awoke to a gun in his face. In the dim moonlight seeping through his bedroom windows, he looked up with shocked and disbelieving eyes at the four men standing over him. His wife lay beside him, her eyes wide with fear, her mouth taped shut. *Oh, God, the children.* He started to rise but was slammed against the backboard. "Please," he begged. "Take anything you want. Just leave my family alone."

"No harm will come to you or your family," one of the hooded men advised him, "as long as you do exactly as we say. Act foolishly and your children will die."

"Where are they? Let me see them!"

"Do you understand, Mr. Coleman?"

Tearfully, Coleman nodded.

"Bring the children here."

The shortest of the four men left the room and returned a minute later with Coleman's teenaged son and daughter. Their hands were tied behind their backs and their mouths were taped shut. They were frightened and sobbing, but otherwise unharmed. The short man shoved them onto the bed next to Coleman's wife. "Don't worry. We'll come out of this OK," Coleman bravely consoled them. Then the leader dragged Coleman to his feet and led him to the downstairs study.

"Activate the computer."

"Activate"? Were these people foreign? Afraid for his wife and children, Coleman did as he was told.

"As a designer of the Internet, you are an expert. Tonight there will be an auction. At this Web address. Several nations will participate. You must manipulate the system. You must make this nation come out on top."

The terrorist typed in a word.

Oh my God, they're Chinese. "Tonight?" Coleman objected, fear cramping his fingers. "That's hardly enough time to—"

"Your wife and children have only sixteen hours to live, Mr. Coleman—if you do not hurry."

Moonlight glimmered on the water. Drake was too exhausted to care. He lifted the girl out of the water and carried her to shore so that she would not cut her feet on the sharp coral. Her naked body was visible through the wet bathrobe. Then he headed back to the shallows and retrieved the prisoner, the man snorting saltwater through his nostrils as Drake hauled him ashore.

They had drifted for hours, passing villages, cliffs, and small marinas, Drake scanning the coast for a safe place to swim ashore. Twice, they had spread out low in the water as a Cuban patrol boat, then a fishing boat had passed by. Finally Drake had spotted a deserted cove.

"Do you have a name?" the girl had asked him.

"Yes. I have a name," Drake had replied. "Yours is Catherine."

On the beach, Drake stripped the man down to his underwear, cutting away his tactical vest and T-shirt. He tossed the pants, shoes, and socks to the girl. The warm wind was a godsend. She dressed quickly in the moonlight while he removed a magazine the man carried in his vest. It bore markings identical to the one he and Jack had found in Maine. He looked at the prisoner with the sudden urge to shove it down the man's throat.

Drake got up and offered the girl some water. She was sitting on the sand with her arms clasped around her knees.

"Are we going to stay here?" she asked.

"Tell me what you know about Elkins."

She told him. It wasn't much. He had contacted her agency in Paris. She had flown to Miami and they had sailed to Providenciales. He had worked for a man named Clayton—they had crashed the space shuttle together, he had bragged one night. Is that true? Is that why they killed him? Is that why they tried to kill me?

"Perhaps we should ask him."

She glanced nervously at the man propped against the tree and shook her head. "He'd be a fool to tell us."

"I think I can convince him otherwise."

"You men are all alike," she said, turning away in disgust.

Drake led her over to the tree. The man looked up at them, his eyes narrowed in fear and mistrust, like hers. He was in his twenties. Sandy brown hair. Mustache.

Drake crouched down, not letting go of Catherine's hand. Then, quelling his anger and in a tone of wry amusement, he said to the man, *"You* have been a very bad boy."

He looked up at Catherine and winked. She relaxed. Slightly.

"Now in case you haven't figured it out yet," Drake said, resuming the conversation, "let me explain exactly the kind of trouble you're in. Those people you and your buddies slaughtered back there—they're members of the Kuwaiti royal family. Which means that the Kuwaitis are going to be falling all over themselves trying to get their hands on you. Now, back in the good old USA, we apply humanitarian ideals to the treatment of prisoners. But in Kuwait? Well, let's just say that it's not a part of their cultural heritage.

"Which brings me to problem number two. You see, if this were Miami Beach, and you felt like playing Let's Make a Deal, we could talk to the D.A. But, unfortunately, we're in Cuba. And when Castro finds out that his oil deal just went down the shitter, he is going to be in a really bad frame of mind. Which is bad news for you, cowboy. Kind of like double jeopardy, you might say.

"So I'm going to make you a proposition: You tell me everything you know about Clayton, and I'll take you back to the USA. But if you hold back or bullshit me in any way, I'll deliver you to Castro myself. Do I make myself clear?"

The man nodded.

"So what's it going to be?

"Maybe you should take the tape off his mouth." Catherine giggled.

Ten minutes later they had the story.

Edward Coleman bent over the keyboard, perspiration dripping down his forehead. Hours had passed. He had accessed the Internet's backbone—the series of computer terminals that act as switching stations, routing packets of information to various locations. As the backbone's principal designer, he knew all the nooks and crannies, all the potential security holes unknown to anyone else. He had called up the auction Web site and had done his best to circumvent the elaborate firewalls designed to prevent tampering. But the firewalls were ingenious, unlike anything he had ever seen before. His only recourse had been to rig the backbone so that any bid coming in, except China's, would be momentarily captured and changed to a random figure between four and six billion dollars before being sent on its way. The entire procedure would occur within a millisecond—if it worked, if his alterations had gone undetected. With the lives of his wife and children on the line, all he could do was pray.

"Hey, are you Jimmy Buffett?"

His mouth agape, Dwight Johnson stared at the naked girl. He was standing atop the right wing of his Grumman Albatross seaplane; the girl was standing on the beach fifty feet away. The fly rod dropped from his hand.

"Why . . . yes!" Johnson stammered with a hopeful smile, scarcely believing his luck. "Why, yes, honey. I sure am!"

Johnson looked up and down the small cove. Palm trees, dazzling white sand, no one in sight.

The girl waded out to the shallows. Not a single tan line marred her perfect body. With a shy smile, she reached down and picked up Johnson's fly rod.

"You dropped this."

"Guess I'm a little nervous. I have a concert tomorrow night. In Miami. At the, uh . . . Orange Bowl! Say, would you like to join me for a swim? Then we could have lunch together, right here on the beach."

"Gee, Mr. Buffett. That'd be great!"

"Your boyfriend won't mind?"

With downcast eyes, she said, "We broke up last year."

He could scarcely breathe. He scrambled along the wing, and slid down the windshield, disappearing through the nose hatch. His head popped up a few seconds later.

"Know what, darlin'? I plumb forgot my swimming trunks."

"That's OK."

For all the sweet music serenading Johnson's heart, he *could* have been Jimmy Buffett. He shucked off his shorts and dove out the cockpit door, his erection slicing the clear water like a centerboard. The girl waded toward him, splashed him once, then playfully dove to his right. With an ardor he had not known since the day he had opened his first copy of *Playboy* magazine, penis in hand, Johnson dove after her, the sight of her strawberry blond pubis burning in his imagination. He wanted to lick her body from head to toe and bury his penis inside her forever. Then his face slammed against something solid.

Flustered, he surfaced, wiping saltwater from his eyes. Arms akimbo, the girl leaned against a ruggedly handsome man dressed in black and wearing some kind of exotic diving rig. The man raised a submachine gun.

"Jimmy, I'd like you to meet James Bond."

Sitting buck naked and weeping at the controls of the Grumman seaplane, Dwight Johnson powered up the engines for takeoff. "You gotta let me go," he pleaded "My boss is going to kill me."

"No can do, sport," Drake replied. "Who's your boss anyway?"

"Chuck Harbaugh," Johnson said, naming the defrocked Baptist minister turned radio and television personality. A phenomenon of the 1990s, Harbaugh's cigar-chomping visage and right-wing politics had made him the millionaire darling of the disenfranchised, a conservative counterpart to Al Sharpton.

Drake looked at the sealed boxes of Montecristos lining the plane's interior. Evidently the right reverend had sent Johnson on a shopping spree not unusual for the times. Few Americans were aware of just how receptive Cuba had become to the number of private American jets that flew into Havana's José Martí airport each week on little side hops from the Bahamas to load up on cigars. The Cubans had a name for the assemblage of privately owned Lears and Gulfstreams. They called it Hollywood Row.

Drake opened a window and tossed the contraband into the sea.

"Hey, what are you doing?" Johnson wailed. "That belongs to—"

"Yeah, I know who it belongs to. That's why I'm throwing this shit overboard."

———————

They were airborne. From the copilot's seat, Drake glanced over his shoulder at Catherine. She was asleep, curled up against a window. Bound and gagged, the prisoner lay on the floor three rows behind them.

Drake glanced at Johnson.

"Still in Cuban airspace?"

"No."

"Plot a course for Bimini."

Johnson did as he was told.

He felt Catherine at his shoulder. "I thought you were asleep," Drake said.

"Bimini?"

"I used to live there. I need to call someone. I can't do it from a cell phone."

"Your girlfriend?"

"Wife, actually."

"Oh." There was a trace of sadness in her voice, and for a long moment she gazed at him in silence. Then she caressed his cheek. "Thank you."

"No thanks necessary."

"I don't even know your name."

Drake looked at her with compassion.

"My name is Philip Drake."

"How long have you been married?"

They were sitting in the middle row of the seaplane, sharing Johnson's lunch.

"A year," Drake said. "How about you?"

Catherine giggled. "Have you ever been to Venice, Mr. Drake?"

"No."

"I went there last year. We stayed at the Cipriani. Beautiful gardens. Saltwater pool. Venice is the city of Casanova, you know. I always thought that he was an old roué, until I read his *Histoire de ma vie.* Did you know that he escaped from the Leads Prison, translated the *Iliad* into Italian, and collaborated with Da Ponte on the libretto for *Don Giovanni*? I think he loved women because they brought him so much happiness. Why should love be otherwise?"

Drake had stopped munching on his sandwich.

She bit off an orange section and leaned against the stainless-steel bulkhead with her legs crossed on the seat. Her straw-colored hair fell past her shoulders in thick strands, fused by the salt. She smiled at him. "Are you a spy, Mr. Drake? Casanova was a spy."

She was toying with him. Drake rolled his eyes and gazed out the window. They would be landing in Bimini soon.

"I'll trade this orange for that bag of potato chips."

Drake looked down at the bag. "OK."

She handed him the orange. "Hey, there're no more chips in this bag."

Now it was Drake's turn to smile.

"My brother used to do that." She reached over and snatched the orange from Drake's hand, beaming in triumph. Then she sat down beside him. "We share."

Drake looked at her as she handed him half the orange. "So what else have you read besides Casanova's *Histoire de ma vie?*"

———

The reggae band was setting up for the night when Catherine and Drake strolled into the Compleat Angler in Alice Town. Other than a couple of salts hanging out in the bar, the Angler was quiet. Catherine wandered about the empty dance floor, gazing at the hundreds of photographs of proud fishermen standing beside giant tuna and marlin twice their size. To the right of the dance floor, another room contained yellowing photographs of Ernest Hemingway. In one of the photographs, Hemingway was standing on the town dock, firing a Thompson submachine gun.

Drake stepped into the bar.

"Well lookee here. If it ain't Captain Nemo hisself."

Drake laughed, gazing with happiness at the bartender, who was holding a new power drill and smiling broadly. "Hey, Melvin."

Catherine walked up beside Drake.

"Shit, I heard you got married. Nice to meet you, little lady."

"It's nice to meet you, too. I'm Catherine." She looked up at Drake, delighted that he didn't say anything.

Drake smiled at her as best he could. "We need a room with a shower. Book us for a week, if you can. And I need to use the office phone."

"No problem, boss." Melvin set the power drill on the bartop and handed Catherine the key. "Room two twenty-one, on the right at the top of the stairs."

Catherine looked at Drake, as though uncertain how to proceed.

"Honey, why don't you take a shower? I'll make the call and be right up."

Catherine turned to Melvin. "Isn't he just the sweetest thing on two feet?"

They watched her stroll out of the bar.

Melvin was shaking his head. "Shit, Phil. She sure is a looker. How come you got so lucky?"

Drake felt a sudden pull in his lower abdomen, wondering the same thing himself. *It would be so easy to follow her up the stairs. Then what would you do? Tell her you love her? Tell her that what happens between two people exists apart from the world? Or the familiar ruse of married men, that you're having problems at home? Is that what you want? To honor Jack's life by telling lies? How do you go on living after that? How do you go on living with Jennifer? What do you say to her? How do you go on living with yourself without becoming the kind of man you always despised?*

Drake smiled at the mystified expression on Melvin's face. "Beats me, Melvin. Looks like there's a god after all. Now how about that phone?"

Melvin opened the office door. "It's right there on the desk, as usual. And the next time you're talking to God, tell him to save a little piece for me."

The door was closed. Drake sat down at the desk. By taking a room for a week, he hoped to throw people off the trail, in case they were being followed. He wasn't taking chances.

He picked up the receiver, dialed, and listened to the connections working through. Then a woman's voice came on the line. It was as though another dimension had opened up.

"Hi."

"Phil? Oh, my God, I can't believe it's you!"

"I miss you, Jen."

"Are you OK?"

"Listen. I'm sending you a package. Express Mail. I need you to hand-deliver it to Walt."

There was a troubled pause on the other end. "Jen?"

She was crying. "Walt's been shot, Phil. He's in Walter Reed. It's very bad. He's not expected to live."

Drake felt his soul crashing to the floor.

"How . . . ?"

"He was with Julia Reynolds. They went out to dinner, and then he walked her up to her room. Someone was waiting inside. Julia's dead."

Drake took this in as Jennifer sobbed on the other end of the line. "Jen. I love you very much."

"I love you, too. Come home. Please."

"Honey, I can't. If I quit now, they win. I'll be all right. You have to trust me. I need you to deliver this package to Adams. Say that you'll do it."

"I miss you so much."

"How's the library coming?"

"They started the foundation."

"Good. I love you, Jen. I have to go now. I'll be careful. I promise." He set down the receiver. *Her words, her voice, the way she curls her chestnut hair around her ears when she's gardening, the warmth of her skin at night: this is what binds me to the world. Think about that and not about what they did to Walt and Jack.*

But he couldn't help thinking about the catastrophe that had befallen his friends, the rage curling like smoke inside him.

She was in the shower, luxuriating in the cool water spraying down on her body. She knew enough not to expect a night of love. He had someone else in his life, and deep in her heart she was glad. It had been a long time since a man had looked at her as a complete woman and not as something to fuck. She knew she was beautiful, that men would pay thousands of dollars for the pleasure of sleeping with her, but they were selfish men with selfish needs— boy-men. Drake was different. It was as though in looking at a woman his quiet intelligence required more than mere physical beauty and a casual relationship to sustain itself—that this was a man who needed to get at the nature of things.

Catherine stepped out of the shower and toweled off. She felt refreshed for the first time in days. She was hungry. Perhaps they could grab a quick bite to eat.

Drake was waiting in the bedroom. He looked flushed, angry.

"Are you OK?"

"Get your things. We're leaving. Now."

"How's he doing?" Lawrence sat down beside Adams and Helen, McKendrick's secretary, and gazed at the panoply of tubes and machines that surrounded the general, and then at the man himself. McKendrick's face was swathed in bandages. The chairman of the Joint Chiefs of Staff was barely breathing. If it hadn't been for the heart monitor, blinking its steady rhythm, Lawrence would have thought that McKendrick was dead.

"Hanging on," Adams replied with guarded optimism.

Helen had been crying. Lawrence placed a hand on her back. She gave him a hug.

"How are you?" Adams asked.

"Okay," Lawrence replied somberly.

The day before, with tears streaming down his face and Elliot by his side, he had identified Julia's body at the morgue. Both men had been shocked by the damage the bullets had inflicted. He had called her father and had broken the news. The old man had sobbed over the phone.

He remembered the day that she had joined him at the CEL Foundation in Detroit, the first of many such occasions. Julia had pulled up a chair beside a shy fifth-grade girl and had helped her with her homework. She and the girl, whose name was Amanda, still wrote to each other. Julia had helped a lot of children that way, tutoring, counseling. Now she was gone.

Had his probe of the Pentagon's operating system alerted the terrorists? He couldn't see how that could have happened.

He gazed at McKendrick without speaking, his heart leaden with sorrow. He had spent most of the day frantically alternating between funeral arrangements and work, time coiling around his body like a python. Then to Adams he said, "Elliot told me you were here. There's a car waiting outside."

They were packed inside the Situation Room: Adams, Lawrence, Elliot, McGuire, Admiral Archer, Margaret Abrams, and President Young. Their eyes were riveted to the twenty-inch monitor on the conference table. Thanks to Adams's arm-twisting, the French had agreed to allow the United States to secretly bid in their place, and the president had put together a cash figure that was going to do nothing to allay the national debt. But under the circumstances, he had little choice. Drake and the girl had disappeared into thin air. Until the intruder reappeared inside the Pentagon's computer network, Lawrence could do little to trace the source of the break-ins. Federal investigators had turned up no other leads on the *Tri-*

dent highjacking or on Julia's murder. Walt McKendrick lay at death's door. The entire unspeakable catastrophe had come down to a few numbers typed into a computer terminal, a few numbers representing a fortune.

The Gatemaster looked up from his computer monitor. "Sir, someone's fucked with the backbone; they're restructuring the bids."

Clayton frowned. Someone was breaking the rules—his rules. "Who's doing it?"

The Gatemaster stared at the screen.

"Well, God damn it. Just a sec . . ."

The Gatemaster typed in a command. "It's China, sir. Shall I declare them incligible?"

Not daring to believe that he and his family might survive, Edward Coleman watched in amazement as the bids appeared on his office monitor. One by one they were coming in under six billion dollars. Iran, Iraq, Pakistan . . . He looked up at the men, seeking mercy in their eyes. He thought of his wife and children, locked in the master bedroom upstairs. He felt as though he were suffocating. Then China's bid appeared on the screen, flashing in victory, a billion dollars higher than the rest.

The leader of the group slapped his associate on the shoulder. Then the associate, as silent as ever, headed upstairs. The leader turned to Coleman, speaking in a calm voice in which the Internet designer detected a note of condolence. "You have done well,

Mr. Coleman. As I said before, we do not wish your family harm. We are not monsters. We will return you to your family upstairs where you will be restrained. Once we are at a safe distance, we will notify the authorities who will effect your release."

Coleman looked at the stairs, then placed his head on the table like a little boy and cried.

Seven billion dollars, Clayton thought. He planted a congratulatory hand on the Gatemaster's shoulder. The Chinese had manipulated the system, but he had let it slide. The point was never about money, anyway. With the Gatemaster at his side, he could get his hands on all the cash he needed. No, the sale of Bright Star was about revenge. And revenge he had gained in spades. Of all the countries to possess Bright Star, China would pose the greatest threat to the United States.

He thought about his former friends in Washington, imagining the panic that would grip their hearts.

Now it was time to make arrangements for the transfer. They could do that via the *Trident*. Smiling broadly, he pulled up a chair next to the terminal. "Send our congratulations to Beijing."

The mood of the men and women inside the White House Situation Room was grim to the point of desperation. After the winner had been announced, the president buried his face in his hands. It was unimaginable that China could have outbid the United States, yet that is precisely what had occurred. Now with

Bright Star about to fall into the hands of the Chinese, the United States was faced with the prospect of war.

Secretary of Defense Richard Elliot glanced at Adams and said, "Mr. President, I believe that it is imperative that we notify the Chinese that under no circumstances will we allow them to launch Bright Star into space, that we will take every measure necessary to protect our own security and the security of our allies."

Gathering himself, President Young looked at his advisors, his face ashen. "Agreed." Then, turning to Adams, the president said, "Every launching facility in China must be monitored. That is our top priority. Our other priority is to seek a peaceful solution to this crisis. We must leave no diplomatic stone unturned. But if the Chinese attempt to place Bright Star in orbit, we must be prepared to act militarily." He looked at the faces around him nodding in stern agreement, then focused on Admiral Archer. "David, as of this moment, I am placing our forces on alert, Defense Condition Two." He turned to his chief of staff. "Margaret, at some point we'll have to make an announcement."

Elliot spoke up, looking straight into the president's eyes. "You should address the nation, sir. We are going to need the support of the American people."

"Charles?"

Adams nodded. "I concur wholeheartedly. The collective will of our nation speaks volumes and will reinforce our declared commitment to recover Bright Star. Beijing must know in no uncertain terms that we mean business."

"Margaret, will you contact the networks?"

"What date should I give them? I assume that we'll want to contact our allies first . . . and issue a private warning to the Chinese."

"Eight P.M., Eastern Standard Time. One week from today."

Back at his office desk at Langley, fully engaged in the crisis that had suddenly swept over the nation like a thunderstorm, Charles Francis Adams thought back to the Cuban missile crisis of October 1962. Filled with grief, frightened for his country, he was searching for answers, culling the vast repository of historical information embedded in his brain, hoping for illumination and insight. No matter what you thought of John Fitzgerald Kennedy, whether you liked or disliked his politics, whether you disapproved of his sexual escapades or believed that they had no bearing on his ability to govern the nation, you couldn't help but admire the clear thinking and extraordinary coolness of mind that Kennedy had brought to those anxious thirteen days of October when the United States and the Soviet Union had stood on the brink of nuclear war. For Kennedy's decision to impose a naval quarantine around Cuba had been bitterly opposed by many of his closest advisors.

Adams shuddered to think of what the Cuban missile crisis might have wrought had some of Kennedy's less moderate successors been at the helm.

With the exception of Chairman Maxwell Taylor, the Joint Chiefs had urged swift and overwhelming air strikes followed by a full-scale invasion of Cuba a week later, even though they could not be sure that they had uncovered all the missile sites. Throughout the crisis, Air Force General Curtis Le May had made his detestation of Kennedy plain, comparing the blockade to "appeasement." Even after Khrushchev had publicly agreed to remove the missiles, the military had pressed for intervention. Had such an invasion occurred, Adams doubted that Khrushchev could have withstood pressure to invade Berlin.

Thanks to Kennedy, and the clear thinking of McNamara, Rusk, Ball, and Llewellyn, moderation and common sense had prevailed. But Adams was aware that fortune also had lent a hand, that many of the Cold War assumptions that had guided Kennedy and his advisors had been wrong. They had believed, for example, that Khrushchev had placed missiles in Cuba as part of a grand Soviet strategy to dominate the world. Adams knew now, thanks to glasnost, that missiles had been placed in Cuba because Khrushchev had made a desperate gamble. Aware that the United States possessed a seventeen-to-one advantage in nuclear warheads, Khrushchev understood far better than his American counterparts that the Soviet Union was losing the Cold War. As much as he delighted at "tossing a hedgehog at Uncle Sam's pants," he had been prompted to act by an obsessive fear that America might invade Cuba. The U.S.-backed invasion at the Bay of Pigs and the successive attempts to undermine Castro's regime had provided Khrushchev with a very clear picture of U.S. intentions toward his client state. Had the Eisenhower and Kennedy administrations been mistaken in taking such a hard-line approach to Cuba? Certainly the Bay of Pigs invasion and the Operation Mongoose fiasco, which had included attempts to assassinate Castro, had only made a bad situation worse.

Yet clearly, in retrospect, there had been occasions in recent American history when taking a hard-line approach had been the proper course of action. The Gulf War provided an excellent example. In deciding to send U.S. forces into battle against Saddam Hussein, President George Bush had made one of the gutsiest calls Adams had ever seen. Although victory was assured from the start, any number of experts had predicted huge American losses. That those casualties had been prevented, that Saddam's forces had been driven from Kuwait, spoke volumes about political and military leadership at its best. Adams's only regret was that President Bush had not stood before Congress and called for a Declaration of War, as the Constitution mandated. Bush's advisors had suspected that the Democratic-controlled Congress might succumb to partisanship and vote against it, a fear that was not without justification. The subordination of the common good to partisanship was the ongoing tragedy of American politics.

Now seated in his seventh-floor office, Adams worried about all the variables beyond his control. If Bright Star could not be recovered through negotiation, if China attempted to place the satellite in orbit, President Young would have no choice but to attack the launch site. American cruise missiles would be targeted against China. And the Chinese would in all likelihood retaliate. If President Young hoped to steer the world away from the brink of nuclear war, he would have to keep his mind open and his thinking clear, and he would have to convince others to do the same—especially his counterparts in China. The fate of the world depended on it.

25 August

Three minutes past midnight, McKendrick awoke from his coma. He blinked, looking out through a thin veil of gauze at the wall opposite him. It swirled for a moment, then slowly became recognizable. *I am staring at a wall.*

He felt woozy. His body ached with a distant pain. *Morphine.* He tried to get up but couldn't move. *Where am I?* In the dream landscape he inhabited he could sense the odor of burning grass after a napalm strike mixed with the smell of burning flesh. *No. There was life after. A boy who became a man. Was that me, or someone else?* Then he knew that there had been two boys. He was one. The other had been named Drake. But he had died. And then the world divided again: no, there had been two Drakes, father and son.

Kissing: the salty taste of a woman's mouth. Wasps.
Why are these faces looking at me? Here, not in memory?

"Can you hear me?" the nurse asked.

Yes I can hear you, but I can't speak.

"Do you know where you are?"

Hell?

"Do you want us to call anyone?"

God. Julia.

Drake's package arrived by Express Mail that morning, as expected. Jennifer read Drake's letter, then booked a noon flight to Washington, departing from Westchester. For once, the flight wasn't delayed.

She took a cab from Dulles to the CIA. A guard stopped them at the gate.

"I would like to speak to Director Charles Francis Adams, please."

The duty officer looked at her with considerable skepticism. "Do you have an appointment, ma'am?"

"Here is my driver's license. I have other identification, if you wish. My name is Jennifer Drake. My husband, Philip Drake, is one of the divers who rescued the astronauts. He asked me to deliver this package personally to Director Adams. It is urgent. I strongly recommend that you call him now."

Inside his seventh-floor suite, Adams was consulting with Dr. Atkinson from Walter Reed over the phone when his secretary stepped into his office. "Sorry to bother you, sir, but there's a woman here, a Mrs. Drake. She has a package that she says her husband sent to her. She says it's for you."

"Would you like anything? Coffee? A sandwich?"

"Tea," Jennifer replied. Adams had told her the good news about McKendrick. She was so relieved. Considering the extent of Walt's injuries, even the smallest improvement was a tremendous sign of hope. If only she could reach Phil.

Adams scanned the letter, his eyes widening with astonishment. He quickly reached for the phone.

"Good news?" Jennifer asked.

Adams looked at her closely. "Very." He could breathe again. He couldn't wait to inform the president that the break that they had prayed for had suddenly materialized. He shook his head in wonder, happy for the first time in days. First the news about Walt, and now this. Maybe their luck was beginning to change. "He never quits, does he?" he said to Jennifer.

Someone came on the line. Adams turned away slightly. "Hello, Richard? Good news: We've got a facility to take down. In Maine."

Jennifer moved toward the window as Adams described the contents of the letter. She thought of the night Drake had fought his way back to her room where she had been kept prisoner aboard the *Avatar*.

No. He never quit when he rescued me.

Something was up. Donnally could sense the excitement of the Special Operations people he ran into along the Pentagon's corridors. He knew that a preemptive attack on Chinese launching sites was in the works. Soon President Young would address the nation, and the whole world would know about Bright Star falling into Chinese hands. But information regarding any headway the

CIA and other federal agencies might be making in trying to un-
cover the terrorists was being closely held—very closely held. Donnally had never seen such strict security.

That morning he had bustled down the Pentagon's busy
E-ring, unsuccessfully trying to elicit information from the officers
he knew, but they didn't know much, either. Ever since Julia and
McKendrick had been shot, the well had run dry.

Well, desperate times call for desperate measures. In the past
he had been exceedingly cautious in obtaining information, carefully gathering bits here and there, never drawing attention to
himself. Now, if he had any chance of collecting Clayton's money,
he would have to become more aggressive. Something was going
on. Were they closing in? He picked up the phone.

"Dawson. One Hundred and Sixty-ninth SOAR," came the
clipped tone over the receiver.

"Hey, Ted. George Harris at NSC. Yeah. Dave Walker asked
me to liase with you fellas. Yeah, just came in. What kind of time
frame are you guys looking at?"

Billy Lawrence was grabbing a sandwich in the commissary when
his beeper went off. He dropped the sandwich and ran back to his
office. The printer was spewing paper all over the floor. The key-
stroke capture program was working like gangbusters. The intruder was back, and Lawrence was surreptitiously watching his
every move. *It's payback time, motherfucker.* With a few deft key-
strokes, Lawrence activated the tracer. *Wait a minute.* Lawrence
stared at the monitor. Instead of opening file after file, searching
for information, the intruder had headed straight for a specific location, a file that suddenly popped up out of nowhere.

So that's how it's done.

Lawrence watched the deft transfer of information with amazement. This was no Aldrich Ames filling a plastic garbage bag with classified files, then walking out through the front door of the CIA. This guy was having it handed to him on a silver platter.

A mole.

The intruder had cleverly routed his signal through half the countries around the globe, and if Lawrence had been using a conventional telephone trace he would have been blocked out by Iran, Libya, and a dozen others. Not like he could call up Qaddafi and say, "Hey, Mu'ammar, would you mind tracing this call for us, please?" Not likely to happen. With the program Lawrence had devised, you could go anywhere, provided you had enough time, communications satellites tending to cause delays.

But there was no delay in locating the source of the information coming from inside the Pentagon. Lawrence picked up the phone. "Get me the secretary of defense. Yes. Bill Lawrence. It's urgent."

Elliot got on the line. "Say, Billy." His voice was strained.

"The intruder isn't searching data bases; he's having it fed to him by a mole."

"Are you certain of this?"

"I saw it happen. And I've tracked the mole's computer. The asshole's in room one twenty-nine."

Flanked by four MPs, Billy Lawrence and Secretary of Defense Richard Elliot strode down the E-ring, prepared to do battle, ignoring the stares and sudden whisperings of Pentagon employees passing by. A short distance away, a door opened and a man stepped out. The man glanced at Elliot, Lawrence, and the MPs and casually headed in the opposite direction. The casual approach didn't work. Donnally's goose was cooked.

"Halt!" an MP shouted. Everyone in the hallway froze except for Donnally, who sprinted for the River Entrance.

He was running for his life, streaking for the vast wilderness of cars that filled the River Entrance parking lot. The men chasing him were spreading out, and Donnally could see reinforcements pouring out of the River Entrance. He ducked down, hiding behind parked cars, scampering on his hands and knees like a dog. He tried the door of a Toyota Tercel. Locked. *Damn!* He scuttled around to a Honda Civic. That door was locked, too. *What the fuck is wrong with these people? Don't they trust anyone?*

He stood and bolted for the highway. It was his only chance. He was running for his life. In panic, he looked back over his shoulder at the MPs in hot pursuit. A bad-ass nigger was leading the pack. And to make matters worse, that nigger was gaining on him, too.

Lawrence was hauling ass, keeping his eyes riveted on the Army officer trying to escape across the parking lot. From the way the traitor was running, Lawrence could tell that the man was out of shape. The guy hadn't sprinted five hundred yards and already his head was hanging, a sign that he was gulping air instead of breathing easy. *Good.*

Running flat out, Lawrence could feel the adrenaline pumping through his veins. Julia had shared his dream. Working side by side, they had built a satellite that would guarantee America's safety, a satellite that would cut the defense budget by half. They had worked together at the CEL Foundation, helping inner-city kids enter the mainstream of American life. Together they had transformed a dream into reality. Now Julia was gone, her face obliterated by a submachine gun. Lawrence burned with anger. *That's right, baby,* he counseled himself. *Keep that fire lit.*

The man was heading for the highway. *No way he's going to make it. I'm gonna rip that fucker apart.* Lawrence sprinted past another parked car, as heat shimmered off the asphalt. They were running on the grass median. It was now or never; the highway was only twenty feet away. Lawrence coiled his body like a lion and leaped through the sultry Washington air.

Donnally looked over his shoulder again. *Oh, God.* His legs felt like paste. His lieutenant commander's uniform dripped with sweat. He ripped the tie from his throat. He was gagging, suffocating on the humidity. Fifty feet away cars were shooting back and forth, many of them slowing as they caught sight of the commotion. People were pouring out of the River Entrance and heading into the parking lot. Donnally felt as though he were being chased by a tidal wave. And what about that spear chucker behind him? *Shit!* Wailing with fear, he raced for the highway. Too late. In a flying tackle Lawrence caught Donnally's heel. Both men tumbled to the ground, Donnally kicking and punching to break free. Lawrence rammed his fist into the Army officer's throat, then grabbed Donnally by the belt, picked him up, and threw him down to the ground with such force that Donnally's right arm snapped. Donnally rolled on the grass, screaming and sobbing in pain. At the sight of the traitor's agonized expression, Lawrence backed away. *The man's down. Enough.*

But as Lawrence looked back at the MPs and the crowd surging toward him, Donnally struggled to his feet and flung himself onto the highway, stepping in front of the first car he saw in a desperate attempt to flag it down.

Gloria Hopkins had been listening to her favorite Lawrence Welk song on the radio when the Army officer leaped in front of her car. Screaming, she slammed on the brakes, but the man disappeared under the hood, the big Buick rising in a hideous lurch as she tried to convince herself that she had run over a log. Panicking, she slammed the car into reverse and ran over the log again.

Lawrence looked away as the air was riven with Donnally's screams. The MPs tried to calm the hysterical woman, who flew out of her car, holding her face in her hands. The crowd surged around. Motorists slowed to a stop and got out of their cars. A siren wailed in the distance. Lieutenant Commander Frank Donnally was still alive when they lifted him from the highway.

26 August

The island lay a mile offshore, surrounded on three sides by shallows and on the east by a deep-water approach. From his vantage point halfway up a Northern pine that stood near the edge of the forest, Drake could see a dock with a Hovercraft moored beside it. Up island and to the right, a helipad spread across a granite promontory. Occupying the center of the island, the slate roof of Clayton's baronial retreat rose above the pines.

Thorne's man had coughed up a wealth of information, including security codes for all the doors and a sketch of the underground facility. Bright Star was being kept aboard the *Trident*, until arrangements could be made with the Chinese. Drake could either enter the underground facility through the clubhouse and work his way down to the cavern or he could negotiate the underwater cave leading directly to the concrete pen where the *Trident* was moored. Working his way through the cave seemed to be the easiest way, except for one minor problem: Clayton had filled the cave with light sensors. Drake would have to negotiate the cave in total darkness.

Finding the entrance at night wouldn't be easy. He would have to grope in the darkness, wasting time and air. Of course, he could wait until noon the next day; with the sun directly overhead, he would have plenty of ambient light at the bottom to spot the entrance. But what would he do once he reached the *Trident*? Clayton's men were sure to be moving about in the afternoon.

Having seen enough, Drake lowered the binoculars, climbed down the pine, and crept back through the forest to the boulder where he had cached his equipment. Blackflies were out in force. The ancient Egyptians used to sleep on towers, according to Herodotus, so that the wind would prevent the mosquitoes from landing. Not a bad idea. Catherine was sitting beneath a gnarled tamarack.

On top of Jack's death, the wounding of the man who had been his father's best friend and who had guided him through childhood was too much to bear. Every time he thought about what the terrorists had done to Walt, he could see the smoke curling up; he could feel himself yielding to impulses that were better left alone. So he shoved it off to one side, knowing that he would have to deal with it later.

Besides, there was Catherine. He had to look out for her.

They ate an assortment of dried fruit and nuts that they had purchased in Bimini and then settled in for the night. They were encamped amid pines whose dead branches ran almost to the ground, a sign that neither man nor beast had visited this patch of ground in years.

"These flies are driving me crazy," Catherine complained. "How come I can't use more bug spray?"

"Because people can smell it. Stay inside your sleeping bag and use the mosquito netting."

She lay down in the bag beside his, grumbling. Twenty minutes later, she was asleep.

Half past midnight Drake slipped out of his sleeping bag and bent down to collect his gear.

"Hey, where in the hell do you think *you're* going? You're not leaving me here?" She looked at him, at first incredulous, then imploringly, thinking of Johnson and Thorne's man sequestered inside the seaplane that Drake had hidden in a remote thicket of brambles.

"I'm sorry, Catherine. I have to disappear for a while. A couple of hours at the most. When I come back, we're outta here."

"When's that going to be? I'm not the camping type."

"You want to walk back to the seaplane?"

"No."

He gathered his gear and headed for the water, the moonlight pouring down through the trees. He didn't look back. Reaching the shore, he climbed down the rocks, his fins slung over his left forearm, and entered the ocean. The cold water was shocking against his face. He checked his air and switched on the underwater scooter that he had brought from Bimini, hoping that Catherine would stay put. He hated to leave her, but what else could he do? She couldn't make the dive. And he had to get inside the *Trident,* where Clayton and his men were storing Bright Star, and pull the disks before they handed the satellite off to the Iraqis or the Chinese. Bright Star was only good once it was in orbit. And as Thorne's man had said, Clayton was planning to hold an auction.

He wondered how long it would take Adams to coordinate an

assault. He had sent Jennifer a sketch of the facility based on what the prisoner had told him. His headset was still functioning; once the assault force positioned itself around the house, he could make contact, or presumably they would make contact with him. Until then, he and Catherine would be on their own.

Gripping the handles of the scooter, the island silhouetted against the harvest moon, Drake took a compass reading and submerged beneath the glimmering water. The scooter purred in his ears. By not having to swim to the island he was saving air and energy. He thought about Jack and the night they had rescued Jennifer aboard Gerhardt's yacht, *Avatar,* at the end of Operation Torchlight. They had worked together as a team, the way they had been trained as SEALs. Now Jack was dead, and he was going into battle alone.

A quarter of a mile from the island, Drake quietly surfaced, checked his position, and submerged again. He descended to thirty feet, staying well above the boulder-strewn bottom. That was the last thing he needed, to slam into a rock. Cold water rushed past his face, and in the darkness he could see the compass dial on the scooter, a miniature globe of luminous green. He swam on, measuring distance by time.

Nearing the island, he abandoned the scooter, relying on the compass on his wrist. He swam without a light, his arms extended in the darkness for protection. Five minutes later he touched a rock wall covered with mussel shells—the island.

He dropped down another thirty feet, keeping his hand on the rock wall, the moon glimmering on the surface above. He circumnavigated the island, checking the compass until he reached the eastern end. Barnacles and sharp clusters of mussel shells abraded his gloves. He moved with steady deliberation, wondering when he would feel the rocks give way to the cave entrance. He checked the gauges on the rebreather. He still had a ready supply of mix. The water had turned darker. Why? He looked up.

The moon had disappeared.

Beads of perspiration trickled down his backbone. Had he inadvertently wandered inside the cave? Praying that he hadn't become lost, he reversed direction, hoping to figure out where the hell he was. He didn't have the time for this maneuver, not when he still had to penetrate 2,000 feet of cave in total darkness. He backtracked, a knuckle of fear lodging beneath his sternum. *Where am I?* Had he gotten turned around somehow? It didn't seem possible, yet there was still no moonlight visible on the surface. *Don't second-guess yourself. Work the problem. Don't let the problem work you.* He kept on. Then with an icy rush he could see a sliver of light wavering on the surface. The moon.

He descended to the ocean floor, one hand on the wall, the other groping for a place to set the small grapple to which he had attached his penetration line. Eventually he came to a pair of rocks lying beside each other. He wedged the hook between them. Something skittered across his hand. A lobster? He tested the line, pulling it in several directions to make absolutely sure that the grapple would stay in place. Then he ascended until he could see the moon again.

The rebreather worked like a dream. With renewed confidence, he swam ahead. Within minutes he was deep inside the cave, engulfed in darkness.

The line unwound smoothly from its spool as Drake crept along over the next half hour, touching granite walls, picturing the cave as a vast, glittering mica-flecked cathedral, reminiscent of Byzantine mosaics or hidden galaxies of stars. He recalled the writings of Benoît de Maillet, the French consul general in Egypt under Louis XIV who, upon exploring the Great Pyramid, had noted that the interior passageways leading to the burial chamber were so blackened with soot from the torches of ancient thieves that one could not distinguish among individual blocks of stone. Then Drake pictured himself spiraling through a black hole—a burial chamber of another sort, a collapsed star whose gravitational field is so intense that not even light escaped—a journey leading to another dimension in time. When he died, would the earth hold him fast? He kept on, his brain dancing from one reverie to another. His face grew numb with cold. He was thirsty. Then in the distance he could see a faint orange glow—the cavern.

He moved quickly now, emboldened by the light. He could see the dark hull of the *Trident*. He swam toward it with a qualified sense of relief, aware of the danger that lay beyond. Before he knew it, he was beneath the dark hull. He drew his .45-caliber sound-suppressed H&K Mark 23 and quietly broke to the surface between the *Trident*'s port hull and the narrow concrete platform along the cavern's far wall. The room was vast, dark, and quiet. The dank air felt wonderful. He could hear the distant hum of a generator, but nothing else—no signs of movement. He slipped out of the rebreather, switching the .45 to his left hand, and pulled himself slowly onto the platform.

Straight ahead along the rock wall, the narrow platform curved toward the underground command center. To his right the black hull of the *Trident* rose three feet above him. There were no closed-circuit cameras, not here in the inner sanctum. The mansion and the three-story underground command center provided a formidable, if not impenetrable, barrier to all intruders. Drake had just pulled off the unexpected.

He had to move quickly now. He crouched beside the *Trident* and scanned the room, concentrating on the elevated wall of glass that housed the observation room. Directly below, a steel security door stood embedded in the concrete wall. All was quiet. Drake glanced at his watch: 2:00 A.M.

He hopped aboard the *Trident* and opened a hatch. Darkness below. He kept the .45 ready, knowing that if he had to fire, the sound suppressor would eliminate only 70 percent of the noise. Not great, but better than nothing. The great thing about a .45 was its stopping power. Especially with the custom loads that Drake carried. There was nothing like it.

He climbed down the ladder, quietly shutting the hatch. Darkness surrounded him. From his tactical vest he withdrew a penlight and switched it on, spotting an array of control panels. Then he felt the cold steel of a shotgun pressing against his cheek.

27 August

She was curled up inside the sleeping bag, not sleeping but listening to the night noises—or rather, wondering why they had stopped. *Why did he have to leave me here alone?* Moonlight filtered down through the pines, and for a minute she thought she could hear the distant sound of laughter coming from the island.

She could smell the ocean. *Different here than in the Caribbean. The smell of salt mixed with the odor of the earth and pine.* Hiking into the promontory, they had startled a moose. The mangy beast had trotted a few feet into the trees, then decided not to give way, lowering its antlers, which seemed as wide as a king-size bed. Slowly they had backed off, taking another route through the wilds.

What were they doing in Paris now? Not worrying about moose, that's for sure. She couldn't wait to get home. She would take a hot bath, treat herself to dinner, take some time off. Would she ever see

Drake again? *What kind of woman does a man like Drake marry? Is she beautiful? She's probably a lot like him—quiet. But maybe not.*

A stick cracked. She lay huddled against the ground. *He said no animals would come through here. It's probably nothing. Could it be Drake?*

She looked up in the direction from which she had heard the sound. Nothing except the silvery trunks of the pines with their dark branches. Nearby, a bird took flight, crossing the moon. She watched it fade into the cobalt sky, never noticing the men crawling up behind her.

"We've been expecting you."

Arms bound behind his back, Drake lay on his side on a blue plastic sheet spread across the floor of Clayton's office. His left arm stung where the wound had been partially reopened.

Blue blazer, polo shirt, gold-rimmed spectacles, brown hair brushed firmly in place, Geoffrey Clayton chuckled softly to himself. "Looks like you got a nasty cut there." Then to the big security man standing near the door, he said, "Get him up."

Thorne grabbed him by the arms and forced him into a chair. Drake winced from the pain. A livid scar ran across the man's cheek.

Clayton sat on the edge of his desk, peering at Drake closely.

"I want to tell you a little story about Thorne here. Back in eighty-three, a gaggle of Beirut sand niggers took a Russian diplomat hostage. The Soviets hired Thorne to handle the problem. Three days later, the head terrorist's family disappeared: wife, children, mother, father—everyone except the brother, whose mutilated body was found on the terrorist's doorstep with a message pinned to his chest. The message offered a trade. An hour later, the Russians got their man back."

He peered at Drake and laughed. "So what shall I tell Thorne to do with the girl? *Hmmm?*" Clayton looked at Thorne and nodded.

Gripping him by the throat, prying his eyelids open as he struggled for air, Thorne hauled Drake out of his seat and dragged him to the desk, where a skinny youth with tousled hair had placed a monitor and a mouse. Drake twisted, desperately trying to wrench himself free. He felt as if his neck was breaking. Struggling against Thorne's weight, Drake screamed in rage as Catherine appeared on the screen. She was naked, standing in a concrete cubicle six feet high, gazing up in abject fear.

"Well? I'm waiting."

"You are fucking dead," Drake hissed through clenched teeth.

"Know how we tracked you down?" Clayton chimed. "One of your Pentagon friends sold you out. The same guy who shot your asshole buddy McKendrick." He looked at Thorne. "Shall we get on with it?"

Drake couldn't move, his air shut off, his body twisted and racked with pain.

Thorne gripped Drake's head with his massive hands and slammed it down on the mouse.

Suddenly Clayton's office was filled with the sound of Catherine's screaming as water surged into the cubicle. She pounded on the walls as the water rose up around her. Drake struggled against Thorne's iron grip. Then Clayton whispered in his ear: "No one fucks with me, boy. Ever."

———

He awoke an hour later in a six-by-six concrete room. He could barely move. His throat felt like a massive bruise. It hurt to breathe.

The room was hot, stifling, wet. Drake rolled to his other side, feeling several stitches pop along his left arm, his hands still hand-cuffed behind his back. He looked up at the steel door, then got to his feet, gritting his teeth against the pain. A single waterproof lightbulb was screwed into the ceiling. There was no way out.

He closed his eyes. Catherine and Jack were dead. He was next.

Then the water started.

Frantic, Drake curled up in a ball and tried to rock to his feet. He fell back and tried again, feeling the water rise up around him. He tumbled back with a splash. He was submerged, lying on his side, holding his breath. *Oh, Jennifer. I love you so much. Forgive me.* His brain throbbed as the world faded away. *If you open your mouth and inhale, it will be over in seconds. No. I am not going to do that.* Squeezing his eyes shut, he concentrated as death closed in. Then the water drained away.

"How's it going?"

Looking up from his keyboard inside the command center overlooking the *Trident* and the subterranean pool, the Gatemaster twisted up an easy grin.

"Drake or the money?"

"The wire transfers," Clayton asked, slipping his hands into his pockets. He was bored.

"They're coming through now."

"The rendezvous?"

"We're set. I just got word from the Chinese."

"Okay, asshole, it's bath time." The two guards laughed. They hauled Drake to his feet, led him to an elevator, and ascended above ground to the first floor of the mansion.

The interior was lavish: oriental rugs, oak paneling, leather furniture. Drake felt stunned. The ambience reminded him of the Rod and Game Club in Otsego, Michigan, to which his grandfather had belonged. The memory seemed to belong to someone else. They exited the mansion through a side door, walked down a grassy knoll to a long dock of pressure-treated wood, and dragged him aboard a Hovercraft, forcing him down into a seat in the passenger area behind the bridge. The pine and salt air smelled wonderful. Thorne had flooded the room three times before he was done, then the kid had taken over.

One of the guards disappeared into the pilothouse and started the engines, the great fans whirling in a synchronous hum, lifting the craft seven inches above the water. The remaining guard sat across from Drake, his MP5 resting on his lap. The Hovercraft swung away from the dock.

Drake looked at the guard. He was young, about twenty-five, and in excellent shape. The Hovercraft was speeding away from the island out to the Atlantic. Drake could hear rock and roll emanating from the pilothouse. The Rolling Stones. *This is your chance.*

Wavering slightly, Drake tried to catch himself, then wavered again and fell off the seat, his head slamming into the steel deck. He groaned. For real.

"Jesus fucking Christ," the guard muttered in disgust. He rose to his feet and kicked Drake in the ribs. Drake moaned again, thinking that his plan had backfired. From the start it had been a low-percentage move, but there was no percentage in where they were taking him; Thorne and the kid had had their fun. But the guard broke off his attack.

Carefully moving behind Drake's head, he lifted him by an arm to his feet. Drake staggered about, rubber-legged. The guard cursed, struggling to keep Drake steady right up until the moment when Drake crouched and delivered a quantum back kick to the guard's balls. The youth dropped to his knees, gasping. Drake spun around and kicked the guard's head like a football, flipping him, semiconscious, on his back. Then Drake stomped the throat, crushing the larynx. The guard died within seconds. Squatting down, Drake grabbed the guard's nine-millimeter, a Glock, his arm throbbing with pain.

Bracing the length of the barrel against his back, Drake moved quickly to the pilothouse door—another low-percentage move. Quietly, he turned the latch and stepped sideways into the room. The remaining guard stood at the helm, grooving to the Rolling Stones number blasting on the stereo. "Sympathy for the Devil." Drake pumped five rounds into the man's back. The guard turned, a stricken expression darkening his face as he reeled from side to side in an exaggerated strut, flailing for his MP5. He collapsed in a heap. Drake rushed to the man's side and kicked away the submachine gun. In the corner, bound and gagged, Catherine lay huddled, staring at him, too scared to move.

Working with his hands tied behind his back, Drake carefully pulled the duct tape from her mouth. When he turned around, she was crying. They both were crying. He knelt beside her. He wanted to cradle her in his arms until the horror of what Clayton had done to her was banished from memory, from both their memories. "Thank God you're alive."

The Hovercraft was heading out to sea, still on course despite no one's manning the helm. Drake stood, examined the unfamiliar controls, then slipped the Hovercraft into neutral with his chin, the craft gliding to a stop in a graceful pirouette. He looked at Catherine. "I need a handcuff key."

Since Mick Jagger was leaking body fluids, Drake decided to search the other guard. He found a set of keys in a trouser pocket, and after a few minutes of fumbling, he freed Catherine's hands. She threw her arms around his neck and kissed his face.

Jennifer.

A moment later his hands were free.

"They found me in the woods. I didn't stray," she said.

"They were expecting us."

"They put me in a concrete room and filled it with water."

"I know. I'm sorry, Catherine. I never should have brought you here."

Inside the pilothouse Drake broke open the first-aid kit, swallowed three Advils, and cleaned and dressed the laceration along his left arm. Then he placed his hands on her shoulders. "I have to go back. If you steer along the coast, you'll be OK. Keep an eye on the gas gauge. There are harbors all along this shore."

"You're not leaving me?"

"I have to."

"You can't leave me alone again."

"You know what will happen if they catch us again?"

He looked at her a moment and turned away. What was he going to do, tie her up? Instead he collected the guards' weapons, stripped the guard in the passenger area of his uniform, and shoved the Hovercraft into gear, continuing out another mile where he dumped the bodies. They waited until nightfall. "I hope you know what you're getting into," he said.

She looked at him in defiance. "I think I have a pretty good idea."

He steered the Hovercraft back to the island, the moon illuminating the tall pines in which they had concealed themselves the day before. Once inside the mansion, they would head straight for the armory. This time they had the element of surprise in their favor.

Approaching the dock, Drake throttled down and swung the Hovercraft around in a perfect eggshell landing. Two men in shorts and T-shirts disappeared through a grove of pines as they jogged around the island.

Drake palmed the MP5 and whispered, "Let's go."

Together, they quickly moved up the grassy knoll, Catherine wearing only a T-shirt, Drake dressed in a uniform and armed with a Glock and an MP5.

The mansion was dark and quiet; the guards hadn't been missed. Thorne evidently allowed his men a good deal of freedom. Drake punched a code into the elevator-access panel, and they descended to the second floor below Clayton's office. The elevator door opened, and at the far end of the corridor a guard walked by, giving Drake no more than a casual glance as Catherine hugged the elevator's right wall, screened by the control panel. The guard wore a side arm. No automatic weapons. *Good.*

Grabbing Catherine's hand, Drake negotiated the corridor without incident, turning right until they reached a heavy stainless-steel door. Drake punched in another four-digit code.

"Where are we?" Catherine whispered.

"The armory."

The door slid open.

They ducked inside, the door automatically closing behind him.

"My God," Catherine said.

Drake felt like a kid in a candy shop. Arrayed along the walls were automatic weapons of every size, shape, and description. Drake exchanged his MP5 for one that was sound-suppressed. He also grabbed a tactical vest and loaded up with lots of goodies: fragmentation and CS grenades, C-4, microdetonators, extra magazines for the Glock and MP5, and two dozen 12-gauge shotgun shells for the modified Benelli semiautomatic shotgun that he slung over his back in a padded case. He found a pair of shorts and a tactical vest for Catherine and handed her a shotgun, showing her how to fire the weapon and reload. His rebreather was there. He grabbed it and slipped it on, hoping it was undamaged. He had an idea, the makings of a plan.

Stack the odds in your favor. Make them come to you.

Drake unwrapped a dozen bricks of C-4. Clayton's underground facility was about to see the light of day.

"What are you doing?"

"Wiring the room with explosives."

"You're what?"

"Come on. We have to find a place for you to hide."

"You're not leaving me alone again." Her voice was firm.

For a minute Drake thought she would stamp her foot. He looked at her, exasperated. "Catherine . . ."

28 August

The Gatemaster awoke. It was five o'clock in the morning, too early to begin the day. But he had to get up. Nature called.

Yawning, he rolled out of bed, stark-naked, and walked half asleep to the bathroom. Not bothering to switch on the lights and with his eyes half shut, he lifted the toilet seat. After all, he hadn't gone to prep school for nothing.

Sugarplums still danced in his head. His bladder, however, was bursting. Soon he'd crawl back to bed, sleeping till noon when he customarily rose for the day. A smug grin creased his lips. Some poor slobs actually had to work in the morning. In the darkness he steadied himself, anticipating the pleasurable release of his bladder. Then with a youthful swagger he took aim and eased his grip, the instant he noticed the thick electrical cord snaking out of the tank. Desperately he tried to shut off the flow, drawing back, screaming in terror. But it was too late. A hideous blue spark leaped up the waterfall like a salmon.

———————

Clayton wanted to gag. The bathroom air stank of charred flesh. They were standing over the Gatemaster's body, having been awakened by screams. Apart from the mess it had made of the Gatemaster's lower anatomy, the violent electrical surge had blown out the young man's eyes. On the mirror to the left, someone had taken a bar of soap and written: "You're next."

With an inward shudder Clayton turned to Thorne, his anger rising. "I thought you said Drake was dead?"

Thorne looked at his men, noticing for the first time that Eddie and Frank were missing. He suddenly felt vulnerable, a feeling he despised. Ignoring Clayton, he picked up his radio and called down to the men guarding the *Trident.* "Any trouble?"

"Everything's shipshape down here, boss. Why? Something up?"

"Drake. He's probably headed your way. We're powering up the *Trident* in ten."

"Got it covered."

Thorne slipped the radio in his back pocket and looked at Clayton, in no mood to be ordered about. He tapped his employer on the chest and handed him a revolver. "You better get your shit together." Then he looked at his men. "Get the assault gear. We're breaking camp now."

Inside the auxiliary power plant overlooking the subterranean pool, Drake looked out through a grating at the two guards watching the cavern. Behind him in the small cement room stood two diesel-powered generators. After having climbed into the room through a ventilator shaft and disabled both generators, Drake had hunkered down with Catherine, letting events take their course. Bright Star lay inside the *Trident* less than fifty feet away. For once, time was on their side. They were almost there.

"How long will it take before they enter the armory?" Catherine whispered.

Suddenly the cavern shook, followed by a low, rumbling boom. Rocks and debris cascaded down everywhere. The observation room window shattered, nuggets of safety glass showering down like a waterfall, bouncing and clicking against the *Trident*'s hull. The lights went out.

"About that long. Wait here."

"Why?"

"I have to kill people."

This time she didn't argue.

Drake flipped on his night-vision goggles and stepped outside. The guard to the right had been badly injured by a flying rock. The guard to the left was standing, trying to orient himself in the darkness. Drake picked up a rock, crept up to the standing guard, and dealt him a sledgehammer blow from behind, crushing the man's skull. Then he sought out the wounded man and did the same. The method was as primal as killing gets, up close and personal. Drake was glad for the darkness.

Like the Gatemaster, these men had killed innocent people without compunction. They had murdered Jack, Julia Reynolds, and a dozen others. They had nearly killed McKendrick, if he wasn't dead already. But as much as Drake despised these men, hunting them down brought little joy. No amount of killing could ever make up for the loss of his friends, or heal the wound in young Andrew's heart. That was the truth about killing; it never brought anyone back. In the end, it only left you with despair.

Thorne took point. He edged into the cavern, the stock of his MP5 pressed against his shoulder in the low ready position. Everywhere his eyes traveled so did the barrel of his gun. Only five of his men had survived the blast. The rest had been ripped apart, along with a sizable chunk of Clayton's facility. In the rocky ceiling, a gaping hole opened straight up through the mansion floor. Rocks, boulders, and office furniture were strewn everywhere.

Thorne and his men moved through the cavern quickly. Along the way, they discovered the bodies of the guards. Thorne examined their wounds. Blunt trauma. No bullet or knife wounds. These men had been killed in the explosion. Maybe Drake was hiding elsewhere, waiting for reinforcements.

The *Trident* was covered with debris but undamaged. Taking two men with him, Thorne boarded the submarine and moved from compartment to compartment, checking lockers, escape trunks, toilet facilities, everywhere, making absolutely certain that Drake was not aboard. In the cargo bay, the satellite displayed no signs of sabotage. Then Thorne and his men powered up the submarine while Clayton climbed aboard and plotted a course. They had everything they needed: food and water to last a month, the coordinates for the rendezvous, and best of all, three and a half billion dollars of untraceable Chinese cash, the down payment for Bright Star, spread over two dozen numbered accounts throughout Europe, Asia, and the Caribbean. They were almost home. Once at sea, they would become invisible. Not even Drake could find them there.

29 August

Six Blackhawk helicopters skimmed the ocean in the semidarkness, zeroing in on Clayton's island. It was the hour before dawn.

Reaching the island, they broke into two groups, the four lead helicopters sweeping over the island fast and low, fanning pines. The other two choppers hovered above the water over the entrance to the cave. From the cabin of one of the Seahawks, a large package dropped to the water, followed by six divers wearing scuba gear. The package contained an antisubmarine net. The divers unbundled the net and submerged. Some of the divers carried mines. Ordered to prevent the *Trident's* escape by any means, they would stretch the net across the mouth of the cave. But if Clayton and his men attempted to run the *Trident* in before the net was secure, the SEALs were to blow the submarine out of the water.

Topside, two platoons of Navy SEALs from Dev Group were taking down the facility. At this stage of the game, there wasn't much of a facility to take down. Every window of the lovely stone mansion had been shattered by the explosion inside the armory. Below the mansion, the underground complex was a dark warren of fractured concrete, twisted tie-rods, and body parts. The SEALs searched the complex for over an hour before relaying the sitrep. The news wasn't good: There were no signs of Drake and the girl. Worst of all, Bright Star and the *Trident* were gone.

Standing on the stage of the family theater, President Young looked out at his advisors as he rehearsed his address to the nation. He was exhausted and looked it, having spent most of the night honing his address. At 4:00 A.M. he had adjourned to the Situation Room. There the news had been bad. The SEALs had found Clayton's facility damaged and abandoned. The *Trident* and Bright Star were missing. So were Drake and the girl. Afterward he had gone upstairs to the family quarters to tell the first lady.

In all the years that he had been involved in politics, he had read about crises in the newspapers, he had watched them unfold on TV, but not until the theft of Bright Star had he become involved in any crisis of such dire import. Now he sat at the very heart of a conflict that could erupt in thermonuclear war. With his wife at his side he had knelt beside his bed praying that his decisions would be the right ones, that the world would not be consigned to the flames. It was the first time he had prayed like that in his life.

In the audience, Adams sat beside Lawrence and, with great difficulty, concentrated on the president's speech. Floating around in the back of his brain was the likelihood that he might have to tell Jennifer that Drake was dead. The thought filled him with anguish.

On the diplomatic front, the situation was not much better.

The Chinese were stonewalling. Adams guessed that they had ponied up a good deal of cash prior to delivery and wanted the goods. In any case, they continued to deny any involvement.

The only good news was that Lawrence had caught the mole, who was recovering in the hospital after having had both his legs amputated. And McKendrick was still alive, the most blessed fact of all.

McKendrick's wounds had been terrible. When he gazed down at his friend, Adams felt torn in a thousand pieces.

In his address to the nation, President Young would solicit the backing of the American people and nations throughout the world. In this endeavor his chances were good at gaining their approval. No one in his right mind wanted China to possess such an insuperable weapon—except, of course, the Chinese.

Militarily, however, the situation was tense. Two naval battle groups were stationed in the South China Sea, and a third was on its way. The previous afternoon, an American fighter had come very close to dusting it up with a Mig. Accidents led to war, and with all that hardware and men facing off in close proximity, accidents were likely to occur. In the midst of the Cuban missile crisis, Castro had shot down an American U-2. Thank God cool heads had prevailed. Adams prayed that they would again.

Perhaps with world opinion against them, China would relent. But China had been an outcast nation for much of her recent history. She was accustomed to operating alone. Her leaders thought nothing of slaughtering their own people. But would they be willing to fight a war they couldn't win, a war that nobody could win? In the end, if reason and diplomacy failed, it would all come down to their sense of self-preservation.

They held on to each other in silence. What else could they do? Time had run out. The toilet trick had worked—too well. In order to disable Bright Star and survive, Drake had to get in and out of the *Trident* unseen. From the moment of the explosion he needed to dispatch the guards, collect Catherine, locate Bright Star inside the *Trident,* and rig the charges. Which is precisely what he had been doing right up to the point when Catherine had rushed to his side from the conning tower to say that Clayton and his men were on their way. He had been standing inside the satellite, pulling the disks and rigging the explosives, when suddenly he had heard her footsteps padding down the control room ladder.

The business with the electric cable in the toilet tank had been designed to spur Clayton and his men to action, to send them running for the booby-trapped armory. It was not designed for revenge. If Drake had wanted the Gatemaster to suffer, he could have pumped a round into the man's stomach. Electrocuted, the Gatemaster had died within the breath of one long, terrified scream. Gut-shot he would have writhed in agony, perhaps for hours, depending on how Clayton or Thorne treated the wound— if they treated the wound at all. In many ways, shooting the man would have been a lot easier. But Drake had needed the effect to be ghastly, terrifying. He had needed the psychological edge.

Now as he sat inside the satellite, with Catherine on his lap facing him, he could only look at her and feel glad that they were alive. They were lost at sea. The *Trident* had been under way for hours.

30 August

From the dilapidated wheelhouse of the Liberian freighter *Brazzaville*, Captain Gregory Mombasa looked at the GPS readout, then examined his charts. He was way off course, about two hundred miles due east of Boston.

"Stop here."

Mombasa did as he was told. Not as if he had any choice. The Chinese commando pressed a gun to his face.

They had boarded his ship three days before. Mombasa had no idea how they had arrived. He had been sound asleep in his cabin when the door had exploded and two armed men had pulled him to his feet.

Now he looked out through the grimy windshield with fading hope. The ocean was dark, almost indistinguishable from the night sky. Under normal circumstances, he would have found the warm salt air to be invigorating. But the Chinese had already killed three of his crew. Sheer terror had worn him down.

———

"See anything?"

Thorne stepped away from the periscope. "They're here. Right on target."

Clayton peered through the lens. The freighter was black against a starry sky, its running lights twinkling in the darkness.

Thorne looked at the five men around him, seated at the controls of the *Trident*. "We're outgunned, so play it cool."

The men nodded. Then he looked at Clayton. "You dial in your combination?"

Clayton slipped on a lifejacket. "You think I'm an idiot?" In the thirty-six hours that they had been at sea, Clayton had regained his swashbuckling arrogance. Drake and the explosion at the facility in Maine were way behind him. He felt like a pirate of yore. He looked at Thorne. "Just make sure you make it to Havana."

Thorne guided the *Trident* alongside the freighter, then brought the submarine to the surface. Two men ran forward to crack the cargo hatch. A loud hiss, and the redolent warmth of salt air filled the control room.

They were being lifted. Inside the satellite, Drake and Catherine braced themselves, listening to the voices around them as the pallet on which Bright Star rested swayed gently back and forth as it was hoisted through the *Trident*'s cargo hatch to God knew where. Thorne's men had wrapped the satellite in plastic. Nevertheless, they could smell ocean; they could hear the sizzle of waves breaking against something solid. A ship? A dock? No way to tell. But

Drake was going to find out at the first opportunity. Squeezed with all their gear inside the narrow confines of the satellite, they had slept little the night before. She sat on his lap, facing him, her legs straddling his, crotch to crotch. His left arm hurt like the dickens. He felt like a baby raptor inside a twenty-billion-dollar egg. There was nothing sexual about it. Nevertheless, he had developed strong feelings for this girl. In another time, in another place, had Jennifer not been in his life, they would have made love. They both knew that. But Drake knew that as much as he was attracted to Catherine, deep in his soul his heart lay elsewhere, with the woman whose naked body he had held in the shower when Jack was still alive.

The voices became louder. Drake looked at Catherine and held his breath. Clayton was arguing with another American.

The other voices were speaking Chinese.

"I wouldn't touch that if I were you," Clayton warned with a supercilious grin.

The hold of the *Brazzaville* stank of manure. Bright Star stood before them on a raised platform, unwrapped. The Chinese officer scowled at Clayton and pointed to the device. "What the fuck is this?" He spoke perfect American English.

Clayton answered in kind. "It's a chastity belt. In case you guys decide to take off with the satellite before making the final payment and fuck me up the ass. Don't try to remove it. The only way it can be disarmed is by punching in an eight-digit code. I know the first four digits of the code; my partner, Mr. Thorne, knows the second half. You need both of us to remove the device. Otherwise Bright Star goes kafflooey. Once we get to Cuba and your man inspects the satellite and we receive the balance due, I will call Thorne and we'll punch in both combinations. That's the deal. Take it or leave it."

Inside the satellite, Drake and Catherine were sweltering. They had removed their tactical vests and shirts, using them as pillows to lean against. Except for the engine hum, the hold was quiet. It had been hours since Clayton and the man had talked. It was time to move. Besides, their bladders were bursting.

Using a small flashlight, Drake quickly checked the charges he had rigged inside Bright Star, then, snapping off the light, silently removed the wide access panel, carefully sliding it down past the explosive belt that Clayton and Thorne had wrapped around the laser satellite. He paused a full minute to make sure no one else was in the dark room. Then he quietly slipped outside.

After being cooped up inside the satellite, the barnyard air of the hold felt like a sea breeze. Drake reached inside and lifted Catherine out of the satellite, feeling her naked breasts against his arms.

They had to find a place to hide. They were heading to Cuba, destined to arrive in forty-eight hours. Once in Havana, Bright Star would be inspected, crated, and loaded aboard a French cargo plane that Beijing had leased through a shell company in Luxembourg.

How they were going to get back to the United States from Cuba without getting caught was a problem that Drake didn't want to think about. Yet he had to. Bright Star had been disabled; he had pulled the disks and had wired the satellite with explosives. All it would take was the press of a button and Bright Star would burst into a million flaming pieces. But how do you do that and make a safe getaway? Especially with Catherine in tow? And what about the *Trident*? He didn't want to leave a classified and undetectable submarine in the hands of the Chinese. If he wanted to disable the *Trident,* he would have to wait until Thorne returned.

He had forty-eight hours to consider the plan from all angles. He was hungry. His arm hurt. He missed Jennifer. It seemed as though a decade had passed.

31 August

They spent the night inside what appeared to be a rope locker, catching up on their sleep. Judging from the cobwebs and dust, it was plain that the storage room had been rarely visited. Drake and Catherine had crawled under a dusty tarp in the back. "Well, it's not the Ritz," Drake joked.

"It's not the fucking lousy Maine woods, either," Catherine replied. She was exhausted.

Cradling his MP5 in one hand and Catherine in the other, Drake had fallen asleep within minutes.

Then she was shaking him awake. He blinked. *Wha?* Hours had passed. He reached for the MP5. Something hot and slimy engulfed his arm up to the elbow.

"Phil! Oh, my God . . ."

Drake flicked on the pen light and nearly had a heart attack.

"Jesus Christ, Phil, it's a god damned African snake!" Catherine lurched to the side as Drake drew the knife from his vest, his heart practically exploding out of his chest as he looked down at his arm and straight into the beady eyes of a python.

The snake had been inadvertently loaded aboard the *Brazzaville* two months before via a broken banana crate that had spent the previous month outside a Namibian barn. For two months the python had lived happily in the dusty rope locker, feeding on mice and rats. Now it wanted Drake's arm for breakfast.

"Oh, my God, I think I'm going to puke," Catherine wailed.

"You think *you're* going to puke? Shit!" Drake bore down with the knife. The python thrashed wildly, slapping him in the face with its tail as it tried to coil its lower half around Drake's neck. "Hold down the goddamned tail!"

"I'm not getting near that fucking thing," she cried in a terrified whisper.

He could feel the python's mouth biting down on his arm. Drake sawed frantically with the knife. The snake's torso was as thick as a ham.

"Phil. Phil! Part of the snake just slithered across my face."

"Good." Drake was disgusted. The python's mouth relaxed as Drake finished sawing the snake in half. Then with a gigantic effort, he grabbed the python by the mouth and pulled it off his arm, tossing both halves of the bloody beast into the opposite corner. Drake looked at Catherine. "Thanks for all your help."

"You're welcome."

Then they were laughing, pulling the tarp over themselves, holding each other and giggling like children. But neither Drake nor Catherine slept that night. Considering the circumstances, staying awake definitely seemed the better part of valor.

At ten o'clock that evening, the freighter's engines throttled down, the drone lessening. They were entering Havana Harbor. Drake gathered his gear, making sure that it was arrayed so that he could grab whatever he needed quickly. Then he made sure that Catherine had her tactical vest securely fastened. "It's made out of Kevlar; it's bulletproof," he told her. He stood and, taking her hand, moved toward the door. For however long it took to get aboard the *Trident,* he would be working on instinct. That is what his SEAL training had been all about.

It took an hour for the Cuban custom agents to arrive. Not that the Chinese officer was expecting trouble. In the past three days, his government had made sure that all the right palms had gotten greased. With the Cuban economy in a shambles, baksheesh was a way of life. In the open hold of the *Brazzaville,* he looked at the two Americans, his face pale in the floodlights. "Now are you satisfied?" Clayton examined the figures on the laptop computer showing his bank balances throughout the world. They had doubled in an hour.

Clayton looked at Thorne, beaming. They would need the money now that the Gatemaster was gone. The big mercenary had arrived by inflatable three hours before, leaving the *Trident* moored at sea with three men on board. Clayton turned to the Chinese contingent, consisting of the eight commandos, the intelligence officer, and a scientist who had arrived a half hour before. He wished he could photograph the event. Then he could send postcards to all his former buddies in Washington. He looked at the Chinese contingent and nodded in satisfaction. "Gentlemen," he said. "We have a deal."

He punched in his half of the code, then stood aside as Thorne did the same. The red light on the detonator blinked off. Thorne removed the explosive chastity belt. Broad smiles lit up the faces of the Chinese. They had spent the past forty years trying to lay their hands on classified American technology. Now they had walked away with the biggest prize of all. Bright Star, the world's most formidable weapons system, was now their possession.

The Chinese officer knew that the Americans would watch China closely in the following weeks. That had been part of the plan. American reconnaissance satellites would hover over Chinese soil and record every movement, despite his country's denials. That is why Bright Star would not be heading back to China. Once the cargo jet had lifted off from Cuba, the Chinese officer would plot a course to another location: a private construction site owned by one of his countrymen. In Brazil.

The afterdeck of the *Brazzaville* was crawling with Cubans and Chinese. Peering through a window in the empty crew's quarters, Drake could see the heavy crane swinging into place over the hold. The crew of the *Brazzaville,* including the captain, had been taken off board and interned by the Cubans. In the distance the Havana skyline sparkled with a thousand lights. Catherine huddled close to Drake. "What's out there?"

"Take a look."

She did. Men were scattered along the deck. Behind them she could see buildings. Less than a week before she had been vacationing aboard a royal yacht on the other side of the island as a guest of Fidel Castro. Now she was trapped inside a rusted freighter that stank of manure. She looked at Drake. "I hope you're going to think of something."

"I have. We wait."

They sat in the crew's quarters with their backs to the aft bulkhead for twenty minutes, Drake racking his brain to come up with another plan, another way out. But there were no alternatives, unless they wanted to pop out of a hatch on the main deck and get their heads shot off. All they could do was wait. But time was running out. Clayton and Thorne weren't going to hang out forever. Soon they would board the inflatable and head into the sunset. Soon Bright Star would be in the hands of the Chinese.

Peeking out the window again, he could see the crane lowering its cable into the hold. Men were moving amidships. Others stood near the gangway. Some sort of official delegation had arrived. He looked at Catherine. "Are you ready for this?"

She peeked out the window. "No."

"When you hit the water, swim to the prop. Don't get too close. It moves, even though the ship is stopped."

She looked at him with a glum expression. "I'd rather take my chances with the snake."

Drake tied a rope around her waist and quietly opened the door. They were facing aft. The deck was momentarily clear. "Okay, sweetheart, this is it. Let's go."

"But—"

They sprinted across the open deck. The midnight air felt glorious. Drake felt sick. He didn't want to look behind him. But he did because he had no other choice. The few Cubans and the Chinese he could see beyond the superstructure were staring into the hold. Drake knew that they wouldn't be looking down for long.

Catherine scrambled over the stern rail, and Drake lowered her to the water. Fast. He heard a splash. *Uh-oh.* One of the Cubans looked up from the opposite side of the hold, and Drake waved. The man stared at him a moment, half blinded by the glare of the floodlights, then looked down again into the hold.

There was no time to tie the rope. Tossing it over the side,

Drake climbed over the stern rail, inserted the rebreather's mouth-piece between his lips, and leaped overboard, the Havana skyline shooting up as he plunged into the harbor. After having hidden inside the steaming rope locker, the water felt cool and invigorating, despite the likelihood of raw sewage being dumped nearby. He surfaced twenty feet from the prop and twirled in the water, spotting Catherine only a short distance away. She was treading water, her blond hair plastered against her forehead.

Across the harbor, Drake could see dilapidated pastel-colored buildings and lighted windows. Nearby, other freighters were moored. In the distance, two enormous steel petroleum tanks glimmered in the moonlight. In another age, the entire harbor would have bristled with the masts of the Spanish treasure fleets.

He slipped on his fins, staying low in the water, and swam to Catherine's side, drawing her to the starboard edge of the stern. Two hundred feet away, two of Thorne's men sat in an inflatable, just as Drake had expected. Thorne would not risk surfacing in the *Trident* close to the Cuban shore. He would keep the submarine positioned over deep water where he could run and hide.

Lifting the MP5 from the water, Drake slowly approached the rubber raft. Catherine stayed behind clinging to the hull near the stern. He kept his eyes off the men, swimming slowly and carefully, ghosting through the water. He would rely on his peripheral vision to detect movement; people can sense when they're being stalked. He swam steadily and quietly, closing the gap, the rebreather on his back, the mouthpiece between his teeth, the barrel of the MP5 raised above the water.

One of the men suddenly stood and stretched. Drake shot the terrorist in the head, then lunged for his partner seated on the inflatable's starboard tube. He caught the other terrorist by the pistol belt and dragged him overboard, driving him down into the water as the man struggled to break free. Drake didn't want the man dead, just docile. He slammed his fist into his groin. The terrorist doubled up.

Drake brought him to the surface. Coughing up water, the man groaned, his features pallid with fear. Drake pressed the barrel of his MP5 into his face. "All right, shitbag. We're going for a ride."

The terrorist didn't argue. Drake started the engine, swung around the stern, hauled Catherine aboard, and headed out into the glassy harbor. From the weather decks of the *Brazzaville* came the sounds of men shouting and the roar of the crane as Bright Star was lifted from the hold. Drake waited until the satellite came into view, reaching its apogee high above the freighter. Catherine gazed up in wonder. Then she saw Thorne at the starboard rail, staring at them, alerted by the noise of the outboard.

"Phil?"

Drake reached for the detonator and pressed the button.

In a tremendous burst of smoke and yellow flame, Bright Star exploded, fiery pieces of the satellite soaring over the Havana skyline. The tranquil harbor flashed with reflected light, pieces of flaming metal raining down everywhere. Drake didn't need to see any more. Nor did he have time. He looked at Catherine and smiled by way of reassurance. Then he turned the engine handle full throttle, keeping the MP5 trained on his half-drowned captive and said, "Your sense of direction better be right on, fella."

In his sumptuous presidential hideaway overlooking Havana Harbor, Fidel Castro was just lighting up one of Cohiba's choicest Robustos when a fireball lit the sky.

He knew Chinese agents were on the island. Was this sabotage? A Chinese *Maine?*

Gnashing his teeth in anger, he spat the ruined cigar to the floor, scrambling for the phone. He was going to thrust someone's balls in a vise for this one. *Hijo de Puta!*

Thorne picked himself up off the weather deck. He looked down to his right hand. Three fingers were missing. He steeled himself against the pain, biting his tongue. He could hear sirens in the distance closing in. The deck was littered with bodies. Several of the wounded were pulling themselves to their feet. The Chinese intelligence officer, a couple of commandos. They were not happy about the situation. Then out of the corner of his eye he saw Geoffrey Clayton crawling toward him on his hands and knees, whimpering like a dog. Out in the harbor several boats raced in their direction, no doubt looking for survivors. Without looking back, he climbed over the starboard rail and jumped.

The MP5 gripped firmly in his right hand, Drake leaped aboard the *Trident.* Catherine followed. They were two miles off the Cuban coast, floating over a deep-water trench. Catherine looked back at the prisoner and tugged Drake on the arm. "What about him?"

"Leave him." Drake knew the man wasn't going to be a problem. If he had any smarts at all, he'd take the inflatable and head for the hills. Which is exactly what the man did.

Riding on pure adrenaline, Drake climbed down the open hatch, raking the control room with fire, killing two men instantly. The survivor scrambled to the rear of the submarine. Drake pulled Catherine down the ladder, ripped the Benelli 12-gauge from its scabbard, and, shoving Catherine to one side of a circular hatch, fired four quick rounds of double-O buckshot down the length of the submarine where the man was hiding, the buckshot caroming off the steel bulkheads, shredding everything it touched, including the man who screamed. Then he tossed a fragmentation grenade down the length of the submarine and slammed the hatch. The *Trident* shook from the explosion. He waited a minute, then looked outside. Smoke filled the control room. He handed the shotgun to Catherine. "Cover me."

"I see someone!" Gabriel Martinez pointed to the man flailing in the water. Hector Gonzalez wheeled the cigarette boat around. As a high-ranking official in Castro's Ministry of Finance, Gonzalez could afford such luxuries as a speedboat. They came alongside the drowning man.

"Help me," the man pleaded.

They pulled him aboard. Big mistake. Thorne broke Gonzalez's neck instantly, twisting his head 180 degrees. Then he shoved Martinez overboard and slammed the cigarette into overdrive.

Drake had one charge rigged; now he was rigging another. It would do no good to blow a hole in a submarine that could be effectively stanched by the mere closing of a hatch. He needed to sink the *Trident*, put it in a place where the Cubans or the Chinese couldn't mess with it—namely in a trench 6,000 feet deep.

In the forward cargo bay he pressed the C-4 against a bulkhead, placing it carefully beneath the heavy steel bench upon which Bright Star had rested. Welded to the floor, the steel bench would help direct the force of the blast. He quickly completed the wiring and set the timer. They had three minutes to get out.

"How much longer?" Catherine asked.

"Don't look at me. Watch the control room." Worried, he turned and looked up at Catherine just as Thorne took aim.

Oh, my God, no.

The sound of a gunshot reverberated in his ears. Catherine screamed and tumbled to the deck as another round slammed into the steel bulkhead behind them. Rolling on his side, Drake poked the Benelli through the circular hatch, fired twice, and tossed a grenade. Shrapnel ripped through the control room as the *Trident* shook again from the blast. With a crackle and hiss, sparks rained down as the electronics shorted out. Then grayish-blue smoke curled through the interior, black around the edges.

Reeling, heartsick, Drake crawled to Catherine's side and ripped open the tac vest. Her T-shirt was soaked with blood. "I didn't know," she said. "Oh, God, Phil, it hurts. Make the hurting stop."

Drake stroked her forehead. He was sobbing. Catherine groaned and tried to turn on her side. "Phil?"

"I'm right here, baby."

She squeezed her eyes shut.

"I'm going to get you out. You just have to hang on."

But she couldn't hang on, even though Drake had bunched her T-shirt into the wound; the armor-piercing round had clipped her heart. Drake cradled her as best he could, tears pouring down his face, in the minute it took her to die. Then slowly he gathered himself and pulled away. He had no other choice. The timers were set.

Was Thorne dead? Was he wounded and lying in wait? With no time left, Drake tossed a smoke grenade into the control room, slipped the rebreather's mouthpiece between his teeth, and charged forward.

The ladder . . .

He dove into the control room and gripped the steel rungs as the first explosion tore a four-foot hole into the aft bulkhead, the second charge ripping through the forward deck, two massive walls of seawater slamming into him with such force that if the MP5 hadn't become wedged in the bottom rung he would have been swept away. The lights went out. The *Trident* was sinking fast. Even in the darkness, Drake could tell. His ears stung from the pressure.

He reached down, pulled a mask from his tactical vest, slipped it on, vented the water, and looked around. A faint glow appeared on the far side of the control room. A light was flickering inside the tiny window of the escape trunk, a miniature flashlight. Then as the *Trident* flooded completely and the bubbles cleared, Drake saw a man grimace with pain as he donned his escape hood.

Thorne.

Drake turned away and cut himself free of the MP5 as the *Trident* began to tumble beneath the sea. Hanging on for dear life, he pulled himself up the ladder, equalizing the pressure in his ears with every breath. He had to get out. Now. With every foot the *Trident* sank he was increasing his chances of oxygen toxicity. The rebreather wasn't going to be much good past five hundred feet. He pulled himself into the conning tower, groping in the dark water for the hatch. It wasn't there. He began to panic. He was exhausted and sick with grief. He stopped and breathed. *No, you are not going to die. Not here. Not now.* He pulled himself up another rung and groped again. Nothing. He moved higher and reached up, stretching to touch something solid. Then he felt the intricate workings of the hatch release. He shoved the lever forward and pressed his back against the hatch, and bracing his fins on the ladder, forced it open. The *Trident* tumbled again, and Drake was ripped from the ladder. Panic seized his heart as he fought to find the ladder again. And then he realized that the tumbling had stopped. He was hovering in open water, the ocean dark and silent as the *Trident* tumbled into the depths invisible below.

Catherine.

Inside the escape trunk, Thorne continued to watch the water trickling up around him. Something was wrong. The water was taking too long to fill the tank. He slipped the Stienke hood over his face, charged it, and waited, the pain from the stubs of fingers gnawing at his senses. He felt sick. He was drenched with perspiration. He wanted to vomit. *Why the fuck was the water taking so long?*

Drake had disappeared. He had directed the emergency flashlight out the window hoping to see another way out. But there was none.

He should have stayed on the cigarette. With Bright Star gone, he'd assumed that Drake had lit out, headed for the hills. He had seen the inflatable receding in the distance. It wasn't until he had dropped down into the control room that he had noticed the bodies and the girl. He slammed his fist against the side of the tank and waiting another agonizing minute before the escape hatch blew open. From a depth of 600 feet, Thorne rocketed to the surface.

The night was gorgeous. The warm tropical breeze caressed his face like the soft hand of a lover. The vault of the heavens glowed with billions of stars. He looked at them in wonder, the tingling and numbness spreading like wildfire across his left shoulder as decompression sickness took hold.

Thorne tried to relax, but within ten minutes the pain was so severe that he felt as though he were being drawn and quartered, which in a manner of speaking he was. He had stayed inside the escape trunk too long. Now deep in his tissues—in his bones, cartilage, arteries, nerves, muscles, and skin—millions of microscopic bubbles came rushing out of solution, contorting his body at the joints, wracking him with the hideous pretzeling effect of the bends.

He was bellowing, begging for mercy. By the time the Cuban patrol boat homed in an hour later, he had lost all feeling in his legs. He had only minutes to live when they hauled him on board.

Drifting in the ocean, having completed the required decompression, Philip Drake also looked up at the stars. It would be years before he would reveal his deepest feelings about the woman who had died in his arms. And when that happened he would reveal them not to a man, not to Adams or McKendrick, but to his wife, Jennifer. For Drake was not ready to die yet. As long as he remained low in the water he would be safe from the Cuban patrol boats. He wore a wet suit and a tactical vest. He was equipped with smoke grenades, a rebreather, fins, and a Glock 9mm. Key West lay thirty miles due north. He would swim the distance if he had to. He would make it back to Jennifer's arms. He would live to see Jack's son grow to be a man. He would survive.

But the same could not be said of Geoffrey Clayton.

As the Cuban security team boarded the freighter, Clayton raised his hands in supplication: "Don't shoot," he begged. "I'm a United States citizen."

But he wasn't anymore. Neither the Justice Department nor President Young would want him back. And once Castro had learned from an anonymous source about Clayton's involvement in the Kuwaiti massacre, the aging dictator wouldn't have let him go in any case. He would have plans for this former American. Maybe the Kuwaiti oil deal could be resurrected after all.

EPILOGUE

On a foggy morning in late September, Charles Baxter, the U.S. ambassador to Great Britain, along with a minister of Her Majesty's Government, drove to Oxford where they found Paul Durand studying in the Bodleian library. A good-looking young man with blond hair who dreamed of attending medical school, Durand was not accustomed to receiving visitors. He had a mother in London who found it hard to travel and a sister who lived in Paris and worked in the fashion business. They were to meet in Munich during his vacation.

Having invited Durand to take a seat in the chancellor's office to which they had adjourned, Baxter quietly told the young Oxford student what he could about his sister's death. There was little that he could do to console the young man, except offer him an envelope on behalf of the president of the United States and a grateful nation. Inside the envelope was a check for two million dollars, the reward that President Young had offered for the arrest and capture of the terrorists.

Durand would go on to medical school. In fact, he would become one of the finest surgeons in Great Britain. And he would marry, spending his nights and weekends helping his wife to raise their beloved daughter, Catherine.

Billy Lawrence would return to Systems Technologies and the CEL Foundation, named after his deceased parents. In his later years he would give away nearly his entire fortune to charitable causes, becoming one of the great philanthropists of the twentieth century. Six months following Julia's death, with McKendrick at his side, Lawrence would hold a memorial service in her memory. Hundreds would attend, but only he and McKendrick would ever know about the letter that he had discovered inside her briefcase. And they would keep Julia's secret forever.

Lieutenant Commander Frank Donnally would recover from his multiple fractures and massive internal bleeding, though he would not be playing golf at a country club or anywhere else. The fact that his legs had been amputated had nothing to do with it. Following his court martial for treason and murder, Donnally would be sentenced to two consecutive life terms at Fort Leavenworth.

And as for Geoffrey Clayton, the terrible swift sword of Islamic justice would fall on a scaldingly hot day in Ramadan. After six months in a Kuwaiti prison, Geoffrey Clayton would emerge a changed man. Malnutrition and disease had racked his body. His execution would come as a blessing.

Almost six months to the day that Drake pulled himself from the water at Key West and returned to Jennifer's arms, Andrew Henderson would sit on his mother's lap staring up at the biggest building that he had ever seen, the Vehicle Assembly Building, now renamed the Jack Henderson Engineering Center in memory of his father. On hand for the dedication would be all the principals who had striven to bring the Bright Star crisis to an end: Lawrence, Elliot, McKendrick, Adams, McGuire, Admiral Archer, Margaret Abrams, and President Young. Commander Pete Miller would sit with his family beside Dave Cameron, Dennis Franks, and Jeremy Sanchez and their families. Flight Director James Kirkwell would preside over the dedication. After the ceremony, the group would gather for a reception at Mission Control, marveling at the Renaissance statue that graced the new lobby, a marble angel with golden wings, eyes cast heavenward in an expression of faith and everlasting hope. And often when alone, standing on his porch or gazing out the windows of his library, Drake, too, would look up at the stars with everlasting hope, whispering the name: *Catherine.*